If These Walls Could Whisper

by

Rod Ling

First Published 2014 by Rod Ling and Mathom House.
Printed by Lightning Source.

Mathom House Publishing,
Mathom House, 152 Carter Lane East,
South Normanton, Derbyshire, DE55 2DZ

All work ©2013 Rod Ling.

Typset and Cover Design by Gumbo Press
(www.gumbopress.co.uk).

The moral right of the author has been asserted

All rights reserved. No part of this publication may be
reproduced, stored in a retrieval system,
or transmitted, in any form or by any means,
electronic, mechanical, photocopying, recording
or otherwise, without the prior permission of the
publishers.

A CIP Catalogue record for this book
is available from the British Library

ISBN: 978-0-9559262-3-5

Dedicated to the many members - past, present and future – of the Moseley School community in Birmingham. Being a part of it for more than twenty years hasn't always been easy but it has played a major part in shaping my life.

Though elements of this book are founded on the research of an actual building, this is a work of fiction. All characters appearing in this work are also fictitious.

All chapters are initially denoted by the use of 'dropped capitals'. Major 'time shifts' are usually indicated by the addition of chapter headings which also give details of the location.

"It's a poor sort of memory that only works backwards,' says the White Queen to Alice."

— Lewis Carroll,
*Alice's Adventures in Wonderland
& Through the Looking-Glass*

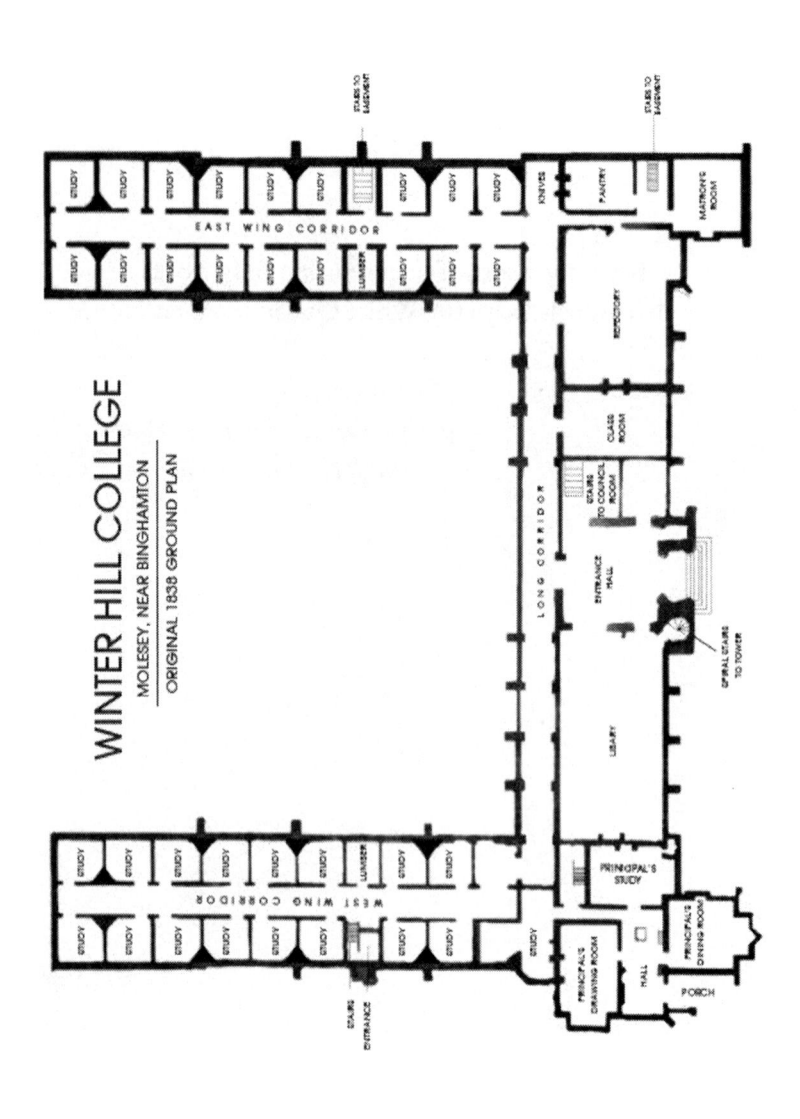

WINTER HILL COLLEGE
MOLESEY, NEAR BINGHAMTON
ORIGINAL 1838 GROUND PLAN

I
Erromanga Island, New Hebrides group, Melanesia. November 1839

Emerging from the doorway to his cabin, Captain Robert Marsham straightened his back, pushed a dark blue, peaked cap onto his head and, at the same time, the tip of his tongue into the disintegrating molar in his upper jaw. Dismayed by the stab of pain that escaped from beneath the blanket of strong liquor, he looked to the starboard side of his vessel. He winced again and trusted to a fresh breeze to prevent his distinguished passenger from detecting the odour on his breath. His agitated fingers found the timepiece in his waistcoat pocket. He noted that the hour was still well before noon. Shifting his weight with practised ease from one leg to the other, he crossed the lightly rolling deck and approached the tall, broad-shouldered man he had conveyed across more than two thousand miles of ocean.

Reverend William John removed his broad-brimmed hat and passed a kerchief across his brow; the early morning sun was already strong and, a large man, he perspired easily. Each of them acknowledged the other with a nod of the head before returning their gaze to the verdant island that rose in a gently sloping cone above the distant breakers and narrow strip of sandy beach.

'Well, there she is at last, Reverend, Erromanga, in all her mickle glory. Not so handsome as your own Raiatea I'll grant, but a welcome sight, nonetheless. When will you go ashore, sir?'

'Within the hour, Captain, with your assistance. My companion, Leota, is, even now, searching the baggage for gifts of metalwork and cloth.'

He raised his right hand to shade his narrowing eyes.

'It is unusual though, for there to be no reception party upon the shore.'

'Oh, they are there, Reverend. Have no fear of that. They are, perhaps, more wary of Europeans than usual. I am told they suffered gravely at the hands of a Dutch vessel in search of sandalwood a year or more since. I believe that a number of natives were killed.'

Deep lines instantly furrowed the brow of the passenger.

'And so we, the *civilised* nations, offer such example to the native peoples of the world. Robert, you would think we were not already faced with sufficient hazard. I am thankful that Mrs John is not with us. Such news would serve only to excite her fears.'

Captain Marsham hesitated and then displacing his sense of unease, cupped his chin and repeatedly drew the thumb and forefinger of his left hand across the grain of stubble.

'Nevertheless, it may be wise to heed her words, even as you imagine them, sir. Our arrival here may not be welcomed … immediately. Will you give me leave to issue the muskets? They may be aged but will ensure that we are approached with caution.'

'No, indeed I will not, Captain. You well know that I have set foot on many islands in the South Seas armed only with my faith and some modest offerings. We will carry no arms but those that are of our own bodies, open wide in greeting. They will thus understand that we intend no harm.'

'Reverend John, I count myself a good Christian man but …'

'Captain, your counsel has been noted but on this matter I will not be moved. I will allow, however, that I would be grateful for the - robust - company of some of your crew. That should provide us with adequate insurance against any misunderstanding as to our purpose.'

He turned in the direction of a sallow-faced, younger man who was crossing the deck with some wariness as it rose and fell beneath his feet.

'Ah, Mr Harris, you are well I trust? Has Leota located our store of gifts?'

'He has, Reverend John, and will join us directly.' The younger man looked at the ship's master and nodded. 'Good-day to you, Captain Marsham.'

The sailor made like response before turning once more in the direction of the deserted shore and raising a battered brass telescope to his left eye. He steadily swept the shoreline of the bay from west to east and spoke as he did so.

'Ah, there is some movement now. I can see a few boys and some of the men to the rear of the strand - but I can see no women as yet.'

'Yes, I think I discern them,' added Reverend John.

'Well, it would appear that some at least are finding the boldness to meet with us. That is promising.'

'But if there are no women, Reverend ... I am uneasy if the women have been instructed to stay away.'

'Nevertheless, Robert, we must proceed as planned. The women are no doubt more cautious. Further delays will serve no purpose.'

'Very well, sir. I will instruct the bosun to prepare the jollyboat. There will be a full load with four of my men to row, myself, yourself and your native.'

'But Captain, I thought it had been agreed ... I must also be included, as escort to Reverend John,' pleaded the younger man, looking earnestly from one to the other.

'There is no room, sir, I'm afraid. Reverend John has already said that he will have need of my men and I will be among them. In my view, you would be well advised to remain here until Reverend John has secured the goodwill of the natives.'

Mr Harris turned to face the man he now considered, after their long voyage, to be his friend and mentor. His expression conveyed everything that was necessary to provoke a response.

'Micaiah, I know that you are eager...'

'I can be of great service to you, sir. I have not been idle during our crossing from Raiatea. I have studied the letters that tell us something of the language and have acquired a few words. I will do your bidding no less faithfully than Leota.'

'There may be hazards ...'

'I am prepared, sir. Leota will be content to stay

aboard the *Camden*, I am sure of it.'

Reverend John reflected that the young man's open enthusiasm reminded him a great deal of himself when he was of a similar age. He smiled softly and nodded.

'Very well, I will speak to Leota. Make haste. You will have need of headwear. We may be exposed on water and shore for some hours.'

He turned to face his host.

'Thank you Captain, we will join you and your men at the stern directly.'

Robert Marsham touched the peak of his cap. 'Very good, Reverend.'

'Oh and Captain, I would be obliged if you could ensure that the men selected are all … clear-headed.'

'Sir? Oh yes, indeed sir,' he assured the famous missionary, briefly pushing his tongue once more into the jagged centre of the offending tooth. 'You need have no concerns on that score. Every single one of them will be stone-cold sober.'

Nearly two hours later the hull of the small boat made rasping contact with the white coral strand. It briefly shuddered and came to an abrupt halt. One man from either side of the craft entered the shallow, warm, crystal-clear water and steadied the boat for their passengers. Once Micaiah Harris had reached the shore, one of the men handed him a large canvas bag containing the items they hoped would help to ensure a friendly reception. He looked up to see some of the natives, at the rear of the beach, moving among the palm trees that fell forward toward them, as though straining to reach the sea.

The young man was struggling to contain his excitement. Here, finally, he sensed his long-awaited opportunity to make a contribution to God's work. He decided that as soon as circumstances permitted, he would strike up the beach and make contact with the strangely-dressed natives. With his mastery of a few words of the native tongue he was confident he could overcome their reserve and delight them with the patterned cloth he was carrying. Then it would become a simple matter to bring them forward to meet the man, his close friend, whose distinguished bearing and great renown would quieten all their fears.

Reverend John, meanwhile, busied himself with instructions for the crew and arrangements for their return to the ship.

'We will encourage the natives to approach as they become assured of our peaceable intentions. Captain, your men should remain close to the boat and do nothing that might cause alarm. I will walk the shoreline in order that they might see clearly that I offer no threat.'

'Very good, sir. But I would ask that you do not stray too far from the jollyboat.'

'Very well, Captain. Mr Harris, be so good as to accompany me.'

Fifty minutes later, though walking slowly with prolonged pauses, the two men had travelled some distance while their progress was tracked by the natives who remained, half-concealed, among the trees and vegetation.

Two small native boys were the first to venture onto the beach. Observing them and eager to initiate some contact, Micaiah Harris smiled and the boys, in turn, grinned and waved in a way that encouraged him to walk in their direction. Reverend John, meanwhile, had dropped onto one knee to examine some large pieces of unusual coral that had caught his eye. He thought they might be of interest to friends and colleagues in England and failed to note that his companion was moving away.

When, after a few moments, he looked up, he saw that his young colleague had extracted some cloth from the canvas bag and was holding it between outstretched arms in front of two native boys. He turned instinctively, to look at the captain and crew grouped together on the beach, the dark shape of the boat behind them moving under the gentle buffeting of the small waves. The outlines of the men shimmered in the intense midday heat.

For a brief moment, Reverend John became aware of a strange, encompassing silence. It seemed to him that time itself had stopped. Slowly, silently, as though in a dream, he began to rise. At the very moment he stood tall, the tranquillity of the scene was shattered by the fearful sound of many heavily-tattooed and bare-chested men, screaming fiercely as they burst from cover and raced across the beach in the direction of Micaiah Harris. In their hands, held menacingly above their heads, was an agitated thicket of bows, spears and dark wooden clubs.

Dropping the piece of coral he was still holding, the Reverend John shouted, 'Run, man!' before turning urgently towards the sea. He could see the crewmen by the boat spring into action. Captain Marsham began shouting and waving, encouraging him to hurry. Three of the crew strained to push the small boat into deeper water.

Harris was overtaken first. Though an athletic man he had, for crucial moments, tried to run holding onto the canvas bag. Thus encumbered, he quickly sensed that his attackers were gaining on him. Terrified, he looked back to see that a small group of natives were attempting to outflank him in his race for the boat. He abandoned the bag and the roll of chevron patterned cloth which unravelled and billowed in the breeze as he headed directly for the shore. Quickly exhausted by the effort of running in heavy footwear on dry sand, he stumbled and fell as he reached the darker, more compacted zone fringing the shore. Within seconds the leading native was above him. The first blow of the square, deeply grooved, hardwood club, crushed a portion of his skull.

William John, some distance ahead, heard a sickening sound and turned to look back. At the same time an arrow pierced the muscle of his right calf. With a cry, he fell into the shallow waters as other arrows passed harmlessly over his prostrate body. Within moments, two other natives, now ahead of the main group, were on him. They hesitated briefly at the sight of his raised arm and the sound of his unintelligible pleas. They ended his life moments before the seawater entered his lungs.

II
Winter Hill School, Binghamton, England. October 2000

'OK, everybody, quiet please! Settle down. Take a seat, boys. Hurry now. Right then, listen! Amir, we are now waiting for you.'

The teacher paused and fixed her gaze on a tall boy of wiry frame towards the rear of the class, then continued.

'We've heard from a number of you now on this assessment about a strong personal memory but I'd like to make room for at least one more reading. I think that it's one of the best and will help take us on to the next task in the programme.'

'Miss, I hope you won't ask me. I can't remember what I wrote!'

Miss Frobisher looked sternly to her left at a small, slim boy whose grin revealed a collection of crooked teeth.

'That's very amusing, Tony, but don't worry, you won't need to remember. I'll make you write it out again at the end of the lesson while the rest of the class go to lunch.'

'Sorry, miss,' replied the boy, his smile now less certain.

'So, the last one we'll have time for is Polly's. Her memory is from two and half years ago, her first day at Winter Hill School.'

A low groan emerged from the back of the room. The teacher turned quickly in the direction of the source. The groaning immediately stopped.

'So, as before, I want you all to listen carefully and then complete a feedback sheet for Polly. Remember you'll be grading her written work for use of vocabulary, syntax; that's the way she puts her sentences together, and interest. You'll also give another set of grades for how well she reads; volume, speed, use of emphasis and last of all, clarity.'

Miss Frobisher now looked at the fourteen year-old girl to her right, seated at a table next to the window. The teacher pressed her lips together and briefly shook her head. As form tutor to the class, as well as their English teacher, she had decided she would have to choose another time to work her way through the list of the girl's obvious transgressions; the streak of bright red, in strong contrast to the otherwise dyed-black hair, the pronounced black eye-liner and hitched-up skirt would all have to wait.

'Ok, Polly. Come out to the front - and take that gum out of your mouth, please. Put it in the bin. How many times do you have to be reminded that this is a 'gum-free' school? I'd also like you to lengthen your tie, please.'

Polly flashed a nervous grin at the girl sitting alongside her and began to manoeuvre the gum with her tongue as she rose, reluctantly, from her chair. She slowly pulled a piece of paper from her blazer pocket, pressed it against her lips and dropped both gum and paper into the bin under the teacher's desk. She moved to stand beside her teacher, undid and re-tied her necktie before finally opening her exercise book.

'Come on, Polly. We still have a lot to get through in this lesson. Now, off you go and please don't hurry. Make sure Maryam at the back can hear then everyone else will be able to as well. Be confident. It's very good writing.'

'Do I have to, miss?'

'Yes Polly, you do and if you like, I'll tell you why; because your work is good, because I know that despite this sullen act, you actually enjoy reading aloud and finally - because I say you must. So, no more time-wasting, please.'

Polly's face contorted in an expression of disdain and resignation. She looked down at her book and began to read.

'A Special Memory; My First Day at School
I would love to go back in time.

'A little more volume please Polly,' the teacher interrupted encouragingly.

If I could, I'd go back to the day when I first walked through the school gates. It is impossible to describe how I felt. I remember looking up at the front of the old building with its huge tower, carvings of stone beasts and ugly gargoyles. I stared at it for a long time. I'd seen it all before but this somehow felt like the first time, *because it was close-up and now it was <u>my</u> school. It had always been a place of mystery to me. If I'm honest, the old college building was a big reason for me choosing Winter Hill.*

My sister, Janine, goes to Swansfield, the girls' school, and my Mum wanted me to go there as well but I said I would only go to Winter Hill. I was surprised when Janine agreed with me. Then I found out that this was not because she wanted to help me; not her. She told me that she didn't want me interfering in her social life and then 'grassing' to our Mum about things she didn't want her to know. So she was happy to tell our parents that I should find my 'own way in life'.

Then my father got involved for once. It takes something very important to get him away from his work! He was a student at Winter Hill fifty years ago. In those days it was a grammar school and you had to pass an exam to get in. Mum says he was too 'politically correct' to admit it, but though he loved the old building, the history and tradition, he was worried about the way the school had changed since it had become a comprehensive. That didn't worry me. I went to St. Luke's Primary and a lot of my friends were going to Winter Hill, especially Lukhwinder, Gemma and Maryam.'

Polly paused and raised her head to look at the reaction from her friends. Amir took advantage of the opportunity to ask why his name hadn't been mentioned and, after some laughter smothered by urgent shushing noises from Miss Frobisher, Polly continued.

'I think that in the end my Dad's opinion was probably the reason why I got my way. My Mum is often 'for' an idea that's different to my Dad's and she thinks it's a good thing for kids to

go to a local school. She also liked the fact that some of my junior school class had chosen Winter Hill.

But when I stood beneath the tower on that first morning with Maryam and Lucky beside me, with our parents waving at us from the gate, I'll admit that part of me wasn't sure I'd made the right decision. The ugly faces of the gargoyles looked scary in close-up. Then a teacher saw us and told us, in a friendly way, that we were in the wrong place and should follow her down to the 'new' building or East wing.

Later, still on that first day, when we were taken into the old building, I remember best the long corridor. It seemed like something from 'Alice in Wonderland', stretching out forever, straight as an arrow, beneath lots of pointed arches. The walls were covered with pictures of buildings which I have now been told are old plans of Winter Hill but I didn't know that then.

That's as much as I can remember of that first day. It was a strange mix of fun, amazement and worry. That's really why I'd like to go back, so that I could live it all again, feel it all again but knowing then what I know now.

But that's impossible. I can't go back in time, nobody can. The only way I can go back is in my mind, using my memory.'

Polly stopped and the teacher started a round of applause in which most of the class enthusiastically joined.

'Well done, Polly. That was very good and I think it has a good ending though something tells me that you might have had some help with it as well - from your mother, perhaps? Never mind, the ideas are clearly yours. Back to your seat now, please, ... we need to move on. Hand in those feedback sheets everyone, as quickly as you can.'

Miss Frobisher collected the hastily-completed sheets

from the front of the rows as they were passed forward. She put them together in a pile on her desk, picked up her notes and, after a brief glance at them, continued.

'Polly's writing leads us nicely into the next piece of work. You've all now written something about an important personal memory. Now I want to set you another task, one that will last for most of the coming half term's homework. As your writing shows, all of you are individuals with your different memories. But there are connections between you as well. Polly's memory, for example, is also part of Lucky's and Maryam's ... and that of the teacher who tried to help them …. and her family's. Their memories of what happened though may not be as clear, as important to them. Can anyone tell me why not?'

A hand went up near the front of the class and the teacher nodded.

'Yes, Charmaine'.

'Because Lucky's mum and dad didn't argue about which school she went to,' said Charmaine pointedly. 'Lucky didn't have a choice, she had to come here.'

'Alright, Charmaine. It sounds to me as though you may be getting too personal but, in a way, I think that what you are saying is right; that different people have different reactions to the same experience. Why is that? Yes, Lucky'.

'Miss, because they *feel* differently about the things that happen to them,' she answered with emphasis and then turned to look directly at Charmaine, sitting behind her. 'And I don't mind if everyone knows that I don't have a dad. He died when I was nine years old and I live with my mum and we may not have much money but I still *chose* to come here.'

'Yes, ok, thank you Lucky,' Miss Frobisher said quickly, choosing to gloss over the obvious tension in the exchange between the two girls. 'I think you're right. Memories are important only when they are connected to some strong feelings or emotions. So, memories can be shared as well as personal, and …' The teacher now looked directly at Lucky and smiled. '... and the people we share our memories with may be living or no longer with us.'

Reassured by Lucky's slight nod of the head, Miss Frobisher turned back to face the class.

'And this brings us to the next piece of work I'm setting today. Look at your worksheet. As it says there, you are to join with no more than three others to make a group. Your task is to find a memory of a place that connects you to the other members of your group and, perhaps, other people outside your group. Then you will research these memories and find out more about the place and people who are a part of it. Does that make sense?'

A low murmur of uncertainty spread through the room.

'So, Amir, your memory, for example, about visiting the car showroom, might be linked to others in your group who also remember something with a connection to cars. You can research among your families and friends and find ways of bringing these memories together in a particular place, like Binghamton. I'm sure I don't need to tell you that Binghamton has a long history of making cars. What can you find out about that history? What kinds of cars, and do these cars have any connection with those personal memories of family and friends' cars?'

'Surjit, your memory was visiting your grandparents in the Gujarat. So your group might take holiday places as the theme. Each of you then finds out more from your parents and other relatives about important holidays or visits back to places from where their families came. That could become a project about the history of migration to Binghamton.'

'But, miss,' interrupted a small girl with long, dark, unruly hair, 'We might do that but I'm working with Susan and her family is from this country'.

'Yes, Jamila, I know that but her family may have memories of moving from another part of the country to here, or even within the city. Migration doesn't just have to mean moving between different countries.

I hope you can begin to see how, starting from one person, we can connect to other people's lives and find out more about the past. And even if you can't see it now, I'm sure that as the weeks pass, it will become clearer. You'll be doing the research but I will be checking on your progress and helping when you need it.'

The door from the corridor suddenly swung open and the atmosphere in the classroom changed immediately, as though a blast of icy air had entered. Mr Pearce, the Head of Year, a tall man with a severe expression, strode into the room, followed by a small, round-shouldered but powerfully built Asian boy, the line of his mouth set in a declaration of mute defiance.

'I apologise for the interruption, Miss Frobisher. But I'm here to ruin your day.'

III
Raiatea Island, Society Islands, Polynesia, March 1839
(9 months before the landing on Erromanga)

Beneath a wide-brimmed grass hat that served to shade his eyes from the intense light and heat of the mid-day sun, William John linked his large calloused hands behind his back and mouthed a silent prayer of thanks. From his elevated position on a rise above the narrow beach, he could view the entire sweep of the bay. Beyond the coral reef, the long-awaited schooner, *Camden,* lay at anchor, her denuded masts rhythmically swaying as the swell beneath her hull hurried towards the shore. At a point where the surging waves began to break, a smaller, laden craft rolled and pitched more vigorously. Aboard the rowboat four oarsmen struggled to keep the prow at right angles to the parallel ridges of white foam in their pursuit of deeper tones of blue and a channel through the reef. At the edge of the placid, turquoise waters of the lagoon, a group of native islanders gathered beside large tarpaulin-covered crates contrasting strongly with the expanse of white coral sand. Close by, distinguishable by their European clothing, a smaller, less animated knot of children and adults waited patiently.

'Will you go down to meet them, William?' asked the woman of her husband, the leader of their small missionary group in the Polynesian islands. She raised the frayed edge of her parasol to glance in his direction.

'I will, Mary, all in good time. There is no hurry for the billows on the reef are strong today. Besides, the men know what to do. I have given instruction.'

She smiled, 'Well, it is a good day, William. The Lord has truly blessed us. My only fear is that some of the more delicate items we requested of our friends in Sydney may have been damaged during the course of the voyage.'

'Fear not, Mary. Whatever the Lord has taken from us he takes for a purpose. For my part, my chief concern is not with the supplies that are landed here but rather with the valuable cargo we are dispatching, destined, ultimately, for England.'

'A year or more away, it is a long journey … ' her voice faded as she turned her eyes toward the horizon.

'Mary, you cannot already be homesick? It is less than twelve months since we were last in England.'

'I assure you, William, that much as I love the work we do here, the ache of longing to see my family and the familiar sights of London and Binghamton, returns after a lot less than twelve months.'

Taking her hand in his, he drew Mary closer to his side.

'We will return when our work here is done and then we shall have many tales to tell and blessings to count.'

'Well, perhaps, William, before that day comes, you will feel able to tell me more about the cargo we are sending, at such trouble and expense, to your friend in Binghamton.'

'Mary, I shall, all in good time. Reverend West has been a constant source of support. To him I owe all that is good in my life.'

His wife turned to look at him intently and waited. His wry smile and shake of the head was soon followed by further explanation.

'Mary, have you forgotten that I was not always the good servant of God I endeavour to be today? Before we met I had fallen into the company of young men who were more interested in the fleeting entertainments offered by the tavern than the enduring joys of faith.

'It was Timothy West who brought me to the light. You must recall his preaching that May morning at the Tabernacle? There is a thread that runs from that day to this; from my apprenticeship at Enoch Salt's ironmonger's shop to our home here on Raiatea. It was he who inspired me to become a missionary. You know that we have corresponded ever since that time. In sending him this precious cargo, I am, in small measure, repaying a debt.'

'The number and size of those crates suggests that you consider the debt to be a large one, William.'

'Indeed I do. It could not be greater. It is comprised of the two elements that matter most to me; my eternal soul and you, who are my soul's companion here on earth.'

Mary squeezed her husband's hand. 'Thank you, William. You have made me a contented wife - and if I do sometimes suffer the weaknesses of worry when you are travelling to other islands or my longing for home, knowing that you are fulfilled makes it all bearable.'

For a few moments they stood in silence.

'Mary, there is another question you would ask of me?'

'No. Why do you say ... ?' she stuttered, sensing immediately that she had responded too quickly. Then, looking up at his weathered face, conveying an expression of such kindly concern, she sighed. 'Yes William, there is,' she conceded. 'I am puzzled by the secrecy concerning this cargo, this 'treasure'. Is it so ... necessary?'

'Mary, anything that is of great value excites unhealthy lusts and desires. I must proceed with caution. My friend was very particular in his instruction. He believes that there are many who would not understand his motives for acquiring these precious items. You know, only too well, that I have not endeared myself to many in our community by my criticisms of attitudes and practices of missionaries here in the South Seas. There are those who would frustrate our plans, were they to learn of them. The Reverend West, it is true, has his ... failings ... and these failings invite censure - but I believe that he is also a visionary and such men are not always understood.'

'He has enemies?'

'Detractors, Mary, and among them are men of our own church. He is a man unafraid of the truth – and such men make enem.... , detractors, as easily as we breathe. So, we must take care if we are to assist him in this work. '

'Of course, William,' answered Mary.

His brow furrowed.

'And I do not wish to excite the native people here either, were they to learn of our plans. With the help of native chiefs like our good friend Tamatoa, the work we have undertaken is proceeding well, but their new faith is not yet secure. Savage pagan beliefs and practices lie just below the surface.'

'But, then, perhaps you should delay your plans to sail to the New Hebrides …?'

'Nine months will soon pass, Mary. I have already delayed the voyage once. The work is important. I thought we were agreed …?'

'But nine months, William, more than two thousand miles distant with all the perils of the sea, illness, frightened natives. Our young sons need their father - and I need my husband.'

'Mary, I know how much I ask of you.'

She looked at him and her face softened. She gently shook her head and spoke softly, as though only to herself.

'Less, probably, than you ask of yourself.'

She struggled to force a new tone of resolve into her voice.

'The Lord spared me last year when I fell ill shortly after I first objected to your plans. I agreed then that if I recovered, you must go wherever your ministry took you. As you have kept your promise to Reverend West, so will I keep mine to you.'

Anxious now to further lighten the mood, Mary quietly squeezed her husband's hand again.

'And as to the matter of the secret cargo, I cannot say that I fully understand your meaning, William, but I will press you no further. You must do as you think fit.' She swung his hand forward with her own. 'Let us go down and join our dear friends on the beach. I wish to be assured that the Lord has been generous. I have asked for more dresses. The ones I have are so worn and faded.'

Her husband responded gratefully to the distraction she offered.

'Mary, you shall have your dresses and I shall delight in your wearing of them, I promise.'

IV
Glover College, Oxford, England, December 1973

With a boldness and verve that anyone who did not know her would have found surprising, the slight figure of Margaret McLaine manoeuvred her bicycle into the middle of the road, through a momentary opening in the oncoming stream of early morning traffic and, swerving to avoid an elderly woman and her dog, between the open and imposing wrought iron gates of Glover College. Dismounting, she easily found a space within the normally congested cycle racks. The vacation that follow -ed the end of Michaelmas term had just begun and a good number of undergraduates had already left the city.

Lifting a worn leather briefcase from her bicycle's large wicker basket, the young woman quickly brushed at her tweed skirt and matching jacket before striding, in her brown leather brogues, past the porter's lodge. She responded to the cheery, accented, 'Good morning, Miss McLaine', with a weak smile, before following the gravel path curving away to her right to approach one of Oxford's celebrated centres of learning.

As she skirted the immaculately manicured, circular lawn, she felt that she had never been happier to visit her old college, her 'alma mater', truly her 'nourishing mother'. Though, at less than a hundred years old, the building was one of Oxford University's least venerable, she never failed to be stirred by the sight of it. The central tower, some eighty feet in height, rose confidently, imposingly, above the front. She experienced a familiar sense of security and calm from the biscuit-coloured stone as it both absorbed the intensity and reflected the warmth of the early morning sun.

To her right, as though a benevolent arm extended to embrace and bring her safely towards the body of the building, stood the chapel. With its immense gothic windows and ornately decorated entrance this wing reached a height only exceeded by that of the tower. Here was the college's pinnacle of architectural excitement and of a design suited to its purpose. Within its walls, bathed in the coloured light that flooded through the stained glass windows, Margaret McLaine, like many young men and women before her, had, only a few years earlier, undergone the most profound spiritual experience.

Beyond the lawn, to her left, rose, in almost equal splendour, the parallel and matching 'arm'. Large elaborately carved stone lettering, composing the declaration 'SCIENTIA POTENTIA EST", revealed its major function; to house, on the first floor, the knowledge of the ages. Margaret considered that for the Victorian industrialists whose wealth had founded the college, 'power' was an obsession. If 'knowledge is power' and in this place, specifically spiritual power, then the twin engine rooms would be the library and the chapel. Designed for contemplation, the former had once nourished her mind as the latter had nourished her soul. She planned to spend a few revitalising hours in both places after her meeting.

Again, Margaret McLaine considered her debt to the college and the wider community of which it was a part. She had been raised a member of the Church of England in her Midlands home town but at school she had come under the influence of a denomination that offered so much more that the predictable comforts of what she now considered to be her parents' insipid faith. They had, at first, been tolerant of and then disappointed by their daughter's growing adherence to what they considered the uncompromising discipline of the dissenting church to which she had become attached. They found that they could do little to prevent their very bright daughter from following her wish to enrol at Glover College when she was successful in her application to Oxford University.

More than five years had passed since then and Margaret felt that her faith had deepened and matured. As a postgraduate student, soon to submit her doctoral thesis on *'The Missionary as Vanguard in the March of Victorian Spirituality'*, she was now at the point of searching for a new direction. This was why she felt so excited and alive on this bright morning. Professor Fielding had phoned only the day before and asked to meet at an early hour. She had arrived with time to spare but as she entered the building beneath the tower's projecting oriel window, swept past the marble bust of the founder to turn and enter a corridor that took her beneath a series of large portraits of 17th century Dissenting clerics dressed in uniform black robes, she now felt weightless in this place of such solemn and serious scholarship.

Professor Fielding had asked her to meet him in the Council Room. At the end of the corridor, a grand stone staircase led up to the library while the passage turned left, along the ground floor of the wing. Here she paused before large double doors, tugged briefly at the hem of her jacket, passed her left hand lightly across her brow to tame any stray hair that had escaped the band at the nape of her neck, placed a small gathered fist against the dark oak and knocked.

There was no reply. She knocked again then slowly turned the large, polished, circular doorknob. The room was empty. Around the walls hung a number of oil paintings in frames so elaborately gilded that they appeared to compete with the pictures themselves for the attention of the viewer. A number of the smaller canvasses were of landscapes and portraits of distinguished benefactors and academics but, as ever when in this room, Margaret was drawn to the dominant full-length portrayal of W.D. King, a tobacco magnate, whose generous bequests in the later decades of the 19th century had been so important to the financial independence of the college.

Margaret was so absorbed in studying this picture that she failed to hear the footsteps behind her.

'Miss McLaine, you are here before me.'

She quickly turned to face the man who had spoken, Professor George Arthur Fielding, Emeritus Professor of Modern Theology and one of her former tutors. Now in his seventies, the professor walked with the aid of a stick, its polished ivory mount enclosed within his large, arthritic, right hand. Though a tall man, she noted how age had worked to reduce his height. His eyes, however, set beneath a generous and unruly mop of white hair, were, as ever, bright with the intensity of energy and interest.

'Professor, it is a pleasure to see you again,' she smiled awkwardly as she reached forward to take his proffered hand.

'The pleasure is all mine, my dear. Please, do take a seat,' he added, steering her around a large table towards one of the heavy, ornately carved chairs in the corner of the room. 'You must forgive me, my dear, if an old man is impatient to come to the point of our meeting.'

'Not at all, Professor. I understand, you are ...'

'Yes, I know, a busy man,' he broke in, 'but that is no excuse for not observing the customs of polite society. I have followed your progress with interest and had regular reports from Dr Sorrell concerning your thesis. I look forward to reading it more fully.'

'Thank you, Professor. I hope you will feel that I have done justice to your teaching.'

'I am confident of that, my dear. However, it is your future, following the completion of your doctorate, which is currently of most concern to me.'

'My future?' Margaret replied, instantly regretting the urgency and volume with which she spoke.

'Yes, indeed, your future - and that of our shared faith.'

He paused to reassure himself that his choice of words had successfully conveyed the desired gravity.

'As you are all too aware, our church, our distinguished and distinct religious tradition, is presently very much at risk. Our membership is declining steadily across the country. We are finding it difficult to recruit for training in ministry, especially for missionary work, because we simply do not have the funds to support our young people. The college here in Oxford is, unhappily, now reduced to admitting some students with no affiliation to our church, simply in order to survive. Our life blood is being drained from us. These are difficult, even desperate times.'

Margaret McLaine nodded in agreement. She was only too aware of the picture the professor was describing.

'There has also been, as you know, the recent ... ,' the Professor paused in order to search for the appropriate word, now uttered with evident distaste, 'merger - with other Independent churches. A few of us, senior members all, have already found ourselves isolated by our resistance to the odious process of ... rationalisation. But, whatever the consequences, I simply cannot accept this dilution of all that is dear to us, that which makes us different, that which provides us with the unique purity of our truth and identity.' He paused again and looked directly at his guest, 'I had cause to think that you might think similarly.'

'Yes, of course. I do agree, Professor. The strength of our church was forged by the persecution and discrimination we suffered in previous centuries. Adversity made us strong. Today's comforts and compromises help to make us weak. I am particularly upset by the way some have suggested that we need to apologise to the underdeveloped nations for our missionary work. I know from my own research how much these men ... and women, have contributed to these societies. We should be proud, not ashamed, of that record.'

'I am pleased to hear you speak in this manner. I felt sure we could rely on you. However, there are, amid the gloom of our decline, some glimmers of light. We are a church that has benefited from the aid of generous persons in the past; men who were steadfast in their wish to see our message spread and our chapels prosper. When I entered the room you were looking at one of them, Sir William King.'

He turned his head toward the portrait. After a few seconds she glanced in his direction and waited, confident that he would continue.

'Yes,' he resumed, 'glimmers of light'... possibilities that have yet to be realised.' His eyes were now focussed intently on hers. 'We would like your help with one such possibility'.

'Anything, Professor ...' she replied with a rising sense of excitement.

V
Winter Hill School

With a final scan of the classroom, interrupted only by Amir when he briefly refused to break eye-contact, Mr Pearce turned and left the room. Not wishing to allow a tumult of gossip to fill the vacuum created by his departure, Miss Frobisher speedily resumed the lesson from the point at which she had been interrupted.

'Settle down everyone!' the teacher ordered then paused for her injunction to take effect. 'So, 9R, you know your task and you'll have the whole of the next half term to complete it. I will give you some time to work on it in lessons but this is your homework for the next seven or eight weeks. Now, in your small groups I want you to talk, quietly, about your shared project and how you plan to take the first steps. I will want to see each group's ideas before the end of the lesson. That gives you just twenty minutes.

Are there any questions?'

'Yes, Sarfraz?'

'When is the next holiday, Miss?'

'At the end of October, Sarfraz. So that's something for us all to look forward to. Yes, Mohammed?'

'So, we can choose who we work with?'

'On this occasion, yes,' she answered before swivelling sharply to look at two boys at a table to her right. 'Don't do that Darren, Josh – unless you want to clear up every scrap of paper that's on the floor when the bell goes.

'Where was I? Remember please, *small* groups; no more than four but I'd prefer three. Discuss ideas and then complete the handout with the questions that I'm sending round.'

Mrs Frobisher turned to a girl sitting directly in front of her, 'Chantelle, would you do that for me?'

'Yes, miss.'

'Thank you.'

Amid the rising buzz of voices Polly stopped chewing on some gathered strands of matted hair, brushed them aside, looked at her friend and softly groaned.

'Well, we'll be a group of two, Lucky, or three, if Muna ever comes back. I've got no ideas though. That will have to be your contribution.'

'So what exactly is your contribution, Polly?' asked the slender, delicately featured girl.

'It was my idea that we work together, Lucky,' Polly beamed.

'Yes, of course; inspirational, Polly. Well done!'

Polly slumped forward to rest her head on her forearms.

'I have no ideas, Lucky. Let's make it something that we can run off quickly. Please. It's all so boring.'

'Polly, we spend hours moaning that the teachers never give us the freedom to explore topics we are interested in and when they do, like Miss Frobisher just did a few minutes ago, you say it's boring!'

'Ok,' said Polly, lifting her head and brightening. 'You're right. I've had an idea. What if we start with my memory of the first day at school and mix it with that family history project I did in year 8. We can get away with just recycling stuff and adding a few extra bits and pieces'

'Do you mean the one about your grand-dad fighting in the First World War?'

'Yeah. Well, he wasn't my grand-dad, he was my dad's uncle, my great-uncle, and the important point is that he trained in the old Winter Hill College building just after the war started.'

'But how does that fit with what miss said about something that connects us, something to do with who we are today because of the past? I can see how it fits with you but not with me - or Muna.'

'Well, the soldiers trained in a building that's part of the school today. It's your school too and you've got memories of being here – that's to do with you. We could also include something about the way the school now has pupils from different backgrounds, different religions. We could use some of your memories about discovering your dad's Hindu culture.'

'Yes, maybe,' said Lucky 'but I'd rather we didn't just repeat what you've already done.'

At this point Miss Frobisher, who had been visiting a number of the tables in turn, encouraging groups to form and appoint someone who would complete the worksheet, interrupted the two girls. Behind the teacher, almost hidden from view, stood the boy who had recently entered the room with Mr Pearce.

'Polly, Lukhwinder, I see there's only the two of you in this group.'

'Yes, miss. We're happy like this. And Muna will be in our group when she comes back, miss. We work well together,' replied Polly, a note of anxiety in her voice.

'Well, I'd like you to agree to add a fourth member,' insisted the teacher, ignoring their obvious lack of enthusiasm. 'Umar hasn't got a group and I know that I can rely on you ...'

'But miss, you said it was best to have no more than three. We've already got our idea sorted and I don't think Umar ...'

'Yuh can figet dat! Me doan wanna be part a yuhr crusty group,' the boy angrily broke in.

'Umar – please – that isn't helpful. Girls, I'm sorry but I'm going to insist on this and Umar if you are uncooperative then I'll be asking Mr Pearce to get in touch with your mother.'

The teacher turned back to the girls with a softer expression. 'Polly, Lucky, there aren't very many people I can ask for help with on this and Umar *has* to be part of a group.'

'Doan worry 'bout me, miss,' interrupted Umar, 'Me doan wanna be part-a group wid a gori an a men-tul cay-us.'

'Umar! That's enough! One more word from you and you'll be back in the support unit full-time. I only agreed to you attending these lessons because you said you liked English and would behave yourself. Do you understand me?'

Umar bowed his head and muttered. The teacher

understood that his stooped posture conveyed not just resentment but compliance as well.

'Right, sit down there, Umar and try to be positive. I know that you have a lot to offer. Girls, don't forget, I want something down on this sheet of paper pretty quickly. Any ideas yet?'

'Yes, miss', the girls uttered miserably in unison as Umar noisily dragged a chair into a position from which it would appear that he was in the group, even if he had no intention of taking part.

'Well, quickly, tell me. I may be able to help.'

'We thought we'd start with Polly's memory of the old college building and how she always thought it was a mysterious place,' said Lukhwinder.

'Yeah, we thought we might do some research on other people's memories and find out about the history of the old building, perhaps, when it was used in the war.'

'Wha' wahr dat den?' Umar asked irritably. 'How cud a school 'ave bin in a wahr?'

'No,' Polly sighed. 'Before it was a school this building was used to train soldiers to fight in the First World War. Don't tell me you don't know about the First World War?'

'Course me know 'bout de stupid wahr.'

'But Polly', said Lucky, 'there's more history than that? The building is even older than the First World War. Wasn't it a religious building first, miss? Why don't we go even further back in history for the project and find out how it started?'

'Well,' added Miss Frobisher, 'looks to me like

you've got some good ideas already. But if you want to know more about the building why don't you speak to Dr McLaine? She knows a lot about the history.'

'Miss McLaine! The Wick ...!' Polly tried desperately to strangle the words as they emerged uncensored.

'Yes Polly, *that* Dr McLaine. The 'Wicked Witch of the West'; was that what you were going to say? I've heard this nonsense before and I'm surprised you can be so silly. Try not to be so narrow-minded. Dr McLaine has a lot to offer you – if you are serious about this. Now, let's get on with it, please - all of you!'

Miss Frobisher turned and moved to an adjacent table.

'Dey say dere djinn in de ole buildin' when yuh here on yuhr own at night,' Umar offered in a more friendly tone.

'Gin?' queried Polly.

'Ghosts, evil spirits' explained Lukhwinder. 'Asian people call them djinns.'

Polly shrugged her shoulders. 'What about my old project, Lucky? We should still use some of that.'

'Well, we can,' responded Lucky. 'It can be part of it, part of the story. What's the matter, Polly?'

Polly had sat upright in her seat with her eyes wide and her mouth momentarily frozen in a perfect circle.

'Yuh-a one strange gori,' muttered Umar.

'I've just remembered something. My dad has got some of my great-uncle's letters written to his parents when he was a soldier in France. There are things in the letters about the time he was here in the building and he talks about ghosts and monks and the time before it became a barracks. Dad says there's a mystery about the letters which has never been solved.'

'That sounds cool. We could say to miss that our memories of the building link us to your dad and then your great-uncle and maybe people before then.'

Umar laughed loudly and slammed the table with his fist.

'Well, yuh gals can do yuh ting wid dis histry stuff, but na wid me. 'N' me tell yuh 'nudder ting, me na goin ta tark ta dat mad wu-mahn, needer. Me doin nutten.'

'Umar why do you do that black guy talk? You're Asian. Anyway I think that you're just scared of the djinns,' retorted Lucky.

Before Umar could respond, the teacher interrupted and asked all groups to hand in their paperwork. Lukhwinder quickly wrote a few words on the worksheet and Polly promised to get hold of her great-uncle's letters and bring them to school the following day.

'Me in de 'pri-zon' tomorra,' said Umar. 'So, yuh can figet 'bout me.'

'Why are you in there anyway?' asked Polly.

'Cos dey say me batter dis kid 'n' canna go ta lessun, cayse me batter him agin. Anyway, if yuh bring de letta, me may wag it tomorra 'n' meet wid yuh,' insisted Umar, getting up from his chair and with a hip-rolling swagger moving towards the door as the bell sounded and the teacher gave permission for everyone to leave.

'First he says he's *'doin' nutten'* then he says he wants to meet us. He's going to be such a pain to work with,' sighed Lucky.

'Yeah, but I agree with one thing that Umar said; we can do this without any help from the 'Wicked Witch of the West'.'

VI
Glover College

Professor Fielding leaned forward placing one pale, tarantula-shaped hand over the other in order to transfer a greater portion of his weight through the length of his upright walking stick. His sunken, rheumy eyes looked directly into those of Margaret McLaine.

'What I have to tell you now has to be treated in the strictest confidence, my dear. These are matters known only to a few. These 'few' are people of great integrity and influence, worthy of the highest respect - but I am not yet ready to reveal their names,' he added with emphasis.

'Of course, I understand,' she replied immediately in an effort to reassure him.

He paused momentarily before continuing.

'As you know, our church had a number of academies or colleges in the last century. Almost all have now closed. Some have been demolished while others have been converted for alternative use.'

Margaret nodded. She recalled reading a book about these 19th century colleges and their work in educating young men for Ministry. At that time their church needed independent institutions because entry to the ancient universities of Oxford and Cambridge was denied to anyone who did not pledge allegiance to the established church, the Church of England.

'One of these, Winter Hill, in Binghamton, is the predecessor to our own Glover College. Were you aware of this? Binghamton is not far from your family home, I believe? You must know the place?'

Margaret nodded in assent. Forty miles from her family home, Binghamton was a large, industrial city. She knew it to have been a major centre for Independent churches in the 19th century.

'I know the city of course, Professor, but not very well,' she replied. 'I have never heard of Winter Hill, however, and I am embarrassed to admit that I was not aware that Glover College was founded elsewhere'.

'There is no need to be embarrassed. The college moved to Oxford and was renamed more than a hundred and twenty years ago. The original, a fine building dating back to 1840, is much altered and now part of a school. It is a boys' grammar at present but I have heard rumours that it too, will shortly be - modernised - and become one of this government's new comprehensive schools.'

'I see, but how does this school offer any hope to our church?'

'In all honesty, I cannot be sure of the answer to that question. But what I can tell you is that some years ago when I was a young lecturer here, Glover College was approached by an antiquarian bookseller in Yorkshire. He had purchased the contents of a private library and it included the journal of a young scholar who attended Winter Hill in the early 1850s. He undertook some research and discovered the connection between Winter Hill and Glover College. When he approached us with a view to a sale, the Principal asked me to deal with the matter and I'm glad that he did.'

'This journal is important then, Professor?'

'Indeed it is. The young man, a Samuel Ferrington, writes about the daily life at Winter Hill, all of which is of some little interest, but just before the journal ends, abruptly, he refers to a meeting with a Reverend West, pastor of Mount Zion Chapel in Binghamton. Have you heard of him?'

'No, I'm afraid I've never heard of the man or his chapel.'

'Well, Reverend West, though once a man of some importance in the Midland counties, is someone whose legacy to our church is now best forgotten. However Ferrington, a friend of West's it would appear, was given something to keep, a letter. He was given instruction not to open it but told that it contained information that might one day lead to the recovery of a 'great prize', a 'valuable treasure', for the benefit and glory of our church. Despairing as I was, of the weak leadership shown by our senior members and believing that we may one day have need of this 'prize' to fund our resurgence as a force in the world, I entrusted only a few close friends with the knowledge of this secret.'

'But what could this wealth be? Where? I am astonished ...'.

'I cannot say where it is or what it is – only that we have very good reason to believe that it still exists somewhere within the building. Believe me, we have looked for it on many occasions, sometimes even helping the school to pay for building alterations so that we could send in people to search without arousing suspicion. To date, we have not been successful'.

'Then the wealth, the treasure, whatever it is, may no longer be there?'

'It may not. But even if the wealth is not there, the secret to its whereabouts must be. For a number of years we have positioned a 'watcher' within the school to, how shall I put it?... safeguard our interests ... but illness has forced the current volunteer to leave his post.'

'But, if I may ask, do we know anything more about the nature of this 'treasure' or 'prize'?'

Professor Fielding felt both irritation and satisfaction. He was irritated because he had hoped to avoid revealing too much detail to his interviewee before she had committed herself and satisfied because her questions confirmed his view that she had the intelligence and directness he required of her.

Momentarily, he shifted more of his weight onto his walking stick, then his feet and slowly emerged from the chair. He turned and walked towards a picture of a pastoral landscape on the wall and stood before it. Carefully placing the stick against the wall, he moved the elaborate, gilt- framed picture aside with one hand, to reveal a metal square inserted into the wall. With his other hand he turned a recessed dial a number of times before pulling on a small handle. An expensively-engineered, heavy metal door swung open. With care and deliberation he reached inside, removed a small leather-bound book and returned to the chair.

'This is Ferrington's journal, my dear, and there is

another item of interest within.'

He opened the worn cover and extracted a piece of paper.

'Do you know who this is?' he asked, handing it to her.

She looked carefully at what was evidently a drawing of a middle-aged man in a wide-brimmed hat, set against a backdrop of tropical palms and native dwellings.

'It is evidently a portrait of a European male. From his clothing and the surroundings, I would guess that he might be a missionary but I have never seen this picture before and the features are not very clear.'

'No, my dear, you would not have seen this before; even a missionary scholar such as yourself. This is a drawing of William John. You are familiar with the name?'

'William John? Yes, of course', she replied. 'The apostle of Polynesia'. He was killed by natives in the late 1830s.'

'That is correct. The drawing is an informal one made by his wife, Mary, who obviously had some raw talent. The reason you have never seen this drawing before has something to do with the informality of the scene'.

The young woman looked again at the drawing and noted that the man had discarded his topcoat and appeared to be carrying a large bladed tool, perhaps for cutting back the undergrowth.

'Yes, we know that John was a strong, practical man, well-equipped for the hardships of missionary life. He was once apprenticed to an ironmonger or blacksmith, I believe. But it is, nevertheless, unusual to see a portrait of such a person without his coat – or even, for that matter, his clerical hat. Formality was expected, even in the tropical climate of the South Seas,' she reflected aloud.

'But there is something else that is unusual. Look more closely ... perhaps at his upper arm ....'

She looked again, under his instruction, and went immediately to the dark area at the top of the man's left arm. Previously she had passed over this as a mark or smudge in the drawing but could now see that beneath the line of his rolled up shirt there appeared to be something, an elaborate pattern, painted on, or possibly etched into, the man's muscular flesh.

'I see it now. Can that really be what it appears to be?' she asked.

'I think so, Miss McLaine. Unusual, is it not, for a man of our faith?'

The professor's words were interrupted by a light knock at the door, which then opened to reveal a young girl carrying a tray with teapot and china cups.

Professor Fielding had already turned with unaccustomed speed, to face the door.

'What the devil? Who are *you* girl? Whatever do you want?'

The girl's bright smile instantly faded. She stuttered a reply to her elderly, irritated, inquisitor.

'Ex… excuse me for interrupting sir, … I'm Lizzie … I'm helping in the kitchens. Mrs Evans says she thought you'd like a cup of tea, you and your visitor, sir. She also says to tell you that there's an urgent phone call from the principal in your office.'

'Oh, really? I don't recall telling anyone about my meeting with Miss McLaine. Well, put the tray down young lady and then leave us, please.'

As he spoke, he glanced in the direction of the safe, the door to which was still visible. Standing open as it was, it prevented the painting from returning to its normal position.

The girl followed his gaze to the wall as she moved to where they were now both standing. Margaret McLaine, seeing the professor's confusion and concern, quickly placed the drawing on the table and went to the wall to fetch his walking stick. As she did so, she deftly closed the door allowing the painting to cover the safe.

She passed the stick to the professor while the girl busied herself with finding a place to position the tray. The professor apologised to his guest, promising to return very quickly and left the room.

Within ten minutes he had returned to find Margaret

McLaine standing at the window, deep in thought, her cup of black tea nestled in one hand with the other lightly holding the thin, white porcelain handle.

'Well, that proved to be a wild goose chase,' the professor grunted with exasperation. 'I can only assume that the principal had decided that the matter could wait after all. Where is that girl, by the way?'

'She left, Professor, I thought it advisable. Can I pour you a cup of tea?'

'Please; white, no sugar. Now where were we …?'

'Professor, forgive me for interrupting you ... I would like to say something. I know that there is much that you have yet to tell me and I am eager to learn but while you have been out of the room I have been thinking.'

'You have, my dear?'

Margaret knew she had reached the most significant point in her life. There could be no doubt about her decision. Here was an opportunity to make herself useful to the community she valued above all else. She understood that this would call for sacrifice and she was prepared for that; in fact, she welcomed it.

'I think I know what it is that you wish to ask of me; that you would like me to secure a post at this school and either find the key to 'the prize' myself or inform you if someone else should stumble upon it. I have yet to understand the missionary connection but feel sure that my training has helped prepare me for the task you have in mind. Professor, I will become your new 'watcher''.

The older man reached forward to take her hand in his.

'Excellent. I am so pleased, my dear. We have such

high hopes for you. Higher than you could ever imagine … but that must wait. Your placement will not be difficult. We will use one of our many levers of influence. And you are correct - there is more for me to tell you. However I want to be sure that you understand one thing above all others; nothing is more important than the concealment of your true purpose and the recovery of our wealth. Anyone or anything that threatens either of these has to be - managed.'

Margaret struggled to conceal a new intensity of excitement, a thrill that she might be required to do that which is forbidden, but for the greater good.

'Do I take you to mean,' she hesitated as she searched for the appropriate words, 'that threats to our quest may need to be 'silenced'?'

Professor Fielding looked again at this young woman with renewed interest.

'I think we understand one another, Miss McLaine. But remember that our actions must at all times be ….. proportionate. We are not Jesuits, after all.'

After a brief pause for her to absorb the subtleties of his words he began to sweep his eyes around the room, to the table, the chairs and the floor. He lifted the tea tray and placed it to one side.

Then the professor turned again to look at her with a furrowed brow and a discernible note of anxiety in his voice.

'My dear, where is the drawing?'

VII
Winter Hill School

The following morning, on her way to school, Polly met Muna in the corner shop. After exchanging views on the 'telly' from the previous evening, Polly took the opportunity to tell her tall, elegant, Somali friend about the idea for the 'shared memory project'. Muna showed little enthusiasm for the task until Polly mentioned the mysterious letter written by her great uncle and her plan to share the contents that day with the group, as soon as they could all meet up.

When they arrived in the top playground they spotted Lucky on the far side and headed in her direction. As they approached, Polly could see that her friend was in an animated discussion with two girls. She was used to this. Lucky was not the most popular girl in the school. Polly had already considered that this was partly because her friend was bright and able to do well without ever appearing to try very hard but also, if she were honest, because Lucky was more than a little 'odd'. Apart from being uninterested in many of the things that many girls at the school spent their time talking about, like clothes, pop stars, 'soaps' and boys, her friend had the habit, every so often, of going into a strange mood, a kind of day-dream. One of their teachers, Mr Thomas, jokingly referred to Lucky's tendency 'to go walkabout'. Others were not so amused or tolerant. They considered her reluctance to share their interests as arrogance. Then there were those who found her behaviour unsettling, even disturbing.

On one recent occasion, after yet another argument with her parents, this time about her wish to have a small tattoo inscribed on her right hip, Polly had sought refuge at her friend's house. Lucky's mother answered the door and told her to go up to the bedroom. When Polly tried the door it wouldn't open. She knew that there was no lock and that somehow the door must have been deliberately jammed. She knocked lightly and called her friend's name but there was no reply. She pushed and eventually felt the obstruction slide sufficiently on the wooden floor to give her the room she needed to squeeze her head through the opening.

The curtains were drawn and in the dim light Polly could see Lucky sitting cross-legged on the floor. Something about the stillness in the room encouraged her to move carefully. With a little more effort she was able to ease herself around the still-wedged door. Lucky did not respond. Her eyes were closed but Polly could see that she held her head erect and was breathing regularly. Scattered about the floor in front of her were photos of her father and mother, together with a few letters and other handwritten notes. Polly resisted the thought that she should fetch Lucky's mum. Instead, she sat down on the bed and waited.

After about ten minutes, Lucky suddenly opened her eyes, flexed her neck from side to side and, seeing Polly sitting in the gloom, smiled softly and stood up. At first her friend would say little about her trance-like experience, only that, if she could find the right time and place, it was possible to 'visit' her father. She said that she missed him a lot and had discovered in the last few months that she had the ability to go back and be with him. She said that each time she did this it became easier and that she could 'stay away' for longer periods – as long as she had some photos and things of her father's to help 'connect' her. Polly had found this idea to be a little creepy and chose not to question her friend any further. Lucky sensed her embarrassment and said no more.

Now, as she came close to where Lucky stood, the girls with her, Charmaine and Miriam, turned and looked coolly at Polly.

'Here come your only friends, have fun, yogurt,' Charmaine drawled before lifting her head in an exaggerated manner and walking away.

'What was that all about? Why 'yogurt'?' asked Polly.

'I wish I knew,' replied Lucky. 'The 'yogurt' thing, I assume, is because someone knows I go to yoga classes; very witty eh? People like Charmaine seem to think that makes me stuck-up, a snob. What a joke? Me? Someone who can't afford more than one pair of shoes, a snob!'

'Forget about them, Lucky. They're just immature idiots. You're not a snob,' Polly said with a smile, 'I'd soon tell you if you were! Look, I've brought that letter I told you about.'

Polly slid her hand into the canvas bag slung across her shoulder.

'We must be careful though, because my dad'll kill

me if it's damaged; says one day he's going to do some research on it himself.'

'How old is your dad?'

'Dunno for sure. He works at the University; fifty something, nearly sixty, perhaps. He's a lot older than my mum. When she wants to upset him she reminds him that she was a student at university and he was one of her lecturers. Anyway, he's always saying he can't retire until I've been to university myself. But he won't miss this for a few days ...'

Polly extracted a card folder from the bag and opened it to draw out a grey envelope marked with War Ministry date stamps. She carefully lifted the flap on the envelope.

'There are quite a few of these. Dad says the first one was sent soon after his uncle left Winter Hill barracks and went somewhere into the countryside to do more training, but this time with real weapons. To begin with they're full of stuff about what a great time they're having but dad says you can tell, soon after they get to France, that he's not so happy, that he's keeping something back, hiding his real feelings from his parents'.

'Chaw, whassat 'bout den? Wha's he hidin'?' interrupted Umar, who had suddenly appeared behind them.

'Umar! Don't do that! I said, my great-uncle Arthur, was hiding his feelings, you div,' Polly responded irritably, before continuing. 'Dad says he was trying to protect them. He didn't want them to worry about him. He was probably seeing some pretty horrible stuff. But he seems to want them to understand something about his life as well, because he keeps writing about who he is and what he'll leave behind if something happens to him.'

'Yeah, me saw dis movie de udder night 'bout fightin' in Zerbia. Dey do sum sair-ree-us fightin' ting dere man, 's cool.'

Polly and Lucky looked disdainfully at Umar. They briefly and unknowingly mimicked each other in shaking their heads.

'So, is this the letter that mentions the mystery?' asked Lucky.

'Yeah and you must all promise not to tell anyone about it.'

Polly turned and looked intently at each of them and they all nodded in assent; 'Yeah, course mahn!', 'Agreed,' from Lucky and a soft 'uh-huh' from Muna.

'I'll read it to you. It's not a long letter. None of them were long. Funny writing they had then but I've got used to it. Dad says that in those days they were taught how to write properly, not like us.'

'Me writin' good!'

Muna quickly added, 'Only when you're using the computer, Umar - but even then you can't spell.'

Umar growled and Polly told them both to 'shut up'.

'Here it is. Listen to this;

August 8th 1916
Dear Mam, Pops, Ellie, Albert, Beatrice, Paul and Josie,

'Crazy names, mahn, an' almost as many kids as yuhr

fam'ly, Muna,' interrupted Umar, which led to the others issuing concerted 'shushes'. Polly continued.

Just a few lines to let you know that I am still safe and well.

The food parsel and letters come yesterday. Thanks ever so. George wants me to thank you to, because he's already eaten half the choccolate! He says he's going to make a ~~speshul~~ special trip to take Pops for a drink when he gets home and bring you, Mam, a lace shawl like the ones we've seen in some of the Frenchy and Belgium villages we marched through.

My boots are a bit of a mess and hurt a couple of hours after I've put them on but I expect they'll get easier soon. Please don't worry about me, I'm fine.

Thanks for the news about Wallys mam. I knew she would take it hard. Wally was always talking about her. We try not to think about him too much which may sound strange but I do miss his larking about.

How are the little 'uns? Behaving I hope? Talking about scamps - how is Patch? I miss the old mutt. Never thought I'd say it but I would love to have him jump up at me now with his muddy paws, wagging his tail and drooling all over me with his wet chops. Give him a scratch from me and please make sure that he stays off Potterton's allotment because I fear what that old fool will do one day if Patch narks him again.

How are Pops early cabbages? I hope he's having more luck getting rid of the caterpillers and bugs than we're having with the Boche! When I think back to a few months ago and we was training in the old college and keen as mustard to be out here, it just don't seem possible. One thing's for sure though - we shouldn't have worried about missing the action. This war is going to go on for some time yet they say, though the top brass keep telling us there'll be a breakthrough soon.

No real news on when we will be home next but it'll probably be a while.

If you should see Maisie Leach tell her 'thanks' for the postcard in your letter. Thank her to for coming down to see us on our perade through the town. Tell her that I <u>did</u> see her waving but didn't want to let anyone down by grinning back at her. That was my mistake. Perhaps you could also say that I'll make sure to visit when I get back.

'Whoa. Maisie Leach eh? He's got de hots feh dis Maisie,' Umar laughed. Polly smiled and paused to glance at Umar with mild surprise at his insight.

'Shut-up Umar,' said Lucky. 'Let her finish.'

There's something else I want you (Pops) to know. When Charlie, Walter, George and me were sharing one of those tiny rooms in the college we found something which had been hidden inside the chimney. It was so cold that winter and there was no coals for the fire so we was trying to stuff an old blanket up the chimney to stop the draft. Well there was this hole in the brickwork and I put my hand in and pulled out a rusty old tin. We don't know how it got there but they say that monks once lived in the building so perhaps one of them had left it.

I threw it onto my bunk and forgot about it for a while but we tried to open it later and eventually managed it. Inside was a piece of folded paper, thick paper it was and obviously old.

We tried to read what it said but most of it was a jumbled up mess of letters and numbers which didn't make any sense, then a short piece of writing, like a poem. George said it looked like some sort of message which got us all very excited.

On the other side in pencil was a note saying that the letter was a clue to the finding of a great prize. The writer hoped that no-one would ever find the tin because if they did then it meant that he had died without solving the mystry and the quest was now for others.

What do you make of that Pops? We thought about who we should tell but decided it was too good a mystry to share with anyone. We never had enough time to do much with it because of the training and chores and then we were moved out to Mollvern.

But now I'd like you to know about it and not just George and me because otherwise the thing may disappear again for who knows how many years? Charlie always said we should try to solve it when we got back but he's not going to be in any state to do that now.

Anyways we agreed to put it back where we found it and perhaps you'd like to know where that is – just in case? The room is the Paul one along on the Philpott house of Auntie Gladys's wing, under the Arthur floor. The hole I hid it in was exactly number 6's age (next week) above the floor and a King Edward distance from the point where the flue joins the outside wall with the window.

Well that's all from me, for now. Please keep sending the parsels and letters. They are a great cumfort. I'll write again soon. Remember me in your prayers. You are all in mine.

Your loving son,

Arthur

PS Tell number 5 that I won't forget the promise. I'm still looking for a good piece of German kit but will definately bring him something back home.

'Wha dat 'bout?' muttered Umar.

'I think he's promised to bring his younger brother something back from the war, a memento; dad says, probably something from a dead German soldier,' suggested Polly.

'Na, me doan mean dat. Dat udder stuff 'bout where de tin is.'

'Yeah,' added Lucky, 'it doesn't make sense; 'The Paul one along'; what does that mean? Read that last bit again Polly.'

Polly did so and then waited as the others looked at one another and exchanged puzzled expressions.

For a short time she enjoyed their confusion, then, she added, through a huge smile, 'I can tell you what it means.'

Polly's friends were now listening intently.

'You see, dad says his uncle was trying to hide his instructions. Look at these stamps on the envelope. See? That says, 'Army Post Office' with a smudged date and the other says, 'Passed by Field Censor.'

'What's a Field Censor?' asked Muna.

'Dad says soldiers' letters had to be read by these army people, called censors, before their letters were sent back to England because they didn't want them writing about things to do with the war.'

'Why not?'

'Because the Germans might capture the letters and learn stuff about the French and British armies and even what they were planning to do next. They were always planning something - like using a new weapon or where to start a new attack.'

'I see,' added Lucky. 'So your great-uncle... what was his name again?'

'Arthur'.

'So Arthur was being careful to hide the information from the censors by inventing his own code.'

'Exactly!'

'Wait a minute Polly! Are you saying that you think the tin may never have been found; that it may still be here in the building?'

'Yes, I am. Well, I don't know for sure, but it could be. You see, not long after this letter got back to England there was another one, from the War Office, telling them that Arthur had been killed in the fighting at a place called Delville Wood, three weeks after his nineteenth birthday. Apparently his mother took everything belonging to her son and shut it up in his bedroom and wouldn't let anyone go in there. Sometimes her other children, including my dad's dad, that's Paul, talked about how she would go into the room for hours and they would sit on the stairs and sometimes hear her crying. It scared them all. Their mum died about ten years later. She was only forty-nine. They say she never recovered from losing her eldest son, it broke her heart.'

'And the letter ... what happened?' asked Lucky

'Well, dad said that when my grandfather read it again it was after the college had become a school, sometime in the 1920s. They made a lot of changes to the wings because they wanted bigger rooms so they could have classrooms. When my dad went to the school in the 50s and 60s he looked but couldn't find anything like the small rooms his uncle wrote about, or any fireplaces, so they never did anything with it, though they did spend some time playing about with the hidden message ...'

'And – did they work it out?'

'Most of it – it was pretty easy really but it was stuff you'd only know if you were part of the family'.

'Me doan get it!'

'Like I said, Umar, you'd have to know about the

family. Look, the coded bits are these; *'the room is the Paul one along'* ... *'on the Philpott house'* ... *'of Auntie Gladys's wing'* ... *'under the Arthur floor'* ... *'and the hole I hid it in was exactly number 6's age (next week) above the floor'* ...' and a King Edward distance from the point where the flue joins the wall which has the window in it.'

'Arthur's mum and dad would have been able to work out what it meant pretty quickly ...'

'N' ennywahn who waant de seecret could tort-cher dem if dey doan tark,' offered Umar but the others ignored him as Polly continued.

'... but I guess the army had lots of letters to read and really weren't that bothered about a silly tin.'

'Or perhaps they never read it,' suggested Lucky. 'Like teachers always say they read your homework but sometimes I think they just put a tick on every page.'

'So, come on then,' said Muna, eagerly. 'Tell us what it means Polly.'

'Well, ok,' replied Polly, pausing for dramatic effect. She was enjoying the way that the others were giving her their full attention. *The room is the Paul one along'* means the *fifth* one along the corridor because Paul was the fifth child in the family. Apparently the parents sometimes called their children by numbers, rather than names; it was a bit of a family joke. Remember the PS when Arthur says he hasn't forgotten his promise to number 5. He's letting his parents know how to decode the instructions.'

'This is great,' enthused Lucky. 'It's beginning to make sense.'

'Yes, but then it gets a bit difficult. Dad doesn't

understand, *'on the Philpott house'*. He says he's never heard of Philpott and can't remember his dad explaining it either.

'What about the others?' Muna said.

"Auntie Gladys's wing', that means the west wing because Auntie Gladys married Tom West …'

'Which is the west wing?' asked Muna.

'That part alongside the road. There's the front of the college facing the playing fields and then two wings that go back to make a kind of a C shape, like three sides of a square …'

'Rectangle, Polly.'

'Whatever, Lucky. The west wing is the one with the two floors and classrooms for our 6th form. The East wing has been made into the gym with the changing room and weights room underneath.'

'Yeah, yeah. G'wan wid de rest, gal.'

'Ok, the next bit is *'under the Arthur floor'*. Well, remember that Arthur was the oldest, so he was number 1, or the first child. So, this means, 'under the 1st floor', in other words, the ground floor.'

'and the hole I hid it in was exactly number 6's age (next week) above the floor.' Well, Josie, who was number six, was exactly three and a half years old a week after the letter was dated. So, Arthur was saying that the hole was three and a half feet up from the floor *'and King Edward distance from the point where the flue joins the wall which has the window in it.'* That's the distance in from the wall. This is the bit I like best; my great grandfather had an allotment and grew a lot of potatoes. Do you know what a King Edward is if you grow vegetables?'

The others shook their heads. Polly smiled and continued.

'A King Edward is a potato, what they call a 'main crop' potato which means that you plant it later than some of the other kinds of potatoes and dig it up in the late summer'.

'But how does that help us?'

'Dad asked grand-dad about this before he died and he said that the distance between rows of main crop potatoes is two feet.'

'So', said Lucky, touching in turn each of the fingers on her left hand with the index finger of her right hand. The tin is hidden in the chimney of the *fifth* room along the corridor on the *west* side of the building, *three and half feet* up from the floor and *two feet* in from the window.

'Well done Lucky – but we still don't know what 'the Philpott house' means,' Muna reminded her.

'Does it matter? I think we can find it without that information can't we? We seem to have everything we need.'

'Yuh sayin' dat we look fa it now, mahn?' asked Umar.

'Why not?'

'Me tink yuh-a figettin' sumting.'

Polly interrupted, 'Umar's right. Dad was a student here, remember. He said that he looked for the fifth room in the west wing and there wasn't one; just classrooms. He says that everything's been changed and there are no fireplaces any more.'

There was silence. They were all deflated by the thought that they could go no further. But Lucky had an idea.

'Ok, why don't we do what Miss Frobisher said and at least speak to Miss McLaine? If she knows so much about the building maybe she can help.'

'I dunno. She's weird. I don't even know where to find her.'

'Oh, come on Polly. What have we got to lose? She's in the old building somewhere. We'll find her and I'll come with you,' offered Lucky. Muna nodded in support.

'Well, yuh can count me out, mahn. Dat wuh-man doan like me – if yuh go, yuh go widdout me pro-teck-shun!'

VIII
Winter Hill College, October 1851

Samuel Posthumous Ferrington lifted the rough serge blanket above his shoulders and gathered the edges tightly beneath his chin with his left hand. Sitting at his desk he coughed weakly then shivered as a single tear landed on the blank page of his journal. The desk was piled high with well-worn texts of Greek, Latin and Hebrew primers and papers that lay scattered beside them. Samuel, however, was not absorbed in his work or interested in adding an entry to his journal. In the small, cell-like, study, he was preoccupied with other concerns.

His room had little in the way of furniture. An east facing window threw some welcome light onto the dark oak desk carefully positioned against the adjacent wall. On the wall opposite the window, a door gave access to the central corridor along which were ranged another fifteen similar studies, eight on either side, for the use of the scholars. An identical wing to the east side of the Front Range provided accommodation for another sixteen students. On the fourth wall, to the left of the door, stood a small bookcase with neatly ordered texts and a fireplace that ran at a forty-five degree angle to return to the exterior wall. In the centre of the room a small, soot-marked, square, woollen rug gave a much-needed, if very faint, note of warmth to an otherwise bare wooden floor.

Despite the cold there was no fire in the grate. Scholars were only allowed coal for both their studies and bedrooms, of identical proportions on the floor above, between the months of November and April. Today was October 5th. Samuel coughed again. He and his fellow scholars had been trained, from an early age, to accept, even welcome, physical discomfort. They were told by their elders that it was to be viewed as a test of their capacity to endure the hardships that were all a part of the life of a dissenting Christian. Nevertheless, he wondered how he, and they, would survive the next few weeks if the wind continued to blow from the north-east.

But today the cold was not Samuel's greatest worry.

He had not long returned from an interview with the College Board held in the first floor room of the central tower that rose imperiously above the roofs of the front elevation. After waiting for nearly an hour on the narrow and steep wooden staircase that gave access to the Council Room, Samuel had been summoned by the morose, elderly college servant. He had stood facing the five seated board members with their lengthy, black gowns gathered about them. Three faces among this gathering of sinister corvids, were familiar to him; two college tutors and the man seated in the centre, the fleshy, ruddy features of the chairman of the Board, Reverend James Angel.

Despite the roaring coal fire in the hearth, the

atmosphere in the Council Room had been anything but warm. Nervous as he was, Samuel had found it difficult to look directly into the penetrating gaze of the Reverend Angel. He focussed instead on a point seen through the windows behind the distinguished chairman's right shoulder. This was the tall, tapering, pointed, stone obelisk that stood at the end of the avenue of young trees that marched across the field towards the boundary of the College grounds.

Reverend Angel had proceeded to question Samuel, very closely, on matters related to the young man's religious beliefs, questions he thought he had answered confidently and fully. What had surprised him was the allegation made by one of the panel that some of his fellow scholars had reported him to the Board for questioning the way in which the church was led. The college principal, Professor Barker, a most severe-looking and slight figure had confirmed that two of his scholars had also raised the matter with him, anonymously.

After further discussion concerning his academic weaknesses, the Board decided that Samuel was to be sent home and asked to reconsider his theological views with the help of his family pastor and father. Flustered and surprised by the severity of the Board's judgement, Samuel had found it difficult to defend himself. All he could think about was the response to this news that he could expect from his parents. He knew they had made many sacrifices to enable him to start, more than a year ago, his five-year training for ministry.

Perplexed, troubled and cold, Samuel now struggled

to hold back his tears. He was still only nineteen years old and felt a very long way from the comfort of his parents' modest but respectable home in Halifax. He looked at the empty hearth and thought how comforting it would be to see the bright, lively features of the servant, Bessie Smith, who had recently begun to help with the tending of the fires and handling the laundry for the scholars. There were few moments of female light-heartedness and laughter in the college, such as those he enjoyed at home with his mother and sisters, but Bessie's occasional visits, with her questions about college life and interest in his views, had always helped to lift his mood.

When the knocking on his door announced the arrival of someone with obvious urgency and authority, he uttered a brief, 'one moment, please', in order to give himself the time to quickly wipe his eyes and cheeks with a handkerchief, blow his nose, close his journal, return the blanket to the closet and straighten his jacket.

He opened the door to find the Reverend James Angel standing before him, clutching some papers beneath his left arm. In a soft, avuncular voice the older man spoke first; 'May I come in Samuel. I believe we may have need of one another'.

'Yes of course, Reverend Angel. Please …' and the younger man stood aside with his arm outstretched in invitation.

'I'm afraid I don't have much in the way of seating …'

Reverend Angel waved his hand dismissively. 'I have been seated all morning Samuel, attending to Board business. I am content to stand. But, please …' and he gestured toward the chair.

'I will stand, sir. I could not sit if you were not also seated.'

Reverend Angel looked quickly around the room. 'It would appear that the option is unavailable anyway, Master Samuel. And it is cold here. Comfort may be a cause of lethargy but we must make allowances for inclement weather. I will see to it immediately.'

'Thank you, sir,' the younger man replied, not only with gratitude but also surprise and puzzlement.

'But now, to our business ... I will not keep you long. I wanted to speak with you about the matter we recently discussed in the Council Room. I cannot easily undo the decisions that the Board has taken but I am, as you know, not without some influence and have always taken an interest in your progress.'

'Yes sir, thank you, sir. I appreciate that.'

'If you will indulge me Samuel, I would like to ask you some further questions and you may find them a little unusual but please try to answer honestly and I will reveal all at a later point.' The older man paused and then asked bluntly, 'Will you do that?'

Samuel quickly agreed but was already more than a little surprised at both the visit to his study by the most powerful man in the college and now by his warm, supportive, words ... not to mention the use of his Christian name.

'I believe that you are acquainted with a colleague and former friend of mine, Reverend Timothy West?'

'Yes, indeed sir, I know the gentleman. He is a friend

to my father and when we first discussed the idea of my training for Ministry, we consulted him as someone who knew Winter Hill College intimately.'

'Yes, I understand that but, as I think you are aware, Reverend West is no longer associated with the college and now has a ministry some distance from here, in the region of the Cotswolds?'

Samuel was unable to prevent his eyes from moving towards his desk as he listened. The letter that Reverend West had given him two weeks earlier, was lying just a few feet from where the Reverend Angel stood.

'When did you last speak with Reverend West, Samuel?'

Samuel paused and looked down briefly at the floor. When he looked up he had reached a firm and bold decision.

'Not since I saw him in the town at his former chapel, Mount Zion, sir. It was the same day as the unveiling of the Reverend John memorial in Key Park cemetery but that must have been at least two months ago, I'm sure'.

'It was indeed, I was there myself. So, you say 'at least two months ago',' repeated the older man. 'And you are sure of this? I still hope to be able to help you in your wish to serve our church, Samuel. I understood that you may have conversed with him more recently than that.'

'Yes sir, I mean, no, sir. I am certain of it. I recall that it was August because the Reverend was making preparation to leave for his new post.'

'Very well, Master Ferrington, if you are adamant on

this matter, I shall pursue it no further. I ask because the College committee has reason to believe that Reverend West is responsible for some … impropriety … and we are gathering information as to his movements from anyone with whom he has been in contact over the last few weeks. I have been told that you were seen in his company but evidently, this is not the case. In any event, these unfortunate matters need not concern you; they relate only to the reputation of our college. I will take my leave of you.'

Reverend Angel moved towards the door and turned to face Samuel as he reached the corridor.

'As to the other matter, I hope that you will reflect on the decision of the Board, Samuel and make reparation for your mistakes. Remember,'- at this point he paused and again fixed the younger man intently with his gaze - 'there is always a way back to the fellowship of our church.'

'Thank you, Reverend Angel. I confess, I am perplexed by the events of today and wish to assert my innocence of all wrongdoing …'

'That is as it may be. The Board has given you the opportunity to speak and will give you further opportunity, if you merit it. Think carefully, Samuel, about *all* that we have discussed. My door is always open. Goodbye.'

With this the Reverend Angel turned and headed down the corridor towards the rooms to the front of the building occupied by the college principal.

Samuel watched him until he had disappeared from view, turned and then walked to the window overlooking the quadrangle. He went back to the corridor, looked along its length once more and firmly closed the door. There were no locks for any of the study rooms but most students had acquired rough, wooden wedges that would hold doors open or, as was more usually the case, closed. Samuel found his and manoeuvred it with his foot until it was jammed securely into position.

Then he went to his desk, opened it, found and extracted the long brown envelope sealed with a button of solid red wax, given to him two weeks before by the Reverend West. Samuel turned the envelope over and over. On the topside was the elaborately handwritten, *Master S.P. Ferrington.* He turned it again and looked at the seal. Reverend West had asked him to keep the letter safe and only open it if something untoward should happen to him or some other, as yet unknown, event take place that would raise a sense of alarm.

Samuel wondered whether the unusual events of the day justified the action of breaking the seal. He knew he had wanted to do so ever since he had received it. Reverend West had only said that the contents concerned the location of a 'great prize' which he had secured overseas for the glory of the church, the nation and the empire. When Samuel had asked about the nature of this prize he had been told that, 'given the feverish nature of current times', it would be best if he were kept in ignorance – and probably for a lengthy period.

Was the 'impropriety' to which the Rev Angel referred his friend's possession of the 'great prize'?

In any case, Reverend West had assured him that opening the letter would not, of itself, provide the answer to his questions. The letter contained a key but only someone with greater knowledge, he had said, could use it to 'open the treasury'.

Samuel felt the length of the envelope again to try and discern the outline of something hard, metallic but could sense only the flexing of paper or parchment.

He considered the events of the day and the way in which his surprise at being disciplined by the Board had been so speedily followed by the visit to his study from the Reverend Angel. Though he had usually found him polite and approachable, with the older man asking regularly after his father, a pastor in Halifax, a personal visit to a scholar's study was very unusual. If his friend's disappearance from Binghamton was connected with the 'key' he now held in his hand, then his chances of avoiding the shame and disgrace that awaited his return home, might be improved by choosing this moment to open the letter.

Within seconds he had broken the brittle wax seal and extracted the paper it contained. When he unfolded it, he read the contents, several times. He repeatedly paced the short distance between window and door before returning the letter to the envelope and then to his desk. He was both excited and worried. In his anxiety, he decided that he could neither leave the letter in his desk, nor risk packing it with his belongings, or even about his person.

His aim now was to return home and write letters to the Board repenting of his errors and asking to be allowed to return. In the meantime he would try to discover the whereabouts of Reverend West in order to make sense of the 'key' he had been given.

But where can I hide the letter?

He decided to look for a place within the room; somewhere that no-one would ever think to look. Having searched, he finally found an ideal location. By reaching up inside the opening to the chimney, he had discovered a number of gaps within the brickwork and one that was large enough to accommodate the width and length of his hand. He then looked for and found the old tobacco tin his mother had given him, in which to keep spare buttons and other small items she feared would otherwise be mislaid. He emptied the contents of the tin, removed the letter, wrote a few notes in pencil upon it, then folded it several times. He closed and then wedged the tin into the largest gap in the brickwork.

The incriminating letter was now no longer directly in his possession. Safely stored, where he believed no-one would ever find it, he felt free to return home and begin the search for the Reverend West. In a few weeks he would return to the same room and reclaim it, hopefully with more information as to its meaning.

Samuel sneezed and began to gather his few possessions together. He would arrange to leave the college the following morning.

The day after his arrival back in Halifax, Samuel contracted what was believed to be a severe case of influenza. Weakened as he was from weeks of living in the Spartan conditions of the college, his condition rapidly worsened. When his symptoms began to alarm his family, they called their physician, who finally diagnosed pneumonia. During the latter stages of his illness when Samuel, in his weakened condition, was tended by his mother, she was further distressed by a strange discovery. High on her son's upper arm, a black inky pattern was etched into his skin. Though the parents tried with all manner of soaps, they could not remove the banded design that covered the surface area of a man's hand. Without explaining the nature of the strange, curling fish-like pattern, Samuel died three weeks after leaving Winter Hill. He was buried in the family grave, close to his chapel in Halifax.

The funeral was attended by his grieving family and friends and three members of his old college; his fellow scholar, Eustace Griffiths, his favourite tutor, Reverend Thomas Henry and the chair of the Board of Education, Reverend James Angel. Samuel's parents were grateful that such an important man as the Chairman of the college should attend.

After the service, they spent some time with their visitor making arrangements to transfer their son's remaining possessions to Halifax. Reverend Angel made many generous statements about the 'great potential' their son had exhibited as a scholar and made light of the recent and 'temporary' difficulties that had resulted in Samuel's return home. When the parents confided in him their concern at the discovery of the strange 'pictograph' on their son's arm, they noted that the Reverend was very interested to know as much detail as possible. He, in turn, briefly considered telling the parents something of the barbarous practice of tattooing; a custom that missionaries working with natives in the South Seas had long striven to suppress. He decided otherwise. Instead he told them that he too was mystified and unable to offer any explanation as to its origin and meaning.

Samuel's distressed parents never visited his rooms in the college. They asked his friend, Mr Griffiths, to bundle together his possessions and send them on to their home. Among Samuel's papers in his desk, Eustace found a leather-bound journal and an envelope with the remains of the wax seal. He bundled the papers and journal into a box but threw the envelope into the hearth, where a fire had already been laid for a newly-enrolled scholar, due to arrive in Binghamton the following day.

The tin, with its contents, lay undisturbed within the flue for the next sixty years.

Polly, Muna and Lucky waited until the lunchtime bell sounded on the day following their decision to search for the hidden letter and then went to look for Dr McLaine. They asked the receptionist in the entrance to the college building where they might find the teacher and after phoning to confirm her availability, they were directed along the main corridor to the doors that would take them into the 'Head's House'. Muna asked why part of the school building was so-named.

'Well my dear, that is a very good question. Not many children have asked me in all the years that I've worked here but I do know the answer.'

The receptionist explained that these rooms were once the living quarters for the principal, the person in charge of the original Victorian college. She told them that this man *('It was always a man, women were not admitted as students or teachers. That was normal at the time.')* lived in the building and his rooms were on three floors. These rooms then became the first head teacher's home when the school opened in 1923. She pointed to the first of a series of framed photographs on the wall above her head.

'There he is, Mr Goodison. He lived there with his wife. The 'old boys' say he was a very strict man.'

'Stricter than Mr Wilby, Miss?' asked Muna.

'Stricter than Mr Pearce,' smiled the receptionist.

'But don't tell him I said so.'

She then explained that the custom for head teachers to live in the school had ended many years ago and that these rooms were now used by teachers and visitors for meetings and sixth form lessons. Some of the smallest rooms were also in use as offices. Dr McLaine's was one of these, on the top floor, accessed by a narrow staircase.

Despite the receptionist's clear directions, the girls had some difficulty in finding the staircase through a narrow passage at the west end of the long corridor. Having eventually found it, they climbed the stairs that twisted around three walls to reach the first floor and paused. The landing gave access to three rooms. Polly tried the handles of the heavy, dark doors. They were all locked. The staircase continued up to the floor above but was now even narrower and gloomier. Though none of them spoke of it, their resolve to continue was weakening. The stairwell was empty and although faint sounds of children at play on fields to the front could still be heard, they all experienced a sense of no longer being part of a busy school building.

'Girls, are you there?' a disembodied, frail but confident, female voice sounded above them.

Polly looked up and responded, 'Yes, miss,' before gesturing urgently to the others to follow her onto the stairs.

'Well, come up then. I'm here for only a short while. You will have to be quick.'

None of the girls had been taught by Dr McLaine but they knew from others that she was older than all other teachers in the school. Someone had said she was so 'old-fashioned' she should have retired years ago but the Head couldn't find anyone to teach the Religious Studies 'A' level course, so he kept her on. Others thought that she was a 'sad old woman' who had 'no life' outside the school and was allowed to stay as an act of kindness. Everyone had agreed on one thing; that she was more than a little 'weird'.

As the girls' heads reached the top of the stairs they could see Dr McLaine through the open door of her small office, sitting at a desk. A slightly-built woman, with white hair pulled close to her head, wearing tortoiseshell-framed spectacles positioned on the end of her nose, she looked up and beckoned, with long slender fingers, for them to approach.

'Be quick girls and if one of you could bring an extra chair from the landing that would be useful; I only have two here.'

Muna picked up a plastic bucket chair and the three girls arranged their seats in the cramped office. There was barely enough room for a desk and a filing cabinet but at least there was plenty of daylight entering through the west-facing, stone-mullioned frame of a small bay window.

'So, how can I help you?'

The girls looked at one another. A silent agreement was made that Polly should speak first.

'Miss, our teacher, Miss Frobisher, told us you are the best person to ask about the old college history. We're doing a project on 'shared memory' in English and we have to explore something that connects us, the three of us – so we've chosen to research the college; from the time when it was first built and during the First World War.'

'I see,' replied the woman in a business-like tone. 'Well, it's certainly true that I know a lot about the college and its history. I should do, I've been teaching here for nearly thirty years. But what exactly did you want to know?'

'Well, when it was built miss, what was it for exactly? Was it a church? Did monks live here?'

'Very well, I'll explain ... er – I'm sorry, what is your name, dear?'

'Polly Venables, miss. This is Lukhwinder Ladwa and Muna Duale. We're all in the same class, 9R', replied Polly.

'How pleasant,' commented the teacher, now looking intently at Lucky. 'Have we met before Lukhwinder? Your face looks familiar ... but no, you can't be the same girl, too long ago ... Where were we? Oh yes, I remember. Well, the original college was built to train young men to become ministers, leaders of their own special church. They lived in the building, in the east and west wings. In the west wing there were sixteen bedrooms on the first floor and sixteen studies beneath, on the ground floor. The east wing had the same number of bedrooms and studies giving rooms for thirty-two young men altogether. These rooms were all identical and quite small; eleven feet wide, by ten feet deep and nine feet high, to be precise.'

'But, miss,' interrupted Lucky, 'we've been down the corridor in the west wing and there's not enough space for sixteen rooms even if they were very small. In the west wing today there's only two offices, the sixth form common room, the corridor into the science wing and some loos – you can't fit sixteen rooms into that space …'

'No, you're right, but let me show you something.'

The teacher opened a drawer and carefully extracted a large sheet of paper that she laid on the desk so they could view it the right way up. 'Please look but do not touch. This is very old. It is the ground floor plan of the college. Can you see how both wings are divided up into very small, square rooms. But there are eight not sixteen studies along the length of the west wing because there were rooms on *both* sides? The corridor was in the middle ...'

'And now it's there, to the side' said Muna, pointing at the document.

'That's right, young lady. When they converted the college to a school after the Great War they knocked out most of the study and bedroom walls and moved the corridor to the side to create the larger spaces needed for classrooms.'

'I see. But it must have been very cold in the wintertime, miss. How would the college students keep warm?' Polly asked in what she hoped was a casual manner.

'What an interesting question? Well, there was no real central heating in the nineteenth century, not like today, though there was a crude boiler in the undercroft for heating those two big radiators in the long corridor on the ground floor. That boiler is still there in fact. But every study and bedroom had a small fireplace and in the winter months the scholars, as they were called, were allowed to have a coal fire in their rooms.'

'So, miss, where are the fireplaces now?'

'Most of them were taken out at the time the alterations were made in the 1920s. In the east wing they took everything out, all the walls, even the ceiling between the two floors. They also removed the chimneys that were identical to those in the west wing. They wanted all the space and perfectly flat surfaces, you see, to install the wall bars for the gymnasium. But the fireplaces in the other wing are still there, at least on the side facing the courtyard. They've been bricked in, plastered and painted but they still exist. They make a 'v' shape protruding into the corridor on both floors – you must have noticed them'.

'Yes, I think I know where you mean but we didn't understand what they were before. It makes sense when you look at this plan. I can see how, if they knocked down all those walls that separated two studies, then two parts of the chimney would come together to make that shape.'

Polly's index finger hopped above the plan pausing at each of the distinct triangular blocks in the wall of the west wing.

'So,' she continued, hesitantly, casting quick glances at the others, 'if we wanted to find where the exact opening to a fireplace was, we would have to make a hole?'

Miss McLaine looked up from her drawing and over the rim of her spectacles, with a new note of interest in her voice, 'Now why would anyone want to do such a thing, Polly?'

'Oh, no reason, really,' said Polly. 'We just wondered what a fireplace would look like ...'

'Yes, how big the opening would be ...' added Lucky.

'... If you wanted to hide something inside the chimney ...' said Muna.

''If you wanted to hide something'? Now what would you hide in a chimney?'

Polly looked with furrowed brow at the others as they turned to look at her. She sighed.

'My great-uncle Arthur was training to be a soldier here in the First World War. A letter he wrote to his parents says that he found something in one of the chimneys,' then, looking intently at each of the others in turn, she stated firmly, in a measured tone, 'but we're not sure which one.'

'What kind of thing, my dear?'

'Oh, nothing important; something to do with a piece of paper he found written by one of the monks. Well, not monk, we know that now - someone who lived in the college. But we don't know what was in it. We thought it would be interesting to find out for my family history – and for our school project.'

Miss McLaine looked down again at the plan on the desk and paused. After a few seconds she looked up with an expression that carried the hint of a smile.

'Well, I hate to disappoint you but I think it very unlikely that anything such as a letter would have survived the last eighty-five years. After the war ended the building was sold to Binghamton Council to be used as a school. They made many changes, as I said, knocking down a lot of the walls in the 1920s. Where they didn't remove the flues they filled the fireplaces making it impossible to reach the chimneys ...'

'What even up to three and a half feet from the floor, miss?' asked Muna.

'Why do you say three and a half feet, Muna?' queried the woman.

Polly interrupted quickly, 'because we thought that would be the right sort of height for a fireplace. We've, er, still got one in our house that's three and a half feet high.'

'Well, I don't know how large the opening to the fireplace would have been but I think it would probably have been less than that.'

With an abruptness that startled them all, the school bell sounded loudly to signal the end of the lunch break.

'There's the bell. I must go and so must you. It has been interesting to talk to you. If you have any further questions then I will try to answer them.'

Dr McLaine returned the plan to her desk drawer as Polly thanked the teacher for her help. When they had retraced their steps to the first floor landing they fell into an excited and whispered exchange.

'Well, now we know why your dad couldn't find the fireplaces, Polly,' said Muna, 'He was looking in the wrong place. So the tin *may* still be there, bricked into one of the walls that stick out in those 'v' shapes.'

'Yes, but this also explains why we do need to understand the 'Philpott clue' – it must tell us which side of the central corridor the room was on.'

'How do you mean?' queried Muna.

'Well, we said that we know everything about where to look, '5th room along the corridor in the west wing' but there are two rooms that could be the one we're looking for; one either side of the corridor. The 'Philpott clue' must tell us which side. The answer should be 'left' or 'right''.

'But 'left' or 'right' depends on the direction you're facing.'

'Yes, I hadn't thought of that.' Lucky paused before quickly adding, 'But wait a minute. When you look at a building you do it from the front, so the left and right are clear. If the 'Philpott house' for example, is on Arthur's parents' road then we should know whether it's to the right or the left from the front and that will tell us which side of the corridor – looking from the front.'

'Yes, Lucky,' agreed Polly. 'That must be right.'

'But even if we do solve that clue we still won't be able to find the tin,' cautioned Muna. 'Miss says it won't be there and anyway, even if it was, we're not going to start knocking holes in the wall - are we?'

'I know someone who would,' said Polly.

The others looked at her before they all said, in unison, 'Umar!'

Giggling with infectious laughter, they descended the stairs and then, where the width of the main corridor permitted, linked arms and made their way down the long corridor in the direction of their next lesson.

The next day the girls and Umar were grouped around a table in Miss Frobisher's English lesson. They had been given fifteen minutes to write a summary of their ideas and research so far. One of them would have to present this summary to the class for comment. Umar, determined that he would not be selected, signalled his lack of interest by casually and repeatedly writing with animated flourishes his 'tag' on a sheet of file paper.

'So, we'll all write something about our memories of coming to Binghamton and joining Winter Hill. That's where we start,' said Lucky.

'But I only came here a year ago,' Muna moaned.

'So where were you before that?' asked Lucky.

'When mum and us kids left Somalia we went to Italy to begin with, then my dad got us papers to come and join him in England. We went to this town, Great Yarmouth, first, where we stayed in a hostel. I remember it was very crowded but good, too, in some ways because all the families helped each other.'

'What did you do?' asked Polly with an emphasis that fell on the final word.

'I spent a lot of time walking by the sea. There was this big path beside a long straight road. It was winter so a lot of the seaside places were closed. Sometimes I'd talk to people. It helped my English though they do talk funny there – a strange 'accent' they call it.'

'Did the people like you?' Lucky asked again.

'Sometimes a white person, usually one of the older ones, used to say racist things. Once I walked into one of the amusement places, arcades, on the sea front and this man started to make fun of my headscarf, asking me if I had any hair on my head, stupid stuff like that. It was very shocking to me ... but others were kind, they brought us things to cook with and food as well. The man who owned the house drove this big posh car. He must have had lots of money.

'But after a few weeks we left there to go to London, where my dad had a job, but he and my mum were arguing a lot so we left him and came to Binghamton. Some of my mum's family live here.'

'Ok, so you didn't know anything about the school when you started, did you?'

'No, not like you, Polly. You've always lived here and your dad went to school here and his uncle was a soldier here and ... it's different for you. You're part of it – I'm not.'

'That's not true. My dad's from India. My mum's white and her parents are from Ireland but this is my school as much as Polly's,' declared Lucky.

'And anyway, Muna,' added Polly, 'Miss says we have to start with something we share - and there's lots of things I don't know about the school and its history. I'm finding out about stuff too, just like you.'

'But, it's not my history, is it? I wasn't born here, my family weren't born here – I was born in Africa.'

'Me born 'ere,' Umar broke in. 'So, it na 'bout whey

yuh was born 'coz me doan tink it my histry eeder, it white peebul histry.'

Without their realising, Miss Frobisher had approached and listened in on part of their exchange.

'Do you mind if I say something?' she asked. 'From what I've heard I think this is a very interesting discussion and sometime I'd like the whole class to hear it. But here's a thought for you - you see, I agree with Umar. It's not about where you were born. Perhaps, it's more about where you feel you 'belong'. But where does that feeling come from? I'm not white either, in case you hadn't noticed! I was born and brought up in Wolverhampton, where my parents still live, though they came to this country from Barbados.'

'Where's that, miss?'

'It's a small island in the West Indies, in the Caribbean Sea. Now, I feel I 'belong' in Wolverhampton but I've lived in Binghamton for eleven years and feel I 'belong' here as well. This is where most of my friends are now. And I've worked at Winter Hill for nearly five years, so I'm part of it and it's a part of me.

'Perhaps by living and working in a place, by making friends and accumulating memories we develop a sense of belonging. It takes time of course and you are all very young but I think that by learning more about each other and the history of people who have been here before, you will begin to feel that you do belong – or at least a part of you does.

'Now, I want you to carry on and be ready to say something in a little while, please.'

The teacher paused and looked at the boy.

'Well done, Umar – I was impressed with how you explained what you felt. It helped me make sense of my own thinking, thank you.'

When Miss Frobisher was no longer within earshot Umar shook his head and growled. 'When teech-ur start pray-zin' me, me know tings na right!'

The others laughed. Lucky added, 'Well you lot can praise me and I won't say you're wrong.'

'What for?' asked Muna.

'I found out who the Philpotts were. Anna and George Philpott were neighbours of Arthur's family and lived at number 34, which is to the right of the Venables at number 36. So the room we're looking for should be on the right of the central corridor as we walk down it from the long corridor.'

'That's great, Lucky.'

'Yeah, well done, gal,' added Umar.

'But how did you find out?' asked Polly.

'Oh, it was no big deal,' replied Lucky, hesitantly. 'Don't worry about it. I just did some digging around on the internet and found the information there. It's not difficult, anyone can do it.'

'Well you'll have to show me how, Lucky,' said Muna. 'I'm hopeless with searches like that. I always end up with websites written by weirdos.'

'Dat ex-splayn it den. Lucky would be in gud cumpny!' retorted Umar.

The following Monday Polly met Lucky in the top playground. The girls exchanged a brief ritual hug with 'air kisses' as their cheeks touched right to right, left to left.

'Did you see anything strange when you came past the college?' asked Lucky.

'No, I don't think so. I wasn't really looking. Why?'

'Something's up. I overheard a group of sixth formers talking about some serious damage in the common room'.

'The common room? What, the sixth form common room?' asked Polly.

'Yeah, you know, where they eat at lunchtime; the corridor that's been opened up, with all those tables in it.'

'Wait a minute. The ground floor, in the west wing?'

'Yes, exactly,' Lucky agreed.

'But that's where we think Arthur's room was, isn't it? What kind of damage? We've got to find out.'

Before Lucky could respond Polly had turned and headed back up the slope towards the building.

'But, Polly,' pleaded Lucky, struggling to catch up with her friend who was already weaving her way around and through small groups of students. 'We're not allowed in there at this time. We'll only get told to leave, or worse, if we bump into Pearce.'

'I don't care,' countered Polly, 'and anyway teachers are always too busy doing other things to worry about us.' Then, less convincingly, she added, 'We'll just have to risk it.'

They entered the college through the student entrance, part of the block added to the building in the 1920s. A flight of steps took them up to the junction with an extension to the long corridor. As they passed beneath the arches they could see to their right the assembly hall and then the courtyard or 'quad' but as it was located on the north and, therefore, cooler side of the building, it was empty at this time. At the point where the corridor turned ninety degrees to enter the west wing they could see the headteacher, Mr Wilby, in conversation with Miss Kaur, their science teacher who was also the head of sixth form, a man they recognised as one of the caretakers and a young uniformed police officer.

'Polly, let's go back and try later,' urged Lucky.

'No way,' Polly replied firmly. 'I'm going to find out what's happened.'

'Where are you girls going?' asked the female teacher, authoritatively, as they approached the corner.

Polly stopped sharply and Lucky stood nervously behind her. 'We've been asked to collect some science equipment for Mr Green, miss. He says he needs it for first lesson and we were told to use the sixth form corridor to save time.'

Lucky looked at Polly with an expression of alarm and amazement, tinged with a degree of admiration. Fortunately, nobody was looking at her when the Head responded to Polly's brazen lie.

'Well, Mr Green will have to wait until you've gone back around the building, I'm afraid. No-one will be going through here today.'

'Sir?' said Polly, straining to look beyond the adults to the closed corridor doors. Through the glass panels she could see some stools connected by red and white plastic tape appearing to restrict access to the right hand wall. 'What's happened? Has there been an accident.'

'No, no accident, young lady – just some deliberate vandalism to the school. The culprits will soon be caught, I hope, and the damage repaired. It's nothing for you to worry about.'

'But what damage, sir? Can I see?' pleaded Polly.

Both teachers replied, 'No', in unison and Miss Kaur again instructed them to leave the sixth form area by the way they had arrived. Lucky pulled at her friend's arm and they began to retrace their steps. By the time they had reached the playground more students had gathered with the accompanying increase in noise levels. Without their being aware of his presence, Umar had spotted them, detached himself from a group of boys and approached.

'Wassup!' he suddenly exclaimed, just inches from Polly's head.

'Umar!' said Polly spinning round to face him. 'Don't do that. It's scary!'

'That's why he does it Polly,' sympathised Lucky and then added, while glaring at Umar, 'but getting upset just encourages his pathetic, childish, behaviour.'

'Wha de matter wid you? Tink you're so clever wiv

your snobby wurds,' sneered Umar. Then, by way of making amends, his expression and tone softened. 'Anyways, me tort you like to know wha' me know.'

'Oh yeah, what do you know?' Polly replied sarcastically.

'Me see yuh come out de bill-din'. Me know wha' happen in de six farm corry-dor,' replied Umar, 'n' me bet yuh doan know dat.'

'What? How could you know?' said Lucky, her irritation giving way to curiosity.

'Coz me bin a look. Me saw da Babylon car a de back o' de science block an' went in from dat side. Yuh can get to de doors on de far side o' de common room 'n' see wha happen. Is some sair-ree-us damage, mahn.'

'Well, go on,' encouraged Polly.

'De walls arl mash up where dem bits stick out inta de corridor. On de side where it stick out, me see brick have bin bashed an' tayken out. Me tink dey-a done de sayem ta boat side but me only see part a it. Dere's load a mess, mahn; brick, plar-ster, dust, load a brick.'

'How high up the wall, Umar?' asked Polly.

'Me dunno; bout 'ere ta 'ere,' said Umar, raising a flattened hand, held horizontally, from his waist to a point just beneath his chin. As he spoke they heard the first bell sound. They had about five minutes to get to their classrooms for registration.

'Well that's very strange,' mused Polly. 'It was only a few days ago ...'

'We'll have to talk about it later, perhaps when we can meet up with Muna? Thanks, Umar. We need to get to registration,' insisted Lucky and the girls turned and began to make their way down the steps that led to the lower school building where the younger students had their form rooms.

Umar, however, moved away in the opposite direction. With less urgency, he made his way against the human tide towards the science block, added in the 1960s to the west wing of the college. Here, in a small room on the first floor, he attended lessons in the Learning Support Unit together with a small number of other pupils. Most had been taken off their normal timetables for a few weeks because their behaviour had caused difficulty for students and teachers. Umar, unlike the others, had been 'resident' for more than six months while the police and probation service investigated a case of criminal assault in which he was involved.

Until the various authorities had completed a series of meetings and written reports, the school was unable to return him to normal lessons. An exception had been made for his English lessons partly because this 'privilege' encouraged his co-operation but also because, unknown to Umar, Miss Frobisher had strongly requested it.

After their release from lessons at the end of school, Polly, Lucky, Muna and Umar met up near the student entrance to the college. They waited until most of the children had streamed out of the building and the teachers had time to reach whatever meetings were taking place that day. Then they entered the building, walked the length of the long corridor, turned right and descended some steps into the west wing. They now knew that the original corridor had been in the middle of this wing and that they were moving through the area that had originally been floor space for the scholars' small studies.

The corridor doors were unlocked, the plastic tape that restricted access to the walls had been removed and the rubble cleared.

As they walked through the wing they could see to their right a succession of the v-shaped buttresses with hardboard taped to the walls. Umar said that these must be covering the areas that had been damaged. Polly tried to recall the original plan of this area Dr McLaine had shown them in her office as they continued along the wing. They soon reached the point where the corridor opened out to serve as a common room and eating area for the sixth formers. Here they could see the entire width of the wing; from the quadrangle wall to that which faced an area of lawn, beyond which was a laurel hedge that screened the building from the road.

'Look,' said Lucky. 'You can see where the old central corridor walls were.'

'Wha' yuh mean?'

'Here,' said Lucky, putting her hand on the upright section between two arches. 'This is part of one of the old corridor walls. They've knocked through to open up the space. And look there,' she said pointing to a column protruding from the wall that ran at right angles to the windows on the far side of the wing, 'you can see part of the other corridor wall.'

'Ok, I see,' said Polly. 'So this area here, between the wall with the arches and the window would have been a study.'

'Yes,' added Muna, 'and where two of those angles meet, which now make the 'v' shape, there would have been another wall so that each chimney could be used by two rooms.'

'Four, if you include the two bedrooms above,' added Lucky.

'And if we measure eleven feet like this,' said Polly, placing one foot after the other, 'starting from the joining point of the 'v' then we'll have the other side wall to the study. There, look! It would be here between the windows. That window would be in the study next to this one and that angled wall would have been the chimney and so on.

'So, come on then. Let's try to work out which of these rooms would have been Arthur's. The letter says it was the fifth along on the Philpott side in the west wing. Well we're in the west wing and Lucky says that we need the right hand side of the corridor as we approach from the main corridor. So that's this side', said Polly pointing to the quadrangle wall.

She returned to the steps they had descended and the others followed.

'If we start here, this is study number one.'

'No, Polly. The first room on this side wasn't a study. I think it was used by the Matron. She kept bedding and other stuff in there, for use in the Principal's House.'

'OK, but how did you work that out, Lucky?' asked Polly.

'Oh, I spotted it on the plan that Dr McLaine showed us.' Lucky looked a little nervous and hurried on to stand beside the next window. 'Anyway, the first study would have been here.'

Polly picked up the sequence as she moved down the corridor. 'Right, so this would be the second, with the other side of the chimney, then this would be the third, but then there's no fireplace?'

'That's because there was a lumber room on this side of the corridor, opposite the door over there, used by the scholars to get to their rooms. A lumber room wouldn't need a fireplace.'

'What's a lumber room?' asked Muna.

'I think it's a kind of store-room. It's probably where the scholars stored the trunks which contained their luggage. Remember they would be in the college for long periods and needed to bring everything with them from their homes.'

'Don't tell me, Lucky,' said Polly, sarcastically. 'You

remembered seeing that on the plan as well. I wish I had your memory.'

'But if Lucky's right and we miss the next window, then study number three would be here. Yes, there's part of the 'v' shape in that space and the next one would be four with the other side of the vee,' Polly stopped walking and held her arms extended, '... and here would be number five.'

'Yes, that looks right,' said Lucky. 'I mean, that would make sense from what we saw on the plan; from the turning point on the 'v' shape back to the wall that would have come out there between the windows.'

'Me measure it – me feet bigga dan yours,' stated Umar pacing between the points indicated by Lucky. 'Nine, ten , eleven, yeah, das right.'

'And the distance from the corridor wall to the window should be ten feet, Umar. Measure that as well.'

'One, two ... eight, nine, ten, das bout right too.'

'Then, that's our chimney,' announced Polly indicating the protruding wall alongside Umar. 'And we should look for a point, three and a half feet from the floor and two feet in from the wall.'

'Yeah, which wud be bout 'ere,' said Umar. 'Jus' where dis boarded up.'

'Let's take it off,' proposed Polly.

'I don't think we should? We might get into ... ,' began Muna.

'Why na?' said Umar pulling at the brown parcel tape that secured the board to the wall.

When he had removed the tape and pulled the board away, they could clearly see a large irregular shaped hole in the wall. Several bricks had been knocked out and thrown back into the space within the opening.

'Well, it definitely was a chimney and if anything *was* here and they were looking for it then it's gone now,' said Polly, miserably.

'I'm not so sure,' said Lucky. 'Not unless this was the last one they looked at because otherwise why damage all the others? I think it's more likely that they didn't find anything. Miss McLaine says that the bedrooms on the floor above were identical. I wonder if they've been damaged?'

'Me go an' look,' offered Umar. 'Wayit 'ere.'

Umar bustled through the doors at the end of the wing, bounded up the stairs before turning at the top and disappearing from view. Lucky looked up at the ceiling, listening for Umar's footfall on the floor above. She suddenly shouted, 'I'm coming too!' and raced after him.

Polly and Muna stared at each other, shrugged their shoulders, and waited.

Within a few minutes Umar and Lucky had returned.

'Nah damage ta de floor above,' said Umar. 'De sayem 'v' shape in de wall but nah 'ole may'd. 'Whoeva do dis jus' wan' dis floor, where de studee was.'

'But there's something strange here,' added Lucky. 'Did you notice that we came down those steps off the long corridor to get into this wing?'

'No, yes – ok I see them,' replied Polly, looking back along the wing corridor. 'So what?'

'Well, so far the size of the rooms has been just as Miss McLaine told us; eleven feet wide, ten feet deep but this doesn't look like nine feet high to me. It looks much higher than that. Upstairs the ceiling is much lower. Is it possible that the floor used to be higher than this and those steps weren't there? Yes of course, that's it! Both the long corridor and this one were once on the same level!'

'But who would lower the floor?' asked Polly.

'I'm not sure. Perhaps when it became a school they wanted more rooms with higher ceilings? This space was going to be used for classrooms, remember. They could get that extra height by lowering the floor.'

'OK but how does that help us? It still looks like we're not going to get the tin. Either it was never here or someone's taken it,' said Muna.

'Don't you see?' said Polly, beginning to understand the significance of Lucky's thinking. 'If Arthur said three and a half feet from the floor and the floor's been lowered then the tin is going to be found at a much higher level. If we measure those steps and add three and a half feet it will be more like six and a half feet. We'll have to get a tape and measure the height of the steps.'

'But we still have the same problem don't we? How do we get to the tin without doing a lot more damage?'

They never had chance to discuss Muna's question before one of the cleaners arrived, pulling a dome-shaped vacuum cleaner. They decided it would be better to leave before they were asked to explain what they were doing.

As they headed down the corridor in the direction of the exit at the end of the wing, the cleaner spotted the discarded tape and hardboard.

'Hey, what's this? What do you lot think you're doing?' she called after them.

They did not turn round but quickened their pace, reached the corner and disappeared from view.

The cleaner muttered as she bent down to pick up the tape, 'damn kids, as if there wasn't enough damage here for one day.'

The next day, to everyone's surprise, all Winter Hill students were told that a series of special assemblies were to be held during the course of the morning. Year 9 classes were to leave their normal lessons and report to the hall at 10.00 a.m. Even before the first assemblies had taken place, rumours were circulating.

'Miss, is it true that Mr Wilby is going to tell us about the damage done to the old building?'

'I really don't know, Polly,' Miss Frobisher replied. 'You appear to know more than me. We'll have to wait and see. Let's just make sure that we get there on time, shall we?'

Polly's class was among the last to reach the hall. Unusually, there were no chairs provided for them. They were instructed by teachers to stand in rows according to their respective tutor groups. Silence moved through the hall like a bow-wave as Mr Wilby strode down the central aisle with a fixed and stern expression, climbed the steps and positioned himself close to the edge of the stage. He surveyed the sea of faces before him and waited a few seconds, as though straining to lift the weight of the words he wanted to utter.

'Year 9, I will not keep you long. This will be a very brief but – important – announcement. For this reason, today, I am asking you to stand.

'Yesterday, some very disturbing and serious damage was done to the internal walls of the old college building. I am not talking about minor, casual damage such as the graffiti we sometimes have to deal with. Someone, or some persons, took great pleasure in knocking through large holes in the west wing walls with what must have been heavy tools. The police were immediately informed when this was discovered first thing this morning. My first thought was that this must have been done by someone from outside the school because, to be honest with you, I wouldn't want to think that anyone here would be so criminally-minded as to inflict such shocking damage on our buildings.

'However, it would now appear that we must consider the possibility that a student, or students, from this school are involved – because last night further damage was done to one of the walls.'

Mr Wilby paused as an irrepressible, low murmur spread through his audience.

'It is unacceptable that such a thing could take place in our school and I am asking everyone to think very carefully about whether they know anything that might help us catch the people, or person, responsible. If you have any idea, whatsoever, then you must speak to me or one of the other teachers. Any information you can give will be treated confidentially.

'I need to tell you now that when we catch the people responsible, we will ask the police to prosecute them.'

The headteacher paused again, before continuing.

'And if anyone in this school should be found to be

withholding relevant information about the culprits, their parents will be asked to remove them from Winter Hill and find another school. Now, please go back to your classrooms and think very carefully about what I have said. Thank you.'

The headteacher left the stage and a new swell of chatter quickly, irresistibly, swept across the assembly hall. Polly and Lucky made little contribution, though each was staring at the other. Both were silently mouthing the words, 'more damage?!"

At break, in the playground, Polly, Muna and Lucky were still talking about the head's assembly and trying to understand what a second assault on the corridor walls could mean. Umar suddenly appeared beside Polly and pulled her in the direction of a quiet, unoccupied part of the playground, some distance from the school buildings. Lucky and Muna followed as Polly angrily tried to loosen Umar's hand from her school blazer.

'Let go of me, you idiot,' she hissed. 'What are you doing?'

'Jus' be quiet gal, 'n' folla me. Me got sumtink fa yuh.'

Umar smiled and released her. The girls, seeing Umar's grin, were sufficiently intrigued to follow him to a position beneath some trees on the bank leading to the upper playground. No-one else was within fifteen metres of them.

Umar reached into his jacket pocket and extracted a rectangular metal object.

'Me tink yuh may whan t'ave dis?'

'A tin? What would I want with that? It's rusty and

gross.' Then looking up at Umar and seeing his huge smile, Polly realised what she looking at. 'My God, a tin, *the* tin, Umar,' exclaimed Polly. 'It was you, last night, the second visit ... it was you!'

'Shh – me sayin nutten bout dat. Keep yuh voice dun. Less jus' say dis come inna me po-zesh-shon.'

'Have you opened it Umar?'

Umar pursed his lips and drew air between his front teeth to issue an extended and disapproving whistle.

'Nah, course naht. Ass yuh greyut-uncle letta, yuh greyut-uncle tin; me tort yuh shud be de one ta o-pen it.'

Polly uttered a soft, 'Thank you, Umar,' looked at the tin and tried to prise open the top. After straining for a few seconds the tension in her hand and arm was released.

''Ere let me,' said Umar, elbowing his way between the girls, who had moved forward and very close to Polly. He took the tin from her hands and, gripping the top with his strong stubby fingers, boasted, 'Me know yuh gals wudn't be able t' do it. 'S mahn's work. Wotch na!'

Polly did as instructed and found herself both wishing that Umar would fail, as she had failed, and hoping against hope, that he would succeed.

She soon discovered which of these contradictory feelings was the stronger when she saw the top of the tin begin to slide upward, then with a sudden movement spring open. She could barely contain her excitement as Umar turned toward her with the tin open before him, inviting her to look at whatever was inside.

Polly paused and looked at the others.

'Well, gwan wid yuh gal or me open de paypur meself,' Umar growled.

Polly reached to extract the folded paper, last seen by her great uncle nearly ninety years earlier. She removed it from the tin, lightly blew some of the dust from the surface and carefully opened it out.

When she had done so, the stiff piece of paper, about the size of a page taken from a school exercise book, revealed a faded, but still legible, script.

'Well what does it say?' asked Muna.

'I don't know,' murmured Polly with a note of disappointment. 'It doesn't make sense. It's just a lot of nonsense and then a few words I can read.'

'Well, we knew it wouldn't be easy, didn't we?' consoled Lucky. 'Arthur told us that in his letter. He said he thought it would be some kind of code and codes can be broken. Let's see.'

Polly turned the piece of paper so that they could all see. They stared at the arrangement of letters and numbers before them;

rarotongamitiaroerromangaei
meoaitutakiatiumaukeraiatea
kadavusuwarrowtongatabusavai
ifasetootaiambrymsamoatanna

viliamutamatoapapeihaleota

2:3:vi,4:ii,1:1:i,1:vii,3:i,4:i,9:iii,2:4:i,4:ii,1:12:i,2:3:vi,3:ii,1:9:i ii,1:iv,10:iii,2:1:v,2:i,1:1:vii,1:vi,2:vii,3:vii*2:iii,13:vi,3:viii,5: i,12:i?,3:i,15:iv,13:i,16:ii,11:viii,4:i,1:ix,12:i,2:iii,2:iv,3:vii,3:

viii,2:4:i,3:ii,1:15:i,10:i*13:iii,13:iv,8:vi,5:vii,2:vii,6:iv,3:ii,2:
4:i,4:iii,1:1:i,9:iii,2:ii,16:iii,1:v,2:3:vi,4:ii,2:i,2:vi,1:10:viii,3:i,
1:i*1:ii,12:i,2:3:vi,3:iv,3:v,1:13:iii,13:i,4:v,5:iv,11:iii,9:iii,2:ii,
1:vii,2:iii,2:3:vi,4:ii,1:11:viii,1:iii,1:ix,15:i,12:i*3:ii,2:3:vi,4:iii
,1:13:i,3:x,8:i,15:i,1:v,2:3:iii,2:vi,1:iv,1:16:iii,13:v,15:i,1:v,2:
3:vi,4:ii,1:10:iii,1:ii,14:v*2:2:i,3:vi,3:iv,1:16:iv,13:i,
3:iv,2:4:i,1:iii,2:vi,1:10:iii,2:2:i,3:vi,3:iv,1:11:viii,4:i,1:ii,12:i,
2:iii*10:iii,2:3:vi,4:ii,1:1:i,4:iv,2:iii,2:3:vi,3:iv,
4:i,1:iv,1:11:iii,7:v,13:vi,13:i,7:iv,2:3:vi,1:4:ii,4:iii,4:iv,8:vi,8
:v,12:i*1:ix,9:iii,2:vii,3:iv,3:iii,14:ii,6:iv,12:i,13:v,
11:viii,3:i,8:i,4:iv,2:4:i,3:iv,1:v,1:12:i,4:iv,9:iii

Finally, they found the two lines that Polly had been able to read.

If I with my maker am, find friend John.
Though the body be lost, grave words live on.

Umar was the first to react.

'Thass raw, mahn. It mek nah sense.'

'It does make sense, Umar. It's just that we can't see it,' Lucky retorted. 'We have to break the code.'

'But how do we do that?' asked Muna 'It's just a mess of letters in the first part followed by a bigger mess of numbers in the second!'

Polly read the couplet aloud.

'If I with my maker am, find friend John. Though the body be lost, grave words live on.' That's the starting point. At least we can read it. But what does it mean?'

'Surch me, gal!'

'*If I with my maker am* ... 'If I am with my maker' is

how we would say it. That sounds like the writer is telling the reader what to do if he is dead. If he is with his 'maker', his God, then he's dead and he's saying to break the code you will have to find his friend, John.'

'Yes, Lucky. *That* makes sense but his *'friend John'* is also going to be dead, since this was written nearly one hundred and fifty years ago,' Muna added.

'Yes, thanks, Muna. I think I could work that out for myself - but listen. It's saying that even if John is dead his *'grave words live on'*. *'Grave'* could mean 'serious' ...'

'Or something to do with where he's buried?' offered Polly. 'But John is such a common name. How would we know which John to look for?'

'We'd have to find out more about the person who wrote the letter. He may have had a special friend called John,' suggested Lucky. 'But it also says, *'Though the body be lost'*. Does that mean he couldn't have been buried because there was no body? Perhaps he has a memorial somewhere like the one for the students killed in the war, in the school entrance?'

'But Lucky that memorial is for the Second World War and - if there was no body, why not?' asked Polly. 'It sounds very strange to me.'

'Well, 'e may 'ave drown or bin killed in ex-splozhon an' him body blown inta tousan' pieces a flesh an' ...'

'Yes thanks, Umar, we get the idea,' Polly interrupted. 'But, he's got a point. Mister Bridges told us in those lessons on the First World War that they never found the bodies of lots of soldiers and they put their names on memorials.'

'Yes, but we're just guessing,' said Muna. 'We need facts and don't know who to look for or where. We need help.'

'Muna's right,' agreed Lucky. 'We need someone who knows about these people, someone who understands the time they lived, their religion, their world. Things have changed so much. It's impossible for us to understand …'

Lucky paused, then, continued.

'You know what this means, don't you?'

'I think I do,' Muna replied.

Polly looked at her friends, who were both smiling at her. Then she understood.

'Oh wait. I'm not sure about this,' interrupted Polly. 'It's a bit of a coincidence, don't you think, that we ask Doctor McLaine about the chimney in Arthur's room and two days later all that damage is done?'

'Polly, are you seriously saying that Miss McLaine smashed up the walls? That's crazy. She may be a bit strange but you've seen her, she's a harmless old woman.'

'I know, I'm not sure, Muna, it just seems very odd …'

'I don't think we have a choice, do we? We'll just have to be careful. We can always show her the little poem and not the rest of it. It's no good to anyone without the jumble of letters.'

'That's true, I guess. OK, Lucky. I'll write that part out again and I'll keep the rest in the tin.'

She began to fold up the paper as the bell sounded for the next lesson.

'Hang on a minute, there's something written on the other side of the paper, in pencil.' She turned the paper over and then back. 'It's different handwriting to the coded part of the letter. Someone else must have written it.'

'What does it say?' asked Muna.

'It's not so easy to read, the pencil is faint ... *Letter from Rev. West ...*'

'Rev. West? Wha' kind a nayem dat?'

'Umar, 'Rev.' is short for 'Reverend'. A 'Reverend' is someone important in the church like a 'priest' - or 'Imam' or 'Rabbi,'' explained Lucky. 'Go on, Polly.'

...*'given to me, Samuel Ferrington and opened October 5th. 1851. I pray that no-one but I ever has cause to read these words. If they do, I have failed and the quest for the 'great prize' falls to another. May God be your guide.'*

'So, hang on; a Reverend West wrote the letter, gave it to Samuel Ferrington who opened it in 1851 and presumably hid it in the chimney where your great-uncle found it many years later.'

'I think that's right, Lucky. Ferrington must have been a student at the college.'

'And that means John was probably a friend of West's. That could help us.'

Polly nodded, feeling more hopeful. Then she looked up and saw a teacher headed in their direction. 'Uh-oh, here comes Pearce. We'd better get to Maths. Let's meet in the college entrance at lunchtime. OK?'

'Dey doan let me out at lunch,' Umar moaned.

'That's to stop you eating all the food,' laughed Polly. Then she added, in a softer tone, 'but seriously,

Umar, thanks. You've helped a lot today - I could kiss you.'

The girls giggled at Umar's obvious embarrassment.

'Me rathur kiss a g'rilla - or Miss McLaayne. Go wey wid yuh!'

The college receptionist, having phoned Dr McLaine, told the girls that she was unable to meet them that lunchtime but suggested an alternative; she would see them in the college library after school that same day. The three girls arrived soon after their final lesson and were told they could enter the library, 'as long as they were sensible and waited quietly'.

When they had reassured the receptionist and been invited to open the library door they were all immediately struck by the size and grandeur of the room they were entering for the first time. To their left, the external wall was breached by four towering stone-mullioned windows decorated with intricate patterns in the glass of the upper tracery. To either side of each of these windows the corrugated folds of enormous curtains allowed the room to be flooded with bright daylight.

Along the entire length of the wall opposite the windows and immediately to their right, were ranged a large number of shelves, the lower sections of which were faced with the neatly-filed spines of many books. Above the shelving and protruding into the space above their heads, ran a gallery with an ornate, cast iron, guard rail. The gallery continued around the wall in which the door, through which they had entered, was positioned and ended in the corner to their left, where a spiral staircase descended to ground level. Close to this staircase, tucked into the furthest corner, was a small door, of which, at this time, they took little notice.

Instead, Muna had drawn their attention to the dark-stained, wooden ceiling with its mock-medieval, hammer-beam supports, decorated, at the lowest point, with ornately carved angel heads, complete with broad, folded wings.

'Well, are you impressed, girls?' asked a voice behind them.

They turned to face Dr McLaine carrying a briefcase in one hand and a collection of papers pressed to her side in the other. 'This is the grandest room in the college. It has always been a library but in the original college it also served as a chapel.'

'A chapel, miss? What's that?' asked Muna.

'A place for Christian services, my dear. It's a place where prayers and hymns and words of worship are sung or said.'

'Like a church?'

'Yes, exactly, like a church, except smaller. There were never more than about thirty students and tutors present and sometimes a few local people as well.'

'In my temple we have a huge room for praying. Sometimes there are hundreds of people,' added Lucky proudly.

'Yes, I have been to a number of Hindu temples - and mosques - in Binghamton. They are very special places. Now shall we sit down and you can tell me what it is that you want?'

Polly produced the slip of paper, on which she had

written the couplet, and spoke as she passed it to the teacher.

'We found the letter that my great uncle Arthur said he hid in the college, miss.'

'Really, how extraordinary. Please tell me exactly how and where you found it?'

Polly shifted uneasily in her seat and looked down at the table.

'My dad had it all the time. He'd kept it as a secret but when I told him I was interested in finding out more about our family history he agreed to show it to me.'

'I see,' commented Dr McLaine with a faint smile. 'And can you tell me what is in the letter?'

'It's a collection of letters and numbers. It looks like some kind of code because it doesn't make any sense but with them are these two lines which we think will help us. We wondered whether you could tell us more about what they mean?'

'I see,' said the teacher. She took the piece of paper, paused and then looked up at Polly. 'So you have found the missing letter. How exciting. Well done. I'm guessing that you would rather not show me the whole thing?'

Polly shifted awkwardly once more on the other side of the table. 'Not yet, miss, if you don't mind. I don't have it with me and er, it's just that ... well, we're not sure ...'

'My dear, I understand. You perhaps want to try and solve the puzzle yourself. Just remember you can't solve it if you lose or damage the letter, so, I do hope that you, or your father, have it somewhere safe.'

'Yes, miss. It's safe.'

'Good. Well let's see if I can help you, then.' The older woman read the paper once more. 'You know, I think I can. Whoever wrote this knew that the coded part might need to be understood by someone after his death, so he's saying that if he is dead, 'with my maker', then you will need the help of his friend, John'.

'Do you know who 'John' is, miss?' asked Lucky, impatiently.

'Perhaps, if we knew who wrote this ... What else can you tell me? Are you sure that this is what your great-uncle found?'

'Yes, miss, we think so. He says in a letter to his parents that he found it when he was training here and then put it back in the same place.'

'And this was in the chimney?'

'Yes, miss. I mean, no, miss. I mean my dad says that he thinks he got it a long time ago ... The only clue we have as to who put it there comes from a note which was also in the tin. It says that a Samuel Ferrington hid the tin and hopes no-one has found it because if they have then he must be dead and the quest is for someone else. He says that the letter was given to him by Reverend West and that it was a clue to finding 'the great prize'.

'The great prize'? Well that sounds exciting, doesn't it?' There was a new brightness in the woman's eyes that the girls may not have seen but each of them experienced the fresh intensity of interest in her voice.

'Well, I do know something about the Reverend West but most of it, I'm afraid, isn't good. He was the leader of one of the big chapels in Binghamton. His chapel, Mount Zion, was part of the religious group - the proper name is 'denomination' - that built Winter Hill College. In fact they say that Winter Hill College was Reverend West's idea, that he persuaded the members of a local family, the Glovers, who had no children, to give up their wealth in order to build it. When the college moved to Oxford from here, they wanted to honour that family and so called their new building Glover College'.

'So what did West do that was so wrong, miss?' asked Muna.

'Well, no-one knows, exactly, but we do know that he was an immoral man, rather too fond of the things that men of faith should not enjoy – you young people do not need to know more than that.'

Polly looked at Muna and briefly considered a challenge to this view, based on their familiarity with the lurid stories in celebrity magazines. Something about the obvious expression of distaste in their teacher's voice, however, deterred her from interrupting.

'I can tell you, though, that he took a lot of the money the Glover family gave him for the college and used it to help his wicked friends and himself. He became a rich man while he was in Binghamton.'

'So he was a thief, miss? What happened to him?'

'When the college authorities found out what he was doing, Polly, they forced him to leave Binghamton in disgrace. They never wrote down the details for us, of course, because they didn't want the scandal to ruin their plans for raising more money. His old friend

Reverend James Angel, the leader of the other big chapel in Binghamton, had to take over as head of the College Trust. West disappeared. Sadly, the extra work on the shoulders of Reverend Angel, who was never a well man, helped to bring about his own early death.'

'Wow, I can see why West wouldn't be very popular. And this is the man who has hidden something very valuable so that he can keep it for himself,' said Muna.

'Yes, that's all very interesting but how does it help us with the clue?' asked Polly.

'Well, it says, *'If I with my maker am'* – 'I' is West, we presume - *'find friend John'*. So, we need to know who this *'friend John'* is.'

'But miss, that's not going to be easy, is it? There must be lots of 'Johns' and they're all dead.'

But Dr McLaine didn't answer Polly's question. Instead, she looked again at the paper, then, raising the finger tips of her right hand and placing them lightly on her lips, appeared to be considering something intently.

The girls, sensing that an important decision would soon be made, exchanged glances and waited.

'Girls, do you know, I think I *do* know who 'John' is? And I think I know where the grave words are to be found.'

'Oh really, miss! Who is he? Where are they?'

Dr McLaine looked seriously at each of them in turn.

'Before I tell you, I would like you to promise me something.'

'What, miss?' asked Polly, sensing that their relationship with the teacher was about to change; that they had something an adult wanted in exchange for the information they were after.

'I want you to promise me that this little ... mystery ... is just between the four of us. I don't think anyone else should know about it and I hope you won't mind if I say that this includes your parents, for the moment, at least. You see, it's a special piece of research that we are doing together and when you work like this you have to protect what you know until you are ready to explain the whole story to others. So, if I tell you something about this note I want you to promise to keep it to yourselves and share it with no-one.

'And there's something else as well. I want you to trust me, girls. I'd like you to give me a chance to show you that I can be a good friend.'

The elderly teacher paused, looked again at each of them in turn and asked, 'Well, what is your answer?'

The girls looked at each other. Lucky's brow wrinkled and she mouthed the word 'Umar' at Polly. Polly shook her head almost imperceptibly and turned to face the teacher.

'We agree,' she said and the other two girls nodded.

Dr McLaine rehearsed the procedure, in which she had been instructed, following the death of Professor Fielding. She had only ever had need of it on a few occasions in nearly thirty years but this was now the second time within a few days. Satisfied that she remembered correctly, she entered the sequence of numbers into her phone's keypad. After a few seconds the ringing tone was interrupted by someone lifting the receiver. A male voice said 'Hello'. She silently counted to ten, said 'Raiatea' and replaced the receiver. Within a few seconds her phone rang.

'Doctor?'

The voice on the phone was definitely his, abrupt and with a distinctly nasal quality that sometimes made it difficult for her to understand what he was saying.

'It would appear that those children, the three girls, have been more resourceful than we ever imagined. They appear to have located the West message hidden by Ferrington.'

'Tell me how?'

'I'm not altogether sure. One of them told me some nonsense about her father having it but I didn't want to pursue the matter in case I further aroused their suspicions. They need me to help them but they are also very cautious.'

'Your proposal?'

'I suggest a change of direction, sir. I think that instead of seeking to search ourselves it might be more productive if we use them to take us forward. I think they will be unable to make progress without me but there is a chance that they may just be what we have been waiting for.'

'Your meaning?'

'Well, this letter they have looks very promising. It appears to have been written by Timothy West and given to one of the college students in his time. But I don't yet know how they knew where to look. There is more that they have not disclosed. Also ....'

'Also?'

'It's difficult to be sure. It's just a feeling ... but one of these girls has something special about her – is it possible that she is 'the one'?'

'Explain.'

'I am thinking of the prophecy, sir, – 'the one who will lead us'. She is very bright. She picks things up very quickly and appears to have some special ability.'

'Special ability?'

'Sir, I suspect that she played a part in finding the letter ... the extra hole that was made in the chimney. And I have the sense that I have seen her before - it was a long time ago. But this doesn't make any sense. I'm sorry. All I can tell you is that I feel that there is something special about her.'

A silence followed that lasted several seconds.

'Very well, I agree to your proposal. I will look again at the prophecy. But be careful, if this is the breakthrough we have been waiting for, there must be no mistakes - and I must be kept informed.'

The line went dead. Margaret McLaine understood the need for secrecy but she felt uncomfortable about the anonymity of her new 'superior'. She often wished that her old professor was still alive. It was her continuing devotion to him and his vision of a new, resurgent, church that had sustained her over these long years of isolation.

I have, it appears, achieved my youthful ambition. I have become a true missionary. I am alone, seeking to bring the light into a dark place; sharing 'the Lord's truth' with an ignorant, misguided people.

'Eaten! By udder hoo-mahn been! Dat na possibull!'

'Umar, it is! That's why the poem says *'though the body be lost'*. Anyway, I looked it up on the internet. It happens in different parts of the world.'

'Na now?!'

'No not now, not really, except for the odd horrible story, someone who's usually a bit mad ...'

'A bi' mad!?'

'But it used to happen in different societies around the world, including islands in the South Seas. They believed that eating some of the flesh of your enemy gave you his strength as well as your own.'

'So, dis John was killed 'n' eaten by dese ...

'Cannibals,' said Muna.

'... cannibal, 'n' dat why dere na body, nar even 'is bones?'

'That's right, but John wasn't his first name, his 'Christian name' they called it. It was his last name.'

'Las' nayem? So, wha' 'is furst?'

'William. William John, and although there was no body they built memorials to him on islands in the South Seas.'

'Sout' Seas? Wey dey den? 'Ow we get dere?'

'It's a group of islands in the seas above Australia. There's lots of these islands. But we don't have to go there ...'

'... because,' Polly interrupted, 'the church he belonged to wanted to remember him in this country as well. He lived in London but had lots of friends in Binghamton who gave him money for his work. One of his closest friends was Reverend West. So when his wife died they buried her here and built a memorial to him at the same time.'

'So, dat wey we-a goin'?'

'This bus will take us there. What did you tell your mum?'

'Me doan tell 'er nutten'. She doan axe me wey me go an' me doan axe her needer.'

'As for my mum, we three are taking part in some school research that has to be done this weekend,' Muna grinned. 'And it's sort of true. But I can't be late getting back, Ramadan starts today and I have to be home before Iftar.'

'Iftar?'

'Yeah, that's just after sunset when we break our fast and eat together,' explained Muna.

'We won't be that long - and of course, Umar,' added Polly in a serious tone, 'remember, you know nothing about this visit. Doctor McLaine thinks that it's just us three involved in this.'

'OK by me. Me whan nutten ta do wid de wu-man. So, wha dis guy, John, doin' in de Sout' Seas, anyways?'

'He was a missionary,' replied Polly and seeing a puzzled expression on her friend's face, continued. 'A missionary is someone who travels to another country to try and convert the people to their religion.'

'Yes, Christianity,' added Lucky.

'Usually,' agreed Polly, 'but not always. Anyway, there were lots of English missionaries in the nineteenth century working in different parts of the world ...'

'... where there weren't many white people. There were, there are, a lot of missionaries in India, my dad's country, and that's why there are Indian Christians there now ... as well as Hindus, Sikhs and Muslims. Mr Smithson says that religion was spread not only by war and armies but also by people like missionaries who think they are teaching 'savage natives' the proper, 'civilised' way to live.'

'Well, don't tell me that you think eating people is OK, Lucky,' said Muna.

'I'm not saying that – but today there's a lot of trouble in India because Hindus still think that Christians are trying to change their way of life, trying to convert them, disrespecting their Gods, their culture, the way they dress, what they eat. The missionaries started a lot of that stuff and sometimes the arguments get nasty and people are killed.'

'Well, that happens between Muslims and Hindus and Sikhs as well,' said Polly.

'Yeah, but me doan care bout none a dat. Me juss wanna find de trezur dis guy West 'ide sumweer.'

The bus stopped close to the imposing stone gates to Key Park Cemetery. The burial ground was small compared to those laid out in the suburbs in later years. Above, to the south, rose the exposed sandstone cliff on which the old upper town of Binghamton was built. This is where the growing town's small jewellery, gun and metal workshops were located, more than one hundred and fifty years before. To the north and east, the cemetery was bounded by roads and to the west, by a railway line. Full and unable to expand, the cemetery, Dr McLaine had explained, was no longer used for new burials. For this reason they were not surprised to find that they were alone except for an elderly, overweight man wearing a flat cap and a long coat, with a satchel slung over one shoulder. He was walking slowly, head down, among the graves, periodically pausing to write on a clipboard he held beneath his left arm.

Polly had been to cemeteries before but never one like this with such a dense collection of dark, grand and ornate memorials, set out in blocks bordered by so many large and equally dark trees. The blotchy bark on the trunks looked to her as though the trees were wearing wrinkled tights. Large, dry, brown autumn leaves covered the ground, making it difficult to see where paths ended and graves began. Some graves were in the form of large, stone chests, some sectioned off by low stone edging with a slab of granite, marble or slate set upright at one end. Some of these large slabs had collapsed and lay face down and fractured. The most imposing graves had tall monuments in the shape of tapering pillars reaching heights of more than four metres. Others in marble, were elaborately tiered, and included detailed and enduring likenesses of the deceased. Almost every gravestone wore a film of green algae.

'Dis playss sair-ree-uhs-ly spooky, mahn,' Umar drawled. 'We shud find wha' we wan' 'n' ge' wey from here.'

'It may not be easy though, finding Mary John's grave.

We've got this map from miss, but I can't really make sense of it, can you?' Polly opened a sheet of A4 paper and held it so that the others could see.

'It says that the grave we want is in L section but with all these leaves, it's difficult….'

'Let's ask him,' suggested Lucky, taking the map from Polly and walking towards the man who had paused beside a large stone tomb, his head now bent over his clipboard.

The others followed at a distance. The man turned to face her as Lucky approached.

'Excuse me. I wonder whether you could help us find a grave?' Lucky asked before adding, 'we are looking for number 212 in L section.'

'Roight, yung layday, L section is just over thur', he replied, in the melodic, local accent. He pointed to an area close to the rear of the cemetery. Lucky could see beyond the graves a wall of rock, displaying some exuberant and garish graffiti rising to meet the brick walls of buildings above, 'but Oi'm not shur which wun is 212. It cud be in the catacombs of course.'

'The catacombs?' asked Lucky.

'Yes, the tombs, buhrial plyces dug into the rock fyce. They used to put bodies in thur and then seal them up. Mowst of them have inscriptions. 'Oos gryve are yow looking for? I now quoit a few of them.'

'Is this your job then?'

'Now, it's not moy job. Believe it or not, I dow this for fun. Oi'm making a record of all the inscriptions on the gryves before ennay mower are damaged or destroiyd. It's unusual thou, to see yung people int'rested in this place, unless they want to take drugs or damage something. Exactly 'oo are yow trying to foind?'

'William John', answered Polly who was now standing alongside. 'He was a ...'

'Misshun'ry. Yes, I now and a very famous wun 'e was too. He's not thur of course, just his 'relict' and one of 'is sons.'

'His 'relict'?' asked Polly.

'Sorry, luv; 'relict' means widow, a woman who has survived the death of 'er 'usband. It's an owld word the Victorians used. The grave is that tall wun with the square base and the carving of an urn and draped cloth. It's among the college gryves.'

'College graves?'

'Yes, sum of the men and wimen 'oo founded Winter Hill College, in Bing'amton; Rev'rend Barker, that obelisk is his monument, he was the first Principal, Rev'rend Angel, the Glover family and sum others.'

'But not Reverend Timothy West?' asked Lucky.

'Now, I don't now that name Oi'm afraid. 'Oo was 'e?'

'Oh, just someone we were told was connected to Winter Hill College. Anyway,' said Polly, impatiently pulling at Lucky's coat, 'thanks for your help. We'll go and explore.'

With all four of them looking in the area the man had indicated, they soon found the large memorial with the inscription and stood before it.

Sacred to the Memory of Mary Elizabeth John
Born November 26th 1799 Died January 9th 1851
Relict of Reverend William John

Beneath this was a further inscription

Also
In Loving Memory of Edwin Tamatoa John
Son of William and Mary John
Aged 80 years
Peace, Perfect Peace
Born; Raiatea April 10th 1826
Died; Hendon December 17th 1906.

'Well, this is it but I don't see how it helps us' said Muna. 'Are these the 'grave words' that 'live on'?'

'I don't know. They may be. I'm going to write this down,' said Polly taking a notebook from her bag.

'P'r'aps dis 'elp,' interrupted Umar from the rear of the memorial.

The others joined him. He pointed to the centre of the block of stone.

'See dose four streak a green, 'n' de hole, waan abuv each streak? Me tink dere was sumting screwed inta de stoan an' it bin taayken off.'

'Oh no,' moaned Polly. 'Another dead end. What now? Lucky, where are you going ...!'

When Lucky returned, a few minutes later, she told them that the name of the man with the clipboard was Dick Roberts and he said that there would have been a bronze or brass plaque on the stone if green stains were present. He also told her that these plaques were often stolen from memorials by thieves who would sell the metal to scrap merchants.

Disappointed, they decided that they could do no more apart from take a picture of the memorial, as they had promised Dr McLaine. Polly also took photos of some of the other Winter Hill memorials. As they left, Lucky waved to the large man who was still moving among the graves. As she and Polly dropped behind the others, Lucky found a few moments to speak privately to her friend.

'It doesn't look very good does it - about the memorial? It doesn't seem to help us understand the code as the rhyme said it would.'

Polly shook her head.

'Perhaps, that's not surprising though - with the plaque stolen.'

'I know,' agreed Lucky. 'But Dick also told me something else.'

'What?'

'He told me that there was a big gathering of people here on the day the memorial was unveiled. There was a chapel in the cemetery in those days. He knows all this because there was a newspaper story about it - and he has a copy of it on his computer. I've given him my email address and he's going to send it to me'.

'So you think there may be a picture of the plaque in the newspaper?' asked Polly. 'That's not very likely is it?'

'No, it isn't, not one that we can read anyway. I mean, there may be but that's not my idea?'

'So how will the article help?'

'Polly, it must have been written by someone who was actually there on the day in 1851. I can use that.'

'Use it? How? What do you mean? You're not making any sense. Sometimes Lucky, I think Charmaine and the others are right – you are a little crazy!'

Later that same day, Polly was sitting in her friend's bedroom.

'This *is* crazy, Lucky. Just because you are able to imagine that your dad is alive doesn't mean that you can actually go back in time. I know you're clever but no-one can do that – it just isn't possible ...'

'Polly', said Lucky, calmly, 'I don't just 'imagine' my dad's face you know. I'm actually there with him and sometimes other people are there as well. I can feel the heat of the sun, the breeze on my face. I can smell roses and the wet coat of our old dog, Ashvin, after he's chased a stick into a stream.'

'But you're just imagining or remembering these things – aren't you?'

'No, Polly, I'm not. When I first started this, I could only watch what I saw happening in front of me. It was like being at a movie. But then I started to take part; now I can speak and others can speak to me – now I'm *in* the movie. All I can tell you is that it is very real.'

'But it can't be real, can it? No-one can travel through time – it just isn't possible. You're the one who knows about science, Lucky.'

'I didn't say that I understood how it works – only that it does – and it means that I can find out about things.'

Lucky paused, sighed deeply, looked directly at her

friend and continued.

'Polly, I lied to you and the others. I didn't work out that stuff about the floor being lowered in the college, in the way I told you.'

'What do you mean? You went upstairs with Umar. You said there was a difference in heights between the first and ground floors.'

'Polly, I already knew and pretended to you and the others that I worked it out, so you wouldn't be upset.'

'So what are you saying? How did you know?'

'Can't you guess? I went back in time, Polly. I used the original plan that Dr McLaine had in her desk ... to connect me ...'

'But how could you get hold of it?'

'I got Umar to 'borrow' the plan from Dr McLaine's desk and made a copy of that. I read some other stuff that Dr McLaine lent me about the early history of the college. It was difficult. I had to make several 'trips' but eventually got back to the right time. I met some of the students, 'scholars' in those days. I even met the young man who used that fifth study. His name is ... was ... Samuel, Samuel Ferrington.'

'So you knew ...'

'Yes, I knew that the floor had been lowered because I walked along the central corridor in the west wing. I even managed to get into the fifth study on the right by pretending to be a serving maid sent to make fires but although I looked in the chimney I couldn't find the letter. Perhaps I was there at the wrong time ... I don't know ... but I do know that I can do this.'

Polly briefly raised her hand to her mouth.

'This is how you worked out the Philpott thing, isn't it? You didn't use the internet … you went back to the time my grandfather was living there. You walked down their road. You might have seen my family, talked to them …'

'I didn't see them. I'm sorry, Polly. It's wrong to lie to your best friend ...'

'But … but if this is true … this is crazy ... and it's amazing, Lucky ... think what you can do with this ... you could find out about all sorts of things ... you could find out the questions before an exam … we could make a lot of money!'

'Polly it doesn't work for everything. I can't 'connect' unless I have something from the time to read, see, touch, smell, taste. I have to be able to feel something about the time I'm returning to. I can't go back and change history and there's something else ...'

'What?'

'Each time I go, it gets a little harder to come back. I begin to like some of the people I meet. When I return it makes me sad ... very sad … because I know that they are no longer living … but I am. So, I don't think I can do this many more times, Polly. But I really want to make this visit and find out what the missing words on the memorial can tell us.'

'Ok,' said Polly quietly. 'If you're really sure about it, I'll do what I can to help but you must take care, Lucky – you're my best friend and I don't want you to get hurt.'

With Polly's assistance, Lucky spent the next few

days collecting everything she could about William John and his wife Mary. They researched the internet. They visited Binghamton Central Library to read biographies and other books about the period, including some on the history of Key Park cemetery. When Dick Robert's email attachment arrived with the copy of the newspaper article, on the unveiling of the memorial to the Johns, Lucky read it avidly, several times.

Eventually, Lucky decided that she was ready to 'connect' and one Sunday afternoon when her mother was at a friend's house, the two girls arranged that she would make an attempt.

Polly helped Lucky prepare the room by turning up the central heating, drawing the curtains, muffling the telephone and closing all the doors and windows. With the papers and photographs beside her on the floor Lucky went through a familiar stretching routine.

'Polly, you must go and sit in the chair now and watch out for me. I will close my eyes soon, begin some breathing exercises and then start to meditate. You must see that I'm not disturbed. If anyone comes to the door, do your best to make sure that they don't make too much noise. Is that OK?'

'Yes, Lucky, I'll protect you, but don't be too long.'

Lucky sat down on the floor in what she told Polly was the 'lotus position' with her legs bent at the knees, her ankles crossed, her back straight, head held upright and hands resting lightly on her knees. Then, she smiled softly at her friend and closed her eyes.

Lucky concentrated on her breathing. She soon became more aware of the weight of her body through the points where contact was made with the floor. She sensed too, the way fresh air was drawn into her body through her nose, filling, expanding her lungs and raising her chest. She counted to eight and slowly released her breath on a similar count. She further slowed the rate of breathing and welcomed the arrival of a suffused, warm light that permeated her body.

In this trance-like condition she began to conjure up a rapidly moving series of images; words read and pictures seen in her research. In a blend of will and intuition she slowed the flickering slideshow, then settled on a single mind-image, a portion of handwriting elegantly crafted by the chaplain at the cemetery on the day the memorial was unveiled. It was part of an exquisitely neat record they had found in the Central Library listing all the burials for the 1850s. Mary John's name was there together with the section and plot number.

By conjuring up this image and focussing intently upon it, Lucky began to see how the ink on the paper connected a sequence of moments and how each moment was fixed in time, linked to other countless moments composed of innumerable sounds, colours and feelings. She began her quest to reclaim a portion, a small thread of such moments, moving back towards them though resistance enveloped her. She relaxed. She knew it was pointless to struggle. She had to find the flow, the counter-current that could take her back as an ocean of time flowed around and through her ... a soundless thunder arrived ... she felt the powerful current take her, as though a single leaf in a tsunami of boiling energy. Somewhere the eddies, the undertow of the time-tide was lurking ...

On hearing a volley of light knocking, Richard Wilby finished typing the sentence on his computer screen and looked up. The door had already opened and his personal assistant stood in the doorway.

'Yes, Kate?'

'Mrs Hussein is here with Umar and his probation officer. They're in reception. Should I bring them through?'

'Yes, please do.'

'Oh, and Mr Pearce also asked me to remind you that he is happy to deal with this one if you want him to. He's had a lot of contact with mother. He says he knows how busy you are.'

'Please tell Mr Pearce, 'thank you' but I think it's important that I handle this. I have a special interest in the welfare of this young man.'

Moments later the group stood at the headteacher's door. He invited them in.

'I'm pleased to meet you, Mrs Hussein,' said Mr Wilby, tentatively offering his hand in greeting. Having learned that not all Muslim women were comfortable with a male handshake he was ready to withdraw but the woman responded with a very brief, light grasp.

'And Mister …?' he now turned to shake hands more confidently with the man who had followed the mother into the room.

'Evans. Roger Evans. Umar's probation officer.'

'I'm pleased that you could be here, Mr. Evans; especially as Umar's social worker couldn't attend this meeting.'

Mr Wilby then turned to face the final member of the small group.

'And Umar, as well. Good. Come in.'

Umar reluctantly entered the room and confronted by his headteacher's hand, proffered a limp one of his own in response.

'Right, please take a seat, everyone. Umar, I'm going to ask you to remain standing.'

The headteacher paused as the adults found seats on the blue sofa. He turned his revolving chair and brought it closer to a position facing them.

'Mrs Hussein, I know from my colleagues that you have made several visits to the school to discuss Umar's behaviour and I appreciate that this isn't always easy for you.'

'I'm a single parent, Mr Wilby and have Umar's younger sister to think about. My health's not been good either – I'm under the doctor at Binghamton General Hospital, you know.'

'I'm sorry to hear that Mrs Hussein but I'm sure you appreciate that we have to run a school here for over a thousand students and Umar is causing us major problems.'

'He causes me problems too, Mr Wilby – I tell him that he has to listen to his teachers.'

'Nevertheless, he doesn't always do that. As you

know, he has already been placed in our Learning Support Unit for the last two months because of his assault on another pupil ...'

''E cuss me furs'!' Umar interrupted.

The headteacher turned to look at him.

'You'll get your chance to speak, young man, but not yet.' Then, turning back to Umar's mother, he continued. 'That's a very good example of how Umar can get it wrong, Mrs Hussein. The fact is, everyone has already agreed that physical violence can never be a solution to a problem and Umar wouldn't have a probation officer if his behaviour hadn't already led him into some serious trouble.'

'But ...'

'Umar, wait,' said the probation officer. 'Let's hear what Mr Wilby has to say. You're not doing yourself any favours at the moment, mate.'

Mr Wilby continued.

'So, if we are all agreed that Umar has already been in serious trouble with the school - and the courts - I have to tell you that I now have reason to believe that he has been involved in some new and serious damage to the school buildings.'

'Damage to the building? I didn't know about that ...'

'Mrs Hussein, I will explain. A few days ago some holes were knocked into the walls of our old building, our college building, I'm sure you know the one I'm talking about, at the top of the hill. The very next day further damage was caused to the wall.'

'But what has this got to do with Umar?'

'Umar was seen in the place where this damage took place, the morning after it happened. I also know that he returned to the area later that day, with others, after school had ended and our security cameras show that he was near the building that evening when the second lot of damage was done.'

"How yuh know dat?' asked Umar.

'Umar, you were seen near the damage in the morning, when the area was already out of bounds. The cleaner said you were in the corridor later that afternoon when one of the covers was removed. She described you very accurately and identified you from a photograph. Further damage was caused that evening and we have CCTV images that appear to show that you, or someone very similar to you, was in the grounds after the gates were locked for the night – I'll admit that the quality of the images, in the dark, is not conclusive.'

'Can I ask a question Mr Wilby?' asked Mr Evans. 'If security cameras appear to show Umar near the building on the second night what do they show when the original damage took place?'

'Unfortunately, Mr Evans, the cameras were switched off that evening for some maintenance work.'

Mr Wilby swivelled to face Umar's mother.

'I hope you can see, with the weight of evidence before me, I have little choice but to ask you, Mrs Hussein, to keep your son at home for the next ten days, and perhaps longer, while I make further enquiries.'

'Yuh-a expellin' me!'

'I'm 'excluding' you, Umar, but your mother may want to think about whether it would be a good idea to find you a place in another school. Things are clearly not going well here and a new start, in another school, may be best for everyone.'

'I'm not a well person, Mr Wilby, as I told you. There's no father around to teach him how to behave.' Her voice breaking, she turned to face the boy. 'You've let me down again, Umar. What am I going to do? Do you want me to get worse? Will that help your sister?'

No-one spoke as she reached into her handbag, removed a tissue and blew her nose. When she looked up at Umar, her expression had quickly changed from despair to anger. 'Right, when we get home, you're grounded!'

'Chaw, yuh carn't stop me ...'

'Umar!' Mr Evans interrupted, then, turning to face the headteacher, 'Mr Wilby you said that Umar would get a chance to speak. Can we hear what he has to say about the reasons why he was taking such an interest in the damage, why he removed the covering and why he *may* have caused further damage to the wall?'

'Of course. Well, Umar?'

'Me sayin' nutten ta yuh. 'S waysst a bret.'

'A waste of breath?' translated the headteacher. 'Thank you Umar, you have just made my point for me. I don't think there's anything more for us to talk about.'

IX
Key Park Cemetery, Binghamton
June 1851

'Bessie, is that you?'

Lucky spun round to face the man who had spoken. Disoriented by the suddenness of her 'arrival' she needed time to compose herself. Scanning the scene beyond, she was relieved to see that she was obviously in a cemetery. The young man, she quickly realised, posed little threat as he nervously fidgeted with a scuffed, black, top hat held in his right hand. He smiled at her, she thought, in a quite foolish manner.

'Bessie, it is I, Samuel Ferrington. Do you not recognise me? Are you not well?'

Lucky looked down at her clothes and was reassured to see that she was wearing the same calico smock with ribbons as the one in the library book left open on her bedroom floor. The young man, she noted, was dressed in a black topcoat over a white shirt and with a black cravat tied at the neck. His trousers however, though also black, were of a different tone to his jacket and at least an inch too short for him. She judged that Samuel was a young man of limited means making a determined effort to dress respectably.

'Yes, of course I recognise you, Master Ferrington.

How are you, sir?' she said making a slight curtsey in his direction. She was surprised. She had no idea as to the origins of this movement. It had simply felt like the thing she must do.

'Bessie, I am the better for seeing you. I do like your bonnet, the blue ribbon is charming.'

He blushed, looked down at his hands repeatedly turning the stiffened rim of his hat through his fingers and hurried on.

'Where have you been of late? Are you no longer employed by the college?'

'No, sir, I am not, but please, tell me, why are you here in the cemetery? This is Key Park is it not?' she said, looking about her in search of recognisable features.

The steep rock face up to the town buildings appeared familiar, though there was a lot more smoke and noise than she remembered. But there was no railway, no busy roads and many fewer monuments and gravestones, though those in place were much cleaner and even, where marble and polished granite were used, gleaming brightly. The greatest contrast lay however, in the absence of trees. Those now in evidence were slender, insubstantial and not much taller than her companion.

'Indeed, it is Key Park. This is the final destination for many distinguished men of our independent churches. I assumed that you were here for the same reasons as I, to attend the unveiling of the John memorial. Unfortunately I was late in arriving. I chose to avoid the Holyhead turnpike and got lost. By the time

I'd recovered my bearings the others had already entered the chapel so I have been awaiting their re-appearance.'

The young man turned to look in the direction of a building the girl now recognised as one she had seen in a book on the history of Key Park.

It was a strange and imposing structure that reminded Lucky of a Greek temple, much like those in her school history book on the ancient world. This one however, was composed entirely of blocks of pink-coloured stone. Those that formed the base were roughly carved and surmounted, to both front and rear, by four, tapering, fluted, Doric columns supporting a triangular pediment and the pitched roof. Although not visible from this position, she knew, from illustrations she had studied, that to the front, large double doors were approached by a series of wide steps up to a terrace, from which the building could be entered.

These steps were reached by a path that led directly from a pair of open, iron gates suspended from large stone piers topped with hemispheres, all of which were constructed from the same red sandstone. Through the railings, finished with large, forbidding spikes, she could see a small number of men gathered together in a knot of conversation. Along the cobbled roadway two young boys tended horses, most of which were connected to small, black, well-polished carriages. Above the horses' heads, the muzzles of which were buried in nosebags, the cold air was repeatedly filled by thin, short-lived, clouds of steam.

'The service will be over soon – look, there they are now,' declared the young man as a party of men and women dressed in uniform black began to appear from around the corner of the building, their outlines contrasting with the lighter stone of the chapel walls.

As the column reorganised and grew in length, Lucky looked in the direction in which the party was headed. To her left, she could see a large object, the upper portion of which was covered by a piece of luxuriant black velvet. She recognised the shape of the concealed stone as the memorial she and her friends had stood beside, only a few days before - even though some of the other, imposing gravestones were not yet in place.

'They are going to unveil the John memorial, Bessie. I must go.'

'Yes, of course, the memorial to William, Mary and Edwin.'

'Bessie, what a strange girl you are. William and Mary, yes - but not Edwin. He is still very much alive. Look there. He is the young man close to the head of the procession, walking beside the dark haired woman with the veil, his wife.'

She looked as he had indicated and realised her mistake. Flustered, she tried to distract him, 'Does Edwin have another Christian name, Mr Ferrington?'

'He does indeed. Tamatoa. A strange name is it not?'

Lucky nodded in acknowledgement, 'It is. It is a strange name.'

'It is from the Polynesian Islands, I believe, given to him by his father. Why do you ask Bessie?'

'No reason, really. Who are the others, Samuel? Please tell me.'

'Well, I do not know them all but there are some

important and very clever men here. William and Mary John had many friends and admirers. There, the portly man just behind Edwin; he is the Chairman of the Board of the College, Reverend James Angel and the one alongside him, the Reverend Timothy West, a very good friend to myself and my family. The frail looking woman in front of them is Mrs Henry Glover. She is the great benefactress to the College and was, I believe, a generous sponsor of Reverend William John. Then, there are some other board members and their wives and some of the tutors, of course. Also, some of these people are from the London Missionary Council, I expect.

'Oh, there, look, you'll recognise the tall thin man; that's Reverend Barker. You know him of course from Winter Hill and behind him, Doctor John Pye Smith, from our sister college in Hackney, London. He is a very learned man, a man versed in natural philosophy as well as religion.'

'What is 'natural philosophy', Samuel? I have not heard of it before.'

'Well ... that is hardly surprising for a serving girl, Bessie. Let me see if I can explain it in simple words you will be able to understand. 'Natural philosophy' first of all concerns an understanding of nature. You know what 'nature' is, don't you, Bessie?'

'I do. I am not that simple,' she replied pointedly. 'But 'natural philosophy', I don't understand.'

'Well, it is the study of nature and the ... physical world ... and the laws by which they are governed. Yes, that is about as clear as I can make it for someone of limited learning.'

'Science.'

'I'm not sure what you mean ...'

'Science, is what we should, will, call it. But it doesn't matter, I interrupted you. You were telling me about Dr Pye Smith.'

'Yes, well, it is said that he and the Reverend Angel have many disagreements on the place of natural philosophy, what you mistakenly call 'science', in the college curriculum.'

'And the two men with Doctor Pye Smith? They all seem to be great friends.'

'Ah, yes, these are very interesting fellows, Bessie, though I fear their brains are too advanced for the likes of me. The tall one closest to us, with the mutton-chop whiskers, is the well-known geologist, Charles Lyell, and the other, the younger man, is the author of some interesting papers concerning the natural world. Darwin, is his name; Charles Darwin. A fellow scholar says that he is a man to be watched, that some of his ideas might be ... discomforting, even dangerous, that he could threaten the church, perhaps all Christendom ... no ... all religion – Mahomedism, Judaism, all religious belief, think of that.'

He paused and looked inquiringly at his companion, 'Are you aware that Christianity is not the only religion in the world, Bessie?'

'I am, more than you could possibly know. But how can his ideas be such a threat, exactly?'

'Well ... that is not an easy question to answer, especially if you are unfamiliar with the subject of theology, Bessie.'

'Someone who is a mere female, you mean,' retorted Lucky. 'Samuel, perhaps the truth is that you do not know the answer yourself?'

'You are a strange girl, Bessie,' her companion replied, once more surprised by her confidence in challenging him, something his sisters would never presume to do.

'Well, I can tell you that it has something to do with natural philosophy, with his ideas about the origins of life in all its varied forms. He seeks to explain this variety as the result of the struggle for survival that is the lot of all living things.'

'Yes, but why is that so dangerous?'

'Because, Bessie,' he responded, surprised once more, but this time by the girl's naivety, 'it proposes that life on earth is shaped by natural forces and not by God alone. For this to be so it is said that the world must be much older than the four thousand years biblical scholars have agreed it to be. Read your Bible, Bessie, and you will better understand the challenge posed by such ideas.'

Samuel shrugged his shoulders to indicate that his tutorial was at an end.

'There, I cannot say more – you have exhausted my knowledge of the subject. Doctor Pye Smith made only a brief mention of it in his lecture on geology … on ancient rocks, last week. No doubt this … theory … though it be ingenious, will prove to be a lot of fuss about nothing. After all, no-one of any scholarship and wisdom can seriously dispute the part that our Lord had, has, and will always have, in the creation of life.'

'I have heard of him.'

'Dr Pye Smith?'

'No, Darwin, Charles Darwin.'

'You have heard of him, Bessie? How so?'

'He will be very famous ... I mean I expect that men like him are already being talked about even amongst the lower orders, sir. But why is he here in Binghamton?'

'He is from the wider circle of educated men who are part of the church and support the college, Bessie. I believe he was in correspondence with William John in the South Seas – something to do with coral, I think?'

'Coral? What is coral?'

'It is a kind of 'rock' made by sea creatures. It can grow into miniature mountains in the warm waters of the South Seas. Mr Darwin is interested in just about everything in the natural world, Bessie. But look, I must go and join my fellow scholars at the memorial ... I believe that Reverend West is about to speak.'

'I will remain here Mr Ferrington, for though I would like to have a close look at the memorial – I will wait until the speeches are finished and people have left.'

'Very well, Bessie. I really must go.'

The young man looked nervously down at the ground before placing his hand in his coat pocket and speaking again.

'Bessie, I have something I would like to give you. I hope you will feel able to accept it.'

He removed his hand from the pocket and opened the palm to reveal a small bracelet assembled from a colourful collection of beads and bright, silvery shells.

'William, it is so beautiful. I would love to wear it. Thank you.'

The girl took the bracelet as his hand, encouraged by the warmth of her response, moved towards her. She briefly examined the colours and shapes before slipping it onto her wrist.

'It was given to me by Reverend West. It was sent to him by Reverend John. I had thought to give it to one of my sisters but the other would only feel aggrieved. By agreeing to wear it you have spared me a great dilemma.'

He looked directly at her and smiled.

'I hope that we will meet again, Bessie. Goodbye.'

Samuel nodded politely before turning to follow a neat, recently raked path, leading to the group of mourners now clustered together.

Samuel did not turn around. Had he done so, he might have been surprised by the suddenly sorrowful expression on the girl's face as she murmured, 'Goodbye, Samuel, I will miss you.'

'You met him again? What did he look like? What did he say? How old is he? What about the memorial? Did you see that? Were you there at the right time?'

'Polly, slow down. I can't answer all these questions at the same time. But yes, I was there on the right day and at the right time. I did see the memorial. It looked just like it does today, except that it was a lot cleaner and the lettering was easier to read.'

'But was the metal plaque there? What did it look like? Does it help make sense ... Oh, I'm sorry Lucky. I should just shut-up and let you tell me in your own way.'

'It's OK, I understand. In your place, I'd want to know everything too. Yes, the plaque was there but first let me tell you about something else - I made a mistake, Polly, because something wasn't there then which is now.'

'What?'

'It's more a case of 'Who?'.'

'What? Who?'

'Show me the notes we made in Key Park cemetery when we were there together the other day.'

Polly reached for her shoulder bag and took out her notebook. Lucky took it from her and leafed through the pages. After a little while she stopped and pointed to some scribbled notes.

'There it is. See, Edwin Tamatoa John, died 1906. I saw him there at the memorial. It was the year 1851 and he doesn't die until 1906.'

'Wow, that's really weird. But why is it important?'

'It probably doesn't matter but at the time I was afraid that my mistake would make Samuel Ferrington suspicious. But let me tell you about the plaque. I wrote it all down.' Lucky opened her own notebook. 'It said, *In commemoration of the life of William 'Viliamu' John, Missionary to the South Sea Islands, Born May 22nd 1796. Martyred on Erromanga July 10th 1839. He is remembered as the Lord's wise teacher and steadfast friend in Raiatea and all the Society Islands. King Pomare II of Tahiti.*'

'Mm – does that help?'

'There's something else Polly. In the top left hand corner there was a strange design which had been stamped into the metal. I don't know how it was done but it looked like some kind of a fish with lots of patterns in it.'

'That's strange. But I still don't see how any of this helps with the secret code. Do you?'

Lucky didn't answer immediately. Instead she flipped back through Polly's exercise book until she came to the piece of paper on which the coded message was written. She removed it and studied it intently for a time. Then she looked back at her own notes on the plaque. She drew a pencil line on the coded paper.

'Lucky? Be careful. What are you doing?'

'I thought so. There's something here, Polly. Look at this. We now have four strange words taken from the plaque and the memorial, Erromanga, Viliamu, Raiatea and Tamatoa. If you look at the mess of letters in the code I think I can find the … Yes!' she exclaimed making a further line with the pencil. 'There's another – and another! This is just like one of those word-searches the teachers give us when they want to keep us quiet at the end of a lesson. Look.'

> rarotongamitiaro**erromanga**ei
> meoaitutakiatiumauke**raiatea**
> ruruturimataratongatabusavai
> ifasetootairotumasamoatanna
>
> **viliamu/tamatoa**papeihaleota

'Yes. So it looks like all these letters make up words that are part of a different language. It must be a language spoken on the island where William John lived.'

'Exactly, Polly. By mentioning his 'friend John', West was leaving us a clue about how to make sense of these strings of letters. We now know that two of the words are places, Erromanga and Raiatea, and two are names, Viliamu and Tamatoa. West knew both appeared on the monument when he left the clue. Tamatoa was the middle name given to William's son, Edwin. I think it must have been in honour of someone he knew in the South Seas.'

'But this is only the start of it. We still need to work out if there are other words. So how do we find the rest?'

'That shouldn't be too difficult, Polly. I can put

different combinations into Google and see what it comes up with. I can do that at home.'

'Yes, but when we've got all these words what do we do then?'

'That must be where the rest of the code comes in. The numbers must help us somehow.'

'But how? This could take forever.'

'You're right. I think we will have to go back to Dr McLaine and see if she can help, again.'

'Must we?'

'Polly, be sensible about this. Whatever you may think she has already helped us with the memorial. With-out her, we wouldn't know about William John and the cemetery. We wouldn't have found these clues. We've got to trust her.'

Polly sighed and looked at her friend.

'Ok, if we can find the rest of the words we'll go and see her. But how do we explain the fact that you found the information on the plaque and your time travel?'

Now it was Lucky's turn to wear an expression of concern.

'Good question. I'm not sure. But one thing, I do know. We mustn't tell her anything about that!'

The next day, Lucky went to find Dr McLaine before school began. Their teacher was busy, however, and so, once again, arranged for the three girls to meet her at the end of the day but this time in the entrance hall. By then, Lucky and Polly had already brought Muna up to date. Lucky had added that she had now found all the words in the list of letters. Her guess had proved to be correct. All the letters in the first part of the text could be broken down into the names of islands in the South Seas. The text in the second part was made up of Polynesian personal names and for this reason the words had been more difficult to find. Together, they had experienced a new surge of excitement and were impatient to discover whether Doctor McLaine could help them further. When they looked for Umar, to let him know about their progress, they were unable to find him and none of the students they asked could help.

That afternoon, as they waited for Dr McLaine under the gaze of the framed photographs of all six former head teachers of the school, the girls spent some time watching an older student being instructed by a teacher. This sixth form girl walked slowly forwards and backwards, without turning, in front of the school memorial.

'Please, sir,' said Muna, after a few minutes. 'What

are you doing?'

The teacher turned to look at her.

'We are rehearsing for the school's Remembrance event this Saturday. It happens every year to mark the anniversary of the end of World War One on November 11th.'

'But what is that ring for?' asked Muna indicating the object held by the student.

'That's a wreath. Two wreaths made of poppies are placed beneath the war memorial every year; one from the students and staff at the school today and another from the Winter Hillians.'

'Winter Hillians? Are they the 'old boys', sir?'

'Well some of them are 'old boys' but it's not just for 'boys', or rather, men. The grammar school that used to be here before Winter Hill became a mixed comprehensive, that was for boys – but since 1974 there have been 'old girls', or women, who now are members as well. You girls can join the Winter Hillians, when you leave the school.'

'So, were they killed in the First World War, sir?' asked Polly, looking up and pointing to the memorial.'

'No, not the First World War. This memorial was unveiled in 1947. These men were killed in the Second World War. Most would have been students here in the 1930's. This building didn't become a school until 1923 and that's several years after the First World War had ended.'

'Yes, that was in 1918, I know. But there were soldiers here during the First World War, sir, and a lot of them died too. My great-uncle was one of them. Isn't there a memorial for them?'

'There probably is, Polly, but not here. Perhaps, there's one in France or Belgium? It depends where he was killed and if they ever found his body. I'm sure that his name will be commemorated somewhere. You'll have to ask your parents about it. Maybe, they'll take you to see it.'

'I'd like to do that. I think we should remember those people as well.'

'Well, I agree. Remembrance is for everyone who has died, or been injured, in war – and, at this school, we also believe, for those in any way *affected* by war. Remembrance Days started with the First World War, so people like your family are a part of it, but it can also include those involved in more recent wars, in Korea, Kosovo, Falklands and places like that.'

'My family have been affected by war,' added Muna. 'If it wasn't for the fighting in Somalia, I would still be living in Africa.'

'And Indian soldiers fought in the war as well,' said Lucky.

'Yes they did. You should talk to Mr Smithson about the Indian troops in both the World Wars. And there were soldiers from Africa and the Caribbean too. So, no-one at this school should ever think that Remembrance is just for older, white people.'

Sir,' interrupted the older girl, 'can I go now? I have to get home.'

'Yes, of course, Nasreen. If you are sure that you know what to do on Saturday? Please get here by ten o'clock, at the latest. We can have a last minute rehearsal. Anyway, I have to go myself.' The teacher looked again in the direction of the girls. 'It's nice to chat to you all. Bye.'

As he left the hall, the teacher paused to allow the approaching Dr McLaine to pass through the door ahead of him. The adults exchanged brief greetings before the neatly-dressed woman moved forward to stand in front of the seated group. She smiled warmly at them.

'Girls, I see that you are all here. Good. I have a question for you. Before we talk about your news, how would you like a special treat this afternoon?'

'What is it, miss?'

'Well, I thought I might take you for a trip up the stairs to the top of the tower. We can take the spiral stairwell through the door in the library. Have you ever been up there before?'

'No, miss!' they all replied in unison. 'That would be so cool,' added Polly.

'On the way down from the top I'd like to show you something – and perhaps we can then discuss what it is you wanted to see me about?'

On top of the eighty foot tower, in the late afternoon sunlight, the girls looked eagerly for familiar features in the landscape spread beneath them. Crossing the roof to stand by an opening in the crenellated wall, Muna pointed north to the gleaming high-rise buildings in the centre of Binghamton. Dr McLaine explained that the city centre, some four miles distant, was so prominent because it had first developed on the high ground above a natural crossing point of one of the number of small rivers that intersected the region.

From this vantage point she was also able to show them how the original perimeter of the college grounds included not only the playing fields to the front but also all the land to the rear, bounded by two of the local roads, amounting to some twenty-two acres, in total. She explained that descendants of the wealthy man who bought the college and grounds, after its first occupants departed to Oxford in the late 1880s, had sold the building and half the land to Binghamton Council in the 1920s, retaining the rest until the 1950s. When members of the family sold the remainder of the plot, a cul-de-sac lined with houses had been built on the site where the first college scholars had once taken quiet, country walks.

It was difficult for them to imagine the scene as

described by their teacher; how the crowded streets in which they lived were once largely fields, woodland and commons populated by farm animals, rutted tracks and the occasional cottage.

'Well girls. I don't know if you noticed them but we passed three doors in the stairwell on our way up here. The first door leads into the gallery in the library, the second door into a level above the staffroom and the last into the college archive room where the Winter Hillians keep their collection of photos, records and documents on the school and college. I thought that, as you are interested in learning more about the history, you might like to see it – and we can sit down in there and talk.'

The girls readily agreed and with final, lingering, looks at the cityscape they reluctantly followed Dr McLaine back into the stairwell in single file.

Within minutes the teacher had arrived at the first door, unlocked it and led them into a square room with windows in each of its four walls. Between the windows, the wall space was taken up with a series of tall storage units, the shelves of which were filled with an assortment of cardboard and plastic boxes, stuffed animals in glass display cabinets, old woodworking tools, cookery equipment, scarves, caps, and other items of school uniform, sports trophies, medals and more.

'What are all these things, miss?' asked Muna.

'Most of the things you are looking at were used by former pupils. Every year the Winter Hillians collect things from the school that would otherwise be thrown away.'

'But why, miss?'

'Well, they believe that these things are, and will be, of interest to people who want to return to their old school, learn about its history and, probably most important of all, re-visit the past. They hold reunions every so often and much of this material goes on display. Some of it is used by the teachers as well, to help with History and English projects. The Winter Hillians have a motto, you know; 'Every school needs a memory; every student needs a future.'

'In there,' she said, pointing to one of the units, carefully stacked with boxes labelled with decade numbers, 20's, 30's, 40's etc. 'there are lots of 'long photographs' of former pupils. And in those storage boxes there,' she added, redirecting her finger to another large container, 'are copies of the school magazine which was published at the end of every school term until the end of the 1970s.'

'Will there be photos of us in here, as well, miss?'

'There probably are some already and there will, undoubtedly, be more in the future. You may find it difficult to understand this at the moment but the day will come when you too will be interested in going back in time.'

Polly looked intently at Lucky who smiled back at her, conspiratorially, before the teacher continued.

'So, in the future, you'll be able to re-visit and perhaps meet up with old friends and share memories of your schooldays. You will all become part of the long story of Winter Hill School.'

'My dad was here, miss, when it was a grammar

school. Would there be something about him in here?'

'When was that, Polly?'

'In the 50's I think, Miss. He was born in 1942.'

'Well I would think there's a good chance but it will take a long time to go through the archive. We have a punishment book for part of the 1950s, so you may find his name in there!'

'What's that, miss?'

'It's a record of every child who was given the cane, the number of strokes, the offence and the teacher who gave the punishment, usually the head teacher or his deputy.'

'What sorts of things did they do?'

'Things that still go on today; fighting, smoking, rudeness. One boy got three strokes for expectorating – you'd call it spitting. But there are lots of the old registers and sports team photos, as well. Then, there are the school magazines I mentioned.'

'What, for all the years this has been a school, miss?' asked Muna.

'Yes, my dear. That even includes the war years when the school was closed at various times.'

'Closed? You mean the kids didn't have to go to school?' asked Lucky.

'Not here in Binghamton, they didn't. The boys were sent away to Cheltenham in case the city was bombed by the Luftwaffe, the German Air Force. But, I'm told, that they still had to go to school there – at least for part of the day.'

'And was Binghamton bombed?'

'It was indeed, especially in 1940 and 1941. One

night, in November 1940, four bombs fell in the school grounds. Two of them caused considerable damage, blowing out windows and doors. One young man, a member of the Home Guard, was killed by the blast. The head teacher, Colonel Goodison, wrote an account of that night. It's in one of the magazines, somewhere.'

'We could write something about that in our project, Lucky. We'd then have something about the Second World War, as well as the First,' enthused Polly.

'Yes, your project,' replied Dr McLaine. 'You said you wanted to speak to me about that. Have you made any progress with the coded message? The last time we spoke, I helped you with some information about William John and the location of the memorial in Key Park Cemetery. Did you find the information you were looking for?'

The three girls exchanged glances in silent confirmation of an earlier decision. Polly spoke first.

'We did, miss. Lucky has solved part of the puzzle, but not all. We still need more help.'

'I see,' replied the teacher. 'Well, you had better sit down and explain. If I can help, I will; as long as our agreement, to talk only amongst ourselves, still holds?'

The girls nodded and muttered their assent and Lucky explained again how the message, written by Timothy West and hidden in the college chimney by Samuel Ferrington, had consisted of three parts; the first block of letters in two sections, the second block made up of letters and numbers and the third, the rhyming couplet she had already helped them to understand.

'So, we agreed,' the teacher went on, 'that Timothy

West left the third part, the couplet, to help anyone who might try to find his hidden prize in the future. Now all you have to do is use the clue he left to decipher the main message.'

'Yes,' replied Lucky, 'and we have got somewhere with the first block but then we got stuck with the rest of it.'

'Well, tell me first about your discovery at the memorial, Lucky.'

'The memorial had a metal plaque attached and on it were some words from another language, the language spoken in part of the South Seas, in French Polynesia or the Society Islands. I saw that some of these words were hidden in the block of letters and using Google on my computer ...'

'Google? What is Google?'

'Google is a search engine that helps you find information on the world-wide web.'

'Oh dear, so this is about computers. I have never been able to get used to them. At my age, I find this very confusing.'

'But it doesn't really matter how Google works or what it is, miss. I just tried putting different combinations of letters into the search box until I found one that was recognised as a word.'

'And did you succeed?'

'Yes – eventually. I found twenty separate words. The first fifteen are all islands in the Pacific Ocean and the last four, in the second paragraph, are all names of people connected to William John. 'Viliamu' means William, 'Tamatoa' was a Polynesian name given to

John's son, Edwin, 'Papeiha' was a native who converted to Christianity and 'Leota' another convert who came to live in London after John's death on Erromanga.

'Can you show me, Lucky? I think I understand but it's difficult without looking at it.'

Lucky reached into her school bag. She handed the paper with the first block of letters to the teacher. They waited silently while she read, for what seemed to be a long time.

> rarotonga/mitiaro/<u>erromanga</u>/ei
> meo/aitutaki/atiu/mauke/<u>raiatea/</u>
> kadavu/suwarrow/tongatabu/savai
> i/fasetootai/ambrym/samoa/tanna
>
> <u>viliamu</u>/tamatoa/papeiha/leota

Eventually Dr McLaine spoke. 'So now it is only the second block; the numbers, that still puzzles you?'

'Yes,' they all replied in unison.

'And am I to be allowed to see that too?'

Lucky looked at Polly. Polly reached into her bag and took out a rusty tin. She opened it and handed the paper within to the teacher. Dr McLaine took it and carefully, almost reverentially, unfolded it.

'Thank you, my dear. So *this* is the original West letter.'

She studied the paper for a few moments.

'Well, there must be some connection between the two blocks. It would be logical that we use one block to unlock the coded message in the other. Let me think awhile ... there is something familiar about these numbers ...'

Dr McLaine's voice trailed off into another silence, interrupted some minutes later by Polly.

'Miss, why would Reverend West go to so much trouble to hide the meaning of the message? If he left clues for others to follow, why not just tell them where to go?'

Dr McLaine answered without lifting her eyes from the paper.

'My guess would be that he only wanted someone like himself to find 'the prize' - if he should be unable to retrieve it himself. He wouldn't want it to be lost if anything should happen to him but, on the other hand, he wouldn't want just anybody who might stumble upon the information to understand its meaning. The code was a kind of insurance policy. By making and then giving it to a young man he knew and trusted, he was safeguarding the secret and trying to ensure that only somebody 'worthy' would find it - if the worst should happen.'

'Someone who would know about the life and death of William John?'

'Yes, which means, someone from the same community, the same church ... ' Dr McLaine's voice trailed off. 'Of course, thank you Polly. You have helped me recall where I have seen such combinations of numbers before.'

Polly leaned forward to look at the piece of paper and tried to contain a strong pulse of excitement.

'Will it help you break the code?'

'I hope so – I'm not sure ...'

Once more the girls sat in silence, eagerly awaiting further information.

'Girls, can you see how each set of numbers, separated by commas, consists of two, or sometimes three, numbers, themselves separated by colons?'

The girls replied in confirmation.

'Among Christians, this reminds me of a way of indicating 'chapter' and 'verse' in the Holy Bible. Look at the first combination, '2:3:vi' The first number, 2, could be the 'book', 3, the chapter and vi, the verse.'

'I don't understand, miss,' commented Polly.

'The Bible is made up of many different 'books' and each of these 'books' is divided into chapters and, they, in turn, are divided into verses. This makes it easier for people to find a particular part of the Bible that they might want to read - or ask others to read.'

'So, we need a Bible?' asked Muna.

'No, I don't think so. It looks like there are only two 'books' here. There are many more books than that in the Bible ...'

'But there are *two* separate sections to the first block!' interrupted Polly.

'That is very good, my dear. I think you may be correct ... The islands could be 'book 1' and the names 'book 2' ... So, if we take the first sequence of numbers, 2:3:vi, and look in 'book 2', the names, then find 'chapter 3' and 'verse 'vee-eye'' which means ...

'Verse six!' said Polly.

'Six?' quizzed Muna. 'Why six?'

'They're Roman numerals,' explained Polly. 'It's just a different way of writing numbers. The 'v' means five and 'i' is one. So 'vi' makes six.'

'That's right, Polly. The numbers you, all of us, use today, Muna, are Arabic in origin but the Romans had a different system that was very familiar to people like Reverend West.'

'But if the 'books' are the two sections, what are the chapters and verses?' asked Lucky

Dr McLaine closed her eyes and smiled. When she re-opened them they could sense the satisfaction in her voice.

"Chapter' is the word in the 'book' and 'verse' is the letter in the word.'

'What?!' 'Sorry?' they exclaimed together.

'Let me show you – it's not so difficult. Lets go back to the first collection of letters and numbers; '2:3:vi'. Agreed?'

'Yes.'

'Agreed.'

'Yeah.'

''2' tells us to go to the second book, which we know, thanks to you, Lucky, is the collection of Polynesian names. The '3' means 'chapter 3'or the third word in that section which is …

'Papeiha,' volunteered Lucky.

'And 'vee-eye' means 'verse 6' which is the sixth letter, 'h'. So every combination of numbers refers to a letter and the letters may then make words.'

'Wow; that seems complicated to me. It must have taken him a long time to work out the code.'

'Yes, that's true, my dear, but remember, he was trying to hide something very valuable from others who might be looking for it.'

'What do those star shapes mean?' asked Polly, pointing to the paper.

'And that question mark?' added Muna.

'I'm not sure, yet. Perhaps that will become clearer when I've had time to decode it all and I can't do that now. I have a meeting I must be at in a few minutes. I will need to borrow this paper, girls - if you still want me to decode the whole message?'

'Oh, yes, we do, but that means ...'

'What if you ... lose it, miss?'

'I assure you that I will look after it, but if you like, I will make a photocopy and return the original letter to you first thing tomorrow morning. Come to my office at about 8.30. I should then have decoded the whole message for you.'

The girls looked at each other. Polly nodded first and the others followed.

'Alright, miss. I'll come to your room tomorrow morning.'

'Good. Now I will fold and return this paper safely to the tin. Then, *I* must lock this room and *you* must go home and complete your homework. We will meet tomorrow.'

Kaye McLaine replaced the receiver and waited. On the count of ten the telephone rang.

'Yes?'

'Sir, I have broken the coded message – with the girl's help.'

'The girl you spoke of before?'

'Yes. She found Polynesian words within the first block of letters and I was then able to make sense of how the second block provided the key to the hidden message.'

'And the message? Does it lead us to the prize?'

'Yes, sir, I believe it does but it is not an instruction that is easy to understand. The decoded message is yet another puzzle.'

'More riddles? Damn that man West!'

'I can make sense of it in parts but some of the key elements have been lost because of changes made to the building. West used features that he thought would be permanent but he miscalculated. One hundred and sixty years is a long time. We will need further help.'

'And where will we find it?'

'From Glover College and, I think, from the children, sir - and particularly this girl, Lucky. I believe that she has some very special abilities and with my assistance, she can be used to recover information that has been lost.'

'Special abilities? Is this what you mean about the prophecy? I thought we were looking for a woman.'

'Yes sir, we were because of the obelisk inscription, *Dux femina facti* – but perhaps we were mistaken. 'Femina' needn't mean 'woman'. If, instead, it is taken to mean 'female', we could perhaps be looking for a girl.'

'I see. Professor Fielding always hoped that you ...'

'What? Me? You mean, he thought ... that I ... that I was, the one?'

'Yes.'

There was a pause while Margaret McLaine made sense of this revelation.

'It never occurred to me. My failure ... all those years ... It must have disappointed him. Really, I don't know what to say. I suppose I should be flattered, sir. But I assure you, I do not have this girl's abilities.'

'Yes, I have heard you say as much, several times. But what are these abilities, exactly?'

Margaret McLaine paused before answering in a slower, more measured, voice.

'I believe that she has the ability to connect with the past. I do not know how.'

'Connect with the past? What on earth do you mean? What are your reasons?'

'The way she worked out that the floor level had been lowered ...'

'But that could have been a simple matter of intelligence; an understanding based on information you'd already given her ...'

'I agree, that is possible, but when I sent her and the others to Key Park cemetery, in search of John's monument, I already knew that an important part of it, a brass plaque, was missing. It has been for many years. Yet she managed to recover the details …'

'That is hardly conclusive. She may have stumbled on a photograph, a written account …'

'Again, it is possible, but unlikely. She can be very evasive and there is something about her manner that gives me the sense, 'How can I put it?' that she has seen unusual things and has been affected by them.'

'Meaning?'

'I'm not sure. She has a sadness about her, a maturity, a gift that is so strange, perhaps, that it has made her different, cut off from others. I'm told that she is very unpopular with most of the students in the school and even some of the staff.'

'There are many pupils, I'm sure, who are unpopular with the staff! I'm not convinced by this. You begin to sound as though you are … attached … to this girl. That would be most inconvenient if it should become necessary to … 'resolve' the issue.'

Margaret McLaine, put her hand over the receiver and took several shallow breaths as she struggled to compose herself.

'I understand, sir. I will be careful.'

'I wish to see the decoded message. We must arrange it immediately.'

'Yes, of course.'

'Then you may continue as you see fit – for the moment. Your proposal is …?'

'Sir, to help her – help us.'

When the bedroom door opened Lucky looked up from her computer screen and met her mother's eyes.

'What's the matter, mummy-ji?'

'Are you in trouble at school, Lukhwinder?'

'No more than usual.'

'Lukhwinder!'

'It was a joke, mummy-ji. What's the matter?'

'One of your teachers is downstairs, a 'Doctor McLaine'. She says that she would like to talk to you – privately.'

'Oh, I didn't expect ...' Lucky paused, looked at the computer screen, then back at her mother. 'It's OK, Mummy-ji. I think I know what it's about. She's helping me with a school project and said she might have some information for me. She does things like this. She takes her job very seriously. I like that about her.'

'OK. Well, EastEnders starts in a minute, then there's a movie I want to see. Can I send her up – if you tidy things up a bit?'

'Yes, of course, we can talk here. I'll take care of her. We can have a chat and I'll tell you what happened later, after your movie.'

A few minutes later, Lucky had tidied her room and sat on the bed, facing her teacher.

'You have a nice bedroom, Lukhwinder – with the

latest technology too.'

Dr McLaine glanced at her out-of-date, faded, computer monitor.

'Yes, miss. Can I ask you a question, miss?'

'Of course you may.'

'Why didn't you meet Polly like you said you would this morning? You said you would give back the West letter. She is worried about it.'

An uneasy silence followed, eventually ended by the teacher.

'Lukhwinder, I will apologise to Polly and explain why I was unable to be at school today. It was my eagerness to work on the code … I forgot all about it. But, my dear …'

An involuntary smile appeared on the face of Doctor McLaine. Her excitement was obvious.

'Yes, miss.'

'I have completed it. I now know the instructions for finding the 'prize'.'

Lucky experienced an unusual sensation in the skin at the back of her neck. She very much wanted to ask questions but sensing that her visitor had something more to say, she resisted the urge and waited.

'But before I tell you and the others, the details, there's something I want to ask you, Lukhwinder …'

'Yes, miss?'

'I believe that you are someone with special abilities and I would like to know more about you?'

Lucky looked down at her hands in her lap.

'There's not much to know, really. I'm an only child living with my mother. You just met her. I like science, history and mathematics. I don't have a lot of friends but those I do have are important to ...'

'Lukhwinder, I think that we have met before, many years ago.'

'Many years ago?'

'Yes, nearly thirty years ago.'

Lucky looked down at her hands again.

'I'm only fourteen, Miss.'

'Yes, I know. So, the only way this could have happened, is if you had some extraordinary ability ... an ability I don't understand, that no-one understands ... the ability to move through time ...'

'What do you want from me!?' Lucky exclaimed.

'What I want, my dear, is for you to help me and for me to help you.'

'How?'

'I want to test my belief in you by asking you to return to a point in my early life. I want you to bring back something, a drawing, that will give me proof of your ability.'

'But why should I do this ... even if I could?'

'Because if you pass this test, my memory will make sense to me. It will be aligned with events as they actually happened. I will have the proof I need and ... I will then give you an opportunity to collect some further, valuable information. You will need this if you and your friends are to make sense of the message and find what you are looking for.'

'I don't understand what you mean. What information?'

'Of course you don't understand,' the teacher

snapped back impatiently before making an effort to return to more measured tones, 'How could you understand? You and your friends have become involved in something that is much bigger than you could ever imagine. But the fact is that we find ourselves in a situation where each of us needs the other.'

'Even if I agree to do this, I cannot go back by simply selecting a particular day. I must have something that connects me, directly, to an earlier time.'

'I guessed as much and I will gladly provide you with that 'connection'. I can describe the scene, that day in 1973 as though it were yesterday. Will that be good enough?'

'Perhaps, - probably, - yes,' replied Lucky, unenthusiastically.

'Then, let us begin. Your mother says that she will not disturb us. You make whatever preparations you need and I will describe the details of my visit to Professor Fielding, at Glover College, in early December, 1973. I remember it well. Then, if you are successful and return with the object I will ask for, I give you an account of the night in November 1940 when Winter Hill School was visited by the Luftwaffe ...'

X
Winter Hill Grammar School, Binghamton, November, 1940

Robin Henry Goodison pulled down on the hem of his tunic and quietly regretted the loss of authority that accompanied an expanding waistline. He recalled that as a young lieutenant in the Lancashire Fusiliers, twenty five years earlier, his uniform had been several sizes smaller yet still gave him greater freedom of movement than the one he'd acquired only a few weeks ago and which had already been so expertly, 'let out', by his wife.

Major Goodison D.S.O., M.C. looked down and ran his fingers lightly over the ribbon bar above his left breast pocket. Then he checked in the drawing room mirror to make sure that his new, blue, forage cap with its two polished brass buttons, was correctly positioned before making his way along a narrow passage to pause before a closed door. He took a deep breath, lifted his chest and adjusted the leather belt on his high-waisted trousers before stepping across the threshold that separated his home from his place of work.

Turning right, he was now at the far end of a long corridor that ran beneath a series of pointed and visually-diminishing gothic arches. Glancing to his left, along the length of the school's west wing corridor, he began to walk briskly forward. He passed a series of windows that looked out over the 'boys' quad', until he came to one that was larger and more distinctive than the others. Here the stone mullions divided the opening into five leaded lights, each of which contained a coat of arms. The major glanced briefly at the coloured glass and noted once more that the significance of four of these crests was still unclear to him.

The fifth coat of arms, however, was very familiar. It consisted of six small, yellow crosses, the stems of which were sharpened to a point to resemble swords. They were set on a red background of the standard shield shape and divided into two groups of three by a diagonal white band running from the top left to bottom right. This crest recurred in stone and glass throughout the building. He knew that it was the original coat of arms for the college and he had personally promoted the idea of adapting it for use as the school badge.

'One of your better decisions, Goodison, even if I do say so myself.'

This badge was yet another reminder, he thought, of how unusual it was for a building such as this to be brought into service as a school. He had tried his best, when appointed just after the Great War, to make alterations, so that it might be better suited to its modern purpose but there were limits to how far he could go. He had overseen radical alterations to the original arrangement of rooms in the two wings but nevertheless, it remained essentially as it was intended to be, a statement to the people of Binghamton and beyond of the prestige and power of the religious community that built it.

He turned right again and entered the panelled entrance hall beneath the tower. He crossed the floor, making a determined effort to avoid sight of the wall to his left, before reaching and opening one of the large double doors. Below him, at the foot of the stone steps, a young man in khaki uniform, complete with cap and armband carrying the bold, black lettering, HG, stood to attention. The soldier saluted enthusiastically and his commanding officer returned the gesture with practised ease.

'This was the thing I was born for, command of men in a time of peril. Compared to this, much of what I do is colourless and often of little worth.'

In his twenties, Goodison, then a lieutenant, had served on the western front. As a young officer he had been decorated for staying at his machine gun post with wounded men when, in the confusion of an enemy attack, most of the trench had been abandoned. He ended the war with the rank of Major. On the strength of his military service, a few years teaching experience and, he was prepared to admit, little else, he had been appointed headmaster of Winter Hill School in 1923. He recalled with a smile the words of the chairman of the appointment panel; 'If you can command a platoon under fire, Major Goodison, then a few hundred boys shouldn't be too much of a problem.'

Now, just twenty years after leaving the army, he had answered the call to arms once more. He had been one of the first to respond to the radio appeal by Sir

Anthony Eden, Secretary of State for War, for able-bodied men, between the ages of 17 and 65, to join the newly formed Local Defence Volunteers. He was, of course, exactly the kind of experienced recruit that the government wanted and had been gratified to learn that he would soon be promoted, as Commanding Officer of the 4th Binghamton Battalion, to Lieutenant-Colonel.

He had been pleased too by the decision, made personally by the new Prime Minister, Winston Churchill, to rename the LDV, the Home Guard. He considered the latter to be more in keeping with the proud traditions of the British Army and less vulnerable to the kind of irreverent humour (Look-Duck-Vanish) from those who took, in his view, inexplicable pleasure from undermining authority.

In November 1940, Major Goodison's new, unpaid duties were many. He knew he would have to spend the next two or three hours in his study that evening, attending to paperwork for the following week. Patrols and training for new recruits and meetings with the Air Raid Precaution wardens had to be organised and more letters written urgently requesting equipment and, particularly, rifles, for his men.

'How can they expect my men to protect this city from invasion forces if they have nothing better than garden tools and the occasional shotgun or an old army revolver, like mine, to serve as weapons?'

Once he had attended to these matters he was happy to reflect that he would then be free to inspect the top of the school tower. At eighty feet above ground, on one of the highest points in Binghamton, it had been the obvious place to locate a fire-watch station. He had personally supervised the construction of a wooden gantry to give it still greater elevation and a view of the surrounding city unimpeded by the mock-medieval battlements. Tonight, as on every night for the last month, he, and some of those under his command, would scan the night sky for German bombers. In the event of a raid such as the horrific one which had recently destroyed much of Coventry, his men would be able to direct, by field telephone, the fire crews and Home Guard patrols to locations where bombs and incendiaries had landed. They were particularly concerned to ensure that the local arms manufactory, an obvious target for enemy bombers, was kept under close surveillance.

'At least I don't have to worry about running the school at present. Thank God most of the boys have been safely evacuated to Cheltenham – gives me time to lick these new recruits into shape.'

Major Goodison strode to the edge of the gravel terrace and surveyed the playing fields before him. He knew the building and grounds had been used for training one of the 'Binghamton Pals' battalions during the time of the Great War. He wondered whether it was just possible that something of the kind would be needed again, though the building, he considered, was even less suitable as a barracks than it was as a school.

He turned and looked up again at the impressive façade of the old college. Whatever problems the building gave him, or might yet give him in the future, he still considered it a privilege to be in charge of it – and living in it.

He returned to the foot of the steps leading into the tower and exchanged salutes once more with the eager young man he now recognised as a former student of the school.

'If I'm not mistaken he was a sickly boy, asthma I think'.

'Meadows, isn't it?'

'Holbrook, sir.'

'Holbrook. Of course it is. Good man. Let's hope for a quiet night again, eh?'

'Yes, sir,' came the enthusiastic reply, 'though it's a clear sky, sir. Good night for a bombing raid.'

'Well, if the Luftwaffe comes, we'll aim to be ready, eh Meadows?'

Failing to see the expression of disappointment on the young man's face, the Major made a deliberate effort to take the series of steps at a brisk pace up to the double doors, their surface wreathed in the ornate ironwork that supported the large hinges. Re-entering the hall, his eyes were drawn inexorably upward to his right; to the decorative carved stone surround to the old memorial. This space had been empty throughout his time as Headmaster because, he'd been told, the original plaque in honour of the founders had been taken to Oxford when the college relocated there in the 1880s. He would like to visit Glover College, he thought, perhaps when he reached retirement age.

As he gazed at the blank stone within the surround, he considered now whether the new conflict with Germany would result in similar numbers of casualties suffered in the Great War. He experienced a tremor of horror at the thought and hoped this would not be the case but generally took a pessimistic view. If his worst fears were confirmed, he sensed that this vacant space would become the location for a new memorial, one to commemorate the young men, former pupils of his, who were, even now, joining the armed forces in defence of their country.

'Light is going. Must get on with that paperwork, I suppose – if I'm going to spend some time on top of the tower.'

A couple of the men on duty that night, Great War veterans, like himself, had been recruited from among the older members of his teaching staff.

Several hours later Major Goodison had completed his paperwork, spent some time on the tower with his men and returned to his office. Taking care to ensure that the door was firmly closed, he reached into the bottom drawer of his desk and removed the rounded form of a small bottle of brandy and a glass tumbler.

'On a cold night like this, my old bones need something stronger than the awful brew they make up top on that paraffin stove.'

He spent a few moments enjoying the slow transfusion of warmth as it travelled the length of his body before replacing the bottle. Reluctantly, he then stretched his arm across the large desk to take a Mint Imperial from a willow pattern dish before placing it on his tongue. He rotated it slowly around his mouth a few times.

'God, I hate to ruin the flavour of good brandy but this certainly does the job.'

Then he cupped his mouth and nose with his open hand and exhaled. Satisfied, he quietly re-opened his office door.

In the dim light provided by the illumination from the entrance hall, he was surprised to find that he could make out the shape of a slight figure in the corridor, standing in front of the large window. He was even more surprised to realise that he was, in fact, looking at a young girl, probably no more than fourteen or fifteen years of age. He noted, too, that she appeared to be sketching something in pencil on a notepad.

'What in the devil is a young girl doing here and how had she got past the sentry? Don't these people know there's a war on?'

He moved forward, trying to keep out of her line of sight. She appeared to be absorbed in making a sketch of something in the glass. When he was still a few feet from her, she sensed his presence and spun round to face him, her eyes wide in surprise and alarm.

'See here, young lady, I would very much like to know …' but his remaining words were extinguished by a wailing sound that quickly built in volume to fill the night sky.

*'Damn! The ARP siren. The blackout. I need to get all the lights off and get onto the tower, **now**!'*

Seeing him distracted by the noise and hesitating in his advance towards her, the girl broke free of her paralysis. She began to walk backwards slowly, then quickly turned and raced down the corridor.

'Stop there! Stop right now!' he bellowed after her, but the girl ignored him. She reached the corner, turned to her right and disappeared into the west wing.

There was little point in following her, he thought. She would have left the building by the door at the end of the wing and be out through the gate and onto the road before he could get anyone to respond.

'Damn nuisance though, local kids taking the opportunity to trespass - and not for the first time. I'd like to know who she is – and where she lives.'

The Colonel glanced briefly at the stained glass panels ...

'Strange, though, to be making a sketch of the window. What could possibly be of interest?'

... and then turned with renewed urgency to re-enter the entrance hall.

A little later, now on the tower roof and with binoculars raised and aimed towards the east, he was unaware of the girl's cautious but determined return. He had, however, left instructions with the young man, Holbrook, to turn off all lights and to ensure that no unauthorised visitors entered the building. When the first of the bombers was illuminated in the broad, agitated beams of the city's powerful searchlights, the crump of the anti-aircraft fire soon followed. The explosions built in volume and frequency as the drone of the approaching bombers also became increasingly audible.

In the corridor below, the girl tried to ignore the bedlam above and the sudden changes in the colours and brightness of the glass as the searchlights swept the sky, throwing excited shadows onto the walls behind her. She moved closer to the windows. The sounds of the siren, the guns and the regular explosion of bombs scared her but she was driven by the knowledge that this was her very last chance to complete the drawing she needed. When an arm suddenly reached around her neck and another round her waist she found herself lifted from the floor. She screamed as the man struggled to hold her frantically twisting torso.

'Let go of me! Let go!'

'Calm down then,' shouted Holbrook. 'Calm down, you little fool …'

The young man struggled to hold the girl and he almost fell as she sought to break free. They both reeled at the sound of the first bomb exploding as it hit the science block extension to the east end of the building, then momentarily froze at the realisation of the danger they were in. After a second's pause their stubborn struggle continued and the young man found himself spun round by the force of the girl's exertions. When the second bomb exploded, close to the rear of the west wing, a series of glass showers burst along the main corridor in a brief high-pitched crescendo. The young man, his back to the decorated windows, took the full force of the blast. The clothing on his back was instantly shredded by the myriad coloured shards.

Together, they stumbled forward and hit the floor. The girl found herself trapped beneath the weight of her assailant. She lay dazed for a few moments, then recovered sufficiently to wipe away the warm liquid she sensed running down her face. She looked at the black stain on her hand and screamed. With renewed strength she crawled out from beneath the lifeless body and staggered to her feet. She looked at the scene of smoke, dust, broken glass and the prostrate body, a large piece of coloured glass protruding from the neck. She shivered briefly in the cold night air, sobbed, turned and made her way through the doors thrown open by the blast and into the all-consuming blackness.

The second day after their visit to the tower with Dr McLaine, Polly and Muna looked for Lucky in the school playground but by the time the first bell had sounded she had yet to appear. By mid-morning break it was clear that Lucky would not be attending school that day. As soon as school was over both girls agreed to visit their friend's house. When they reached her house and knocked, the door was opened by Lucky's mum who told them that she had kept her daughter off school because she looked very ill that morning and had caused her considerable worry. Thinking that it may help to lift her spirits, Mrs Ladwa agreed to let the girls visit Lucky in her bedroom.

When her mother had left, Lucky told her friends about the events of the previous evening; the visit to her house by Dr McLaine and the 'connections' with Glover College in 1973 and Winter Hill Grammar School in 1940. Both Polly and Muna sensed that Lucky was close to tears by the time she had finished. They thought, too, that she looked very tired and, having been told of her adventures, could understand why. They suggested that she should stay in bed the following day but Lucky insisted that she would join them in visiting Dr McLaine. Now that she had proved herself to the teacher, Lucky had no intention of missing the moment when they would finally get the details of the decoded message.

The following day the girls shared a sense of eager anticipation as they made their way through the empty entrance hall, along the corridor and up the stairs to Dr McLaine's office.

On the closed door, at the top of the stairs, they read a handwritten note. 'Girls, meet me on the playing field in front of the college steps at the beginning of lunch, tomorrow. Please arrive as soon as you can after midday.'

'Tomorrow?' said Muna, disbelievingly. 'Tomorrow's Saturday. The school will be closed.'

'Of course, I remember now,' said Lucky, 'Miss told me when she visited my house the other night that she might not be in school the next day because she still had something to do. I forgot all about it. She must have left this note yesterday. 'Tomorrow' is 'today'.'

'But it's still a bit strange,' commented Polly. 'Why close to midday? Lessons don't end until twelve twenty.'

'It looks like she wants us to get there as soon as possible after the bell. We'll have to get our lunch later,' added Muna.

'OK, well – it looks like we don't have much choice, do we? Let's meet her at lunch time as she asks.'

By ten past one, patrolling the perimeter of the playing fields and surrounded by the excited cries of other pupils either chasing one another or a football, the girls were feeling both dejected and annoyed.

'I know what Umar would say, if he was here now,' complained Muna. *Dat witch has cheated us, mahn. She teef our stuff 'n' now she gawn.'*

'Yeah,' said Polly joining in, *'me tell yuh gal, neva trust a teecha ... it just play-n foolishness.'*

'Very funny, you two,' said Lucky 'but that doesn't make sense. Where can she go? The prize should be here in this building and she knows that we're going to be here looking for her? Anyway, where is Umar? I haven't seen him for days?'

'Haven't you heard, Lucky? He's been suspended by Wilby. Perhaps they discovered that he broke into the school to get my great-uncle's tin.'

'Let's hope he doesn't tell them anything about us,' replied Muna.

'I didn't know about Umar but I don't think we need to worry. He is one person you can trust not to talk. Umar would find it hard to forgive himself if he correctly told a teacher what day it was. Anyway, there's not much we can do now about Dr McLaine. That's the first bell. Let's meet again at her office after school.'

At the afternoon registration, however, the girls form tutor, Miss Frobisher, asked the class in earnest tones to be seated quickly so that she could take the register as normal before reading a whole-school message from the headteacher, Mr Wilby. The class, sensing from their teacher's voice that they were about to learn something important, fell into an unusually quiet and expectant mood.

With the register completed in near-silence, Miss Frobisher then took a bundle of sealed brown envelopes and a sheet of paper from her desk drawer. She asked the class to pay close attention because she would probably be unable to read the head teacher's message more than once.

She took a deep breath, then, began to read;

'Dear students,
Before the end of school today I thought it important to announce to everyone some very sad and upsetting news.
I was informed by West Midlands police late this morning that Doctor McLaine was killed in a road traffic accident at some time earlier today. It would appear that she was cycling to school when a vehicle collided with her. The police are still looking for the vehicle and appealing for any witnesses to come forward.'

Miss Frobisher, her own voice breaking, paused while some of the class uttered gasps and turned to share expressions of shock and surprise. Then she continued.

'I know that, at this painful time, the Winter Hill School community will pull together and support one another. Doctor McLaine has been a much-respected member of the teaching staff for nearly thirty years. We will greatly miss the benefit of her wisdom and experience.
I would ask you all to attend school as normal after the weekend. In the meantime, whatever your faith, please remember Doctor McLaine and her family and friends in your thoughts and prayers. I'm sure that Doctor McLaine would want us, after a short period of mourning, to continue as usual for the benefit of all our students. In due course, we will announce plans to commemorate her life as a teacher, colleague and friend.

A copy of this letter will be given to you to take home to your parents.

Richard Wilby.'

When they had collected their letters, Lucky met with her friends outside the school. Many of their classmates were huddled together in small groups, still unsure as to how to react to the news. Lucky steered Polly and Muna away from the others and towards a quiet spot beneath an old beech tree.

'I don't know what to say, what to think.'

'None of us do, Lucky,' agreed Polly, putting her arm around her friend's shoulder. 'You must have been one of the last people to see her alive.'

'I don't know. When she left my house it was about 8.30. She said something about having to catch a train. I thought it strange because it was so late. That's why I looked at my watch. Where could she have gone?'

'You realise what this means don't you?' added Muna.

'Go on,' said Polly.

'We've lost her decoded version of West's message. She never made that copy for us. And she had the letter in the tin."

'Well I'm not so sure any of that is important any more,' said Polly miserably.

'But, It might be, Polly – if the coded letter and her death were connected in some way,' Lucky added.

'What do you mean, connected? How? Why should they be?'

'I don't know. I can't think. Everything has

happened so quickly.'

'Well, let's think it through – but not now, it's too much. And please, Lucky, don't go saying things like this to your mum or the police – we could all get into real trouble if you do.'

Several weeks passed after the announcement of Doctor McLaine's death. Still hoping to recover the West letter, Lucky, Polly and Muna had asked Miss Frobisher questions about Dr McLaine's family and what might happen to her possessions but had met with no success. The end of year holiday came and went without further news. Then the new term began and the three girls feared that they would probably never see the West letter or the decoded message, again.

By early April, 2001, when the weather had turned warmer and the days had lengthened, one morning found Lucky and Polly crossing the playground that lay between the two school buildings. Close to the college, they heard someone call their names and turned to see Miss Frobisher walking purposefully toward them.

'Girls, I'm glad I've seen you. I have a suggestion to make. I'm taking some of our best GCSE and A level students to Oxford after the end-of-term holiday to get a taste of what life is like in one of the top universities. Just before her death, Dr McLaine, 'God bless her', arranged for us to visit one of the colleges, Glover College. Apparently she used to be a student there. She sent me a note, the day before she died, asking whether you could be invited as well. She thought it would help with that shared memory project. I know we've moved on to other work now but I remembered that she was quite insistent and I thought you might still be interested. We weren't sure we should go ahead with the visit after the terrible accident but I know this was important to her and I think we should respect her wishes. So, as there are still a few places left if you are interested, what do you say?'

'But what exactly would we do there, miss?'

'Well, Doctor McLaine thought there were some parts of their college building that would fascinate you and - she also said that she has arranged for you to see some of the documents in the Winter Hill archive kept in the Glover College library.'

'You mean they would let us see their historical records?'

'Yes, Lucky, but I have to be with you to make sure that you don't do anything silly, like covering their documents with chewing gum,' she said pointedly, smiling at Polly.

Polly chose to ignore the remark.

'But how will we know what to look for? It will take too long to read everything, won't it?'

'Well, apparently Dr McLaine had already thought about that as well. She knew the archive better than anyone and made a list of the things she thought would be most interesting for you. I have it with me, somewhere.'

Miss Frobisher took the A4 diary that she had under her arm and began to leaf through some papers that had been inserted into it.

'Ah, here it is. Let me see, yes; album of photographs for Winter Hill College 1838 – 1870 , 'A History of

Winter Hill College', with some page number references, the original plans of Winter Hill College, 1837, and the Ferrington Journal, also with page numbers.'

'The Ferrington journal!?' Lucky asked glancing at Polly.

'Yes. But she also said that you will definitely need the help of the librarian, a Mrs Almer, to find these documents and to show you other parts of the College that may be interesting.

'I have to say, girls, you are very, very, fortunate to be allowed to look at the private archive of an Oxford College. Dr McLaine must have had great faith in you. I hope you appreciate that.'

Lucky and Polly agreed that they were, indeed, very appreciative and would speak to their parents about getting permission to join the excursion. Both were very confident that this wouldn't be a problem.

Although only Polly and Lucky had been included in the invitation, the girls asked whether Muna could be given a place as well and Miss Frobisher agreed. However, on the morning of the journey to Oxford, Muna rang Polly to say that she wouldn't be able to go as her mother was unwell and that she was needed to look after her younger sister and brothers. Polly suspected from the tone of disappointment in her friend's voice that she may have been covering up for the real reason. Nevertheless, she knew that there was little she could do but agree to pass on the message to Miss Frobisher.

By the time Polly met Lucky and the two had walked to the school gates to catch the minibus, most of the year 11 and 6th form students were already aboard. The seats alongside Miss Frobisher were still empty, however and, as the minibus headed down the motorway, they found her in a more relaxed and talkative mood than she appeared most days in the classroom.

'Are you religious, miss?' asked Polly when the conversation had turned to the history of Winter Hill and Glover Colleges.

'I'm interested in religion, yes. I'm a Baptist. I don't go to church every week or anything like that but I do go when some important event takes place and sometimes with members of my family, especially my mum. She goes every week without fail. She thinks that I'm a 'lost cause' and nags me to go more often. So, compared to her, I'm not very religious at all.'

'What's a Baptist, miss?' asked Lucky. 'Is that different to the people that built the Winter Hill College?'

'Oh yes, Lucky. You see there are lots of different churches or denominations within Christianity. But they share a lot of the same ideas; they all believe that Jesus was the son of God, that the Bible is God's word. They all believe in prayer, in worshipping God, following the commandments - but they also have many differences.'

'What kind of differences?'

'Oh my goodness, I don't know enough about this! One big difference is between the Catholic and the Protestant Christians.'

'Yes,' interrupted Polly 'my Nan says that she's a member of the Church of England and that England is a Protestant country.'

'Well, I think your Granny may be forgetting that there are and have been, for a long time, lots of different Christians and not all are Protestants. Anyway, we now live in a multi-faith country with Hindus, Muslims, Jews and lots of other people who have no religion at all.'

'So, it's a bit like we were taught by Mr Hill about Muslims. There are different kinds of them as well; Sunnis, Shi-ites ..? '

'And Sufis,' added Lucky.

'Yes, I suppose so,' agreed the teacher. 'Religious belief is seldom uniform, the same, within one country, never mind between countries or across the world.'

'But one hundred and fifty years ago when Winter Hill College started there weren't all these different religions in England then?'

'No, not in England then, that's true, but there were still lots of different types of Christians. You see, religion was a much, much bigger part of people's lives in those days and they often had arguments about their beliefs and these arguments led to splits.'

'What kinds of arguments?' asked Lucky.

'Well, as I said, first there were the Catholics and some people in Europe argued that the church led by the Pope in Rome was corrupt and its teaching difficult for the ordinary people to understand. So, a new kind of church arose, the Reformed or Protestant church, because they were protesting about the need to reform the old ways.'

'But these Protestants split as well?'

'Yes, there were many Protestants who were very strict in their beliefs about being different to Catholics and others who were much closer to the old Catholic Church. One important and very strict group of Protestants were known as Puritans.'

'Puritans?'

'Yes. They wanted what they called 'purity' in the way they worshipped God.'

'Purity? What does that mean? I know what 'pure' gold is but what does it mean to have a 'pure religion'?'

'You do ask difficult questions, girls.' Miss Frobisher paused before going on, 'I suppose it means following the Holy Book, the Bible – as it is written – literally. You know the Bible can say some very strong things about the way that people should live and the Church of England was prepared to compromise or soften its views when dealing with powerful people like kings and queens.'

''Fundamentalist' would be the word today,' interrupted a voice from the front.

'Yes, Mr Burbidge, 'fundamentalist' would be a good word – a word that is used today about people of any religion who are very certain that *their* faith is the *one* true path to God and the afterlife.'

'Is it bad to be a fundamentalist?' asked Polly.

'Another good question. I would say that such people are at risk of seeing the world in ways that are 'black and white'. Do you understand what I mean by that?'

'I think so, miss,' answered Polly.

'If you have a very simple view of the right way to live; the way it says in your holy book, then you are less likely to be open to other people's ideas.'

'Like in politics, miss, when you have to listen to boring arguments between MPs about the way to run the country,' suggested Lucky.

'Exactly, Lucky. A good analogy. Fundamentalists usually feel their beliefs, their way of life, are under attack and so become very 'fixed', inflexible, in their opinions. They will often be prepared to suffer great hardships, make great sacrifices, in some cases even give up their lives.'

'That makes them brave people?'

'Yes, they are often brave, very brave – but perhaps they can also be dangerously brave.'

'So what happened to the Puritans?' asked Polly.

'Well, they split as well and gradually changed into different churches or denominations. The word 'Puritan' was dropped and replaced by new words like Independents and Dissenters.'

'Dissenters?'

'Yes, dissent means to speak against something that has authority. If Mister Wilby says teachers should cane all children who misbehave and I dissent – I hold a different opinion. Dissenters disagreed with the King and the Church of England and were punished for it.'

'So, were the people who built Winter Hill and Glover College, Dissenters?'

'Yes, they were. But words like Dissenters or Independents cover lots of different kinds of churches and not just the group that built those two colleges. But that particular church was once very powerful indeed - and wealthy.'

'So what happened to it?'

'Well, people moved away from religion and these Independent churches became much smaller and less powerful. Now most of the Independent churches are joined together to make the United Reformed Church.'

'If you ask me, which you haven't, we'd be better off without all religions,' the voice in front of them interrupted again. All three looked forward to the back of the driver's head which was half turning to indicate his wish to be heard.

'That's a little extreme, Mr Burbidge.'

'Is it, Miss Frobisher? It's religion and extremism that seem to go together, if you ask me. Science, not superstition, is the way forward.'

'So you would discount all the positive achievements of religion over the centuries?'

'What achievements?'

'Well, education for a start. We're on our way to a college which educated young men when there was very little opportunity, especially in Binghamton, more than one hundred and fifty years ago. Or are you saying that education is unimportant?'

'No, but are we talking about education or indoctrination? Seems to me, it's more like the latter as long as they are promoting their own narrow view. There are plenty of times when the church has stood in the way of knowledge and progress through science.'

'Like when, sir?' asked Lucky.

'Like when the Catholic Church threatened Galileo because it didn't like the idea that the sun and not the earth was at the centre of the universe. Like the persecution and burning of heretics. Like the refusal of church leaders to accept the Darwinian theory of evolution. Like Creationist Christians in America today. There are lots of examples.'

'OK, OK; I'm not saying that you don't have a point about the conflict between religion and science but …'

'But what, Miss Frobisher?'

'But all I'm saying is that it's not the whole story. Religion has brought enlightenment, understanding. Some of the most humane people, good people, were also religious; people who brought light to places dark with ignorance.'

'Now, you're starting to use those religious metaphors. Do you mean places like those that the missionaries visited; colonising people's beliefs, while the military colonised their land.'

'But also bringing schools, literacy, medicine, science, technology….. I agree that religion has sometimes brought conflict and misery. All I'm saying is that a powerful idea, any powerful idea can be used in ways that are both good and bad. On balance, I believe religion has had a positive influence. Look, don't we take that next exit to get onto the Oxford bypass?'

By the time the minibus had negotiated the junction, roundabout and the exit onto the A34 in the direction of Oxford the exchange between the two teachers had cooled, with each considering it unwise, given how quiet and attentive the students had become, to continue.

Thirty five minutes later, they had negotiated the traffic on the Ring Road, the Banbury Road and central Oxford and were driving through the ornate, open gates of Glover College.

Mr Burbidge brought the minibus to a halt beside the porters' lodge. A window opened and a middle-aged man, wearing an impassive expression, slowly leaned forward, ran his eyes along the length of the bus, looked at the student in the front passenger seat and then made a rotating gesture with his right hand.

The student wound down the window.

'You must be the party from Winter Hill School,' the man commented without warmth.

'That's us,' replied Mr Burbidge, smiling.

'So you're from our parent college?'

Miss Frobisher leant forward between the two front seats to join the exchange.

'That's right. Glover College started in Binghamton. Doctor McLaine was one of our teachers for many years. She arranged this visit just before …'

'I knew Doctor McLaine. Saw her recently. She was a frequent visitor. Great loss. It's a shame she ever left here. You are expected. Park the minibus in front of the library wing on the other side of the green and make for the doors at the foot of the tower. I will ring Miss Thomas, Schools' Liaison. She will meet you there. I'd be grateful if you could keep your youngsters off the grass.'

The window closed.

Mr Burbidge turned to his colleague, pushed his bottom lip up and over the top, shrugged, muttered, 'thanks for the friendly welcome', and drove into the grounds. He parked the minibus, as directed, while Miss Frobisher gave the students a pep talk about the behaviour expected of them during their visit. They then made their way along the gravel path that took them past the large stone lettering, SCIENTIA POTENTIA EST, on the wall of the library wing, in the direction of large double doors beneath the tower.

'Watch where you step, Jamal,' said Miss Frobisher, as one boy moved towards the edge of the path. 'Oxford colleges are very proud of their lawns. They don't like people to walk on them'

'It's just like our building, miss,' a girl commented, looking up at the stone facade.

'Well yes, it is similar, Nadia. Not exactly the same but I think all the Victorian colleges built by this denomination followed a similar plan, with a central tower, a central range and two wings - that either go back from the front, as with our building, or come forward, as with this one. The front here is much plainer though – fewer monsters, strange beasts or scary gargoyles.'

'There's one,' Jamal remarked, pointing to a projecting stone depicting a dog-like animal with a large snake curled, several times, around its body. The dog's fearsome teeth held the snake's head in a savage grip.

'You're right, Jamal. That is scary.'

As she spoke, two women emerged from one of a pair of heavy, dark, oak doors and smiled in greeting.

They were of similar height and build but different ages. Gay Frobisher made eye contact automatically with the older grey haired woman to the right but it was the younger one who spoke first, in a clipped, professional, manner.

'Welcome to Glover College. My name is Thomas, Gretel Thomas. I'm Director of Schools' Liaison and this is Mrs Jenny Almer, our librarian.'

The adults exchanged handshakes.

'Thank you, I'm Gay Frobisher, this is Mike Burbidge and these are our eager students.'

'Yes, well it will take a while for us to learn everyone's names, I'm sure, but please come inside and we'll talk about how we are going to organise the day. Dr McLaine was insistent that we did all we could for you. We hope that you will find the visit useful. But to start with we have some refreshments for you, in the refectory, so if you agree, we'll go there first.'

Without waiting for a response, Miss Thomas turned and walked back towards the building. The rest of the party followed. Once they were all inside the entrance hall, Miss Thomas paused and turned to face the group.

'Glover College, as I'm sure you all know, started life in your building in Binghamton and moved here in 1886. So, as you get to know our building, you will see some objects and features that came from your city. That brass tablet on the wall to your left, for example, commemorates the Glover family who gave much of the money that made it possible to build your college, Winter Hill. If you look there, at the bottom of the plaque, you'll see that the man who made it had his workshop in Binghamton.'

Lucky turned to Polly, standing beside her and whispered, 'That must be the memorial that would have been on the wall in our entrance hall.'

'What? Where the war memorial is?'

'Yes. They took it down and brought it here when they moved. Our memorial didn't go up until after the end of the last world war. Don't you remember that teacher telling us about it just before we went up the tower with Dr McLaine?'

'And this marble bust,' continued the speaker, looking directly at Lucky with a disapproving expression, 'commemorates one of the great men of our faith tradition, Reverend James John Angel. You'll see that his name is carved beneath, on the plinth, but in Latin, *Jacobus Johannes Angelum*. Now if you'd like to follow me up the stairs to your right, we'll give you something to drink.'

As they moved through a door in the left hand wall and climbed the stairs to the first floor they passed beneath the portraits of men dressed in black robes, contrasting with white lace neckbands.

'Who are these men, miss?' asked one of the students walking beside Gretel Thomas.

'These paintings are of church leaders from the 17th century. They were ejected from their churches because they refused to follow the rules of the established church, the Church of England, when Charles II became King. If you remember, his father had been executed at the time of the English Civil War.'

'Who won the war, miss?'

'The Parliamentarians, of course. Don't they teach you that in your history classes today? These were the people who believed that the country should be ruled by laws decided by Parliament and not by the King. The leader of the Parliamentarians was Oliver Cromwell.'

'Oh, yes, I've heard of him.'

'Good. We have several pictures of Cromwell in the college. He was a great Englishman, leader of the Puritan Revolution and a great hero to those from the tradition of the church that built your college and ours.'

The party emerged onto the first floor corridor and entered a large room obviously set out for eating, with long rows of tables and accompanying chairs. Sunlight flooded the room through the many tall, arched windows. The visitors were informed that the large portraits lining the walls were of former principals. At the top end of the room, on a table covered with fresh white linen, there were grouped bright aluminium flasks, jugs of orange squash, glasses and china crockery.

Above the table there hung another portrait.

'Look, Polly,' commented Miss Frobisher, as they approached the table, 'a female face at last.'

'Yes,' responded the librarian, Jenny Almer, who stood alongside her. 'That is a portrait of Elizabeth Glover. Miss Thomas mentioned the memorial to the Glover family downstairs in the hall. Elizabeth was the most important member. Without her money and energy it is unlikely that either of our colleges would exist.'

'I see. It is good to know that women are a part of the history.'

'Speaking of the contribution made by females, Miss Frobisher, would these young people be Polly and Lukhwinder, by any chance?'

'Yes. These are the girls that Dr McLaine said you might be able to help with their project. I hope that's still OK?'

'Yes, of course. They are the reason I'm here. I am more than happy to help them. Dr McLaine explained to me what it was she wanted them to see in the library archive.'

'Will you need me to be there as well? I think I should probably help Miss Thomas with the others but I don't want to impose ...'

'No, don't worry. I will look after them. In fact, if it's OK with you, I'll take them with me now.'

'That's fine with me. Girls, we'll meet up later. We'll find you in the library, perhaps. I hope you have everything you need for making notes.'

'Yes, miss,' Polly replied, patting her shoulder bag, before turning to follow the librarian, who looked quickly around, smiled at them nervously and then opened a door in the wall beneath the Glover portrait.

They entered a small, panelled room dominated by a large, ornately carved, stone fireplace. The furniture included several comfortable leather armchairs and an old, heavily-carved, oak table but apart from themselves, the room was empty.

'Polly, it's our building!' exclaimed Lucky looking up at a picture on the wall.

'Yes, girls. That's another item brought to Oxford from Binghamton. It's a very fine watercolour. You are now in the Senior Common Room of the College. This is where the lecturers, the teachers, relax. I expect you have a staff room at school?'

'Yes, of course, miss.'

'We cannot stay here long, girls,' whispered the librarian as she checked to see that the door was safely closed. 'And you must take care.'

'Why? What do you mean?' Polly replied, instantly struck by the woman's new, lower and more serious, tone.

'Glover College is not all that it seems, my dear. There are people here who worked closely with Dr McLaine. They are interested in you and may come to know, or already know, of your presence here today.'

'What do you mean? Why should anyone bother about us?'

'I cannot say more. It is not my place. In any case, I know very little. Look, I do know Doctor McLaine asked me to give you this.'

The librarian reached into her leather shoulder bag and removed a cream envelope sealed with a bright red button of wax. She handed the envelope to Polly.

'Dr McLaine said that you would understand the contents.'

Polly looked hard at the envelope and began to run her fingers over the wax seal.

'Please, don't open it here. I wanted to give it to you as soon as possible. It is now your responsibility. I will take you to the library and show you what you need to see.'

'But why did she give this to you? Why didn't Dr

McLaine give it to us in Binghamton?'

'There wasn't time. She gave it to me the night before she died!'

Without returning to the refectory, the girls and their escort left the Staff Common Room through another door that opened onto the first floor corridor. They retraced their steps to the entrance hall and crossed it to enter the ground floor corridor opposite. This took them beneath the gaze of yet more portraits of black robed clerics to another, grander, stone staircase, supported as it turned and gained height, by a series of pillars surmounted with plain gothic arches.

They followed the librarian to double doors on the floor above where they paused while she used a security card to give them access. They entered, turned sharply to the right and were suddenly confronted with a view of the entire library. Lucky could not help but utter a gasp of surprise.

'This is amazing!', she murmured, looking up, wide-eyed, at the wreathing, colourful, floral panels in the ceiling, then at the series of book-lined bays, ranged along both sides of the wide central hallway and repeated in a gallery floor above, then at the slender wooden pillars, radiating finally into a series of delicately carved arches that supported the ceiling.

'You like our library?'

'I think it's wonderful. I should so love to be a student here,' whispered Lucky, absorbing further details, like the large, arched window that filled much of the furthest wall, flooding the space with light; the parade of paintings on the gallery railings of yet more black-robed men; the scrolled Latin mottoes, she didn't understand, in the stencilled ceiling panels and alongside, the strange images of men, from whose mouths large amounts of foliage was either emerging or entering. Lucky couldn't be sure which it was.

'Well, maybe you will be, one day. Let me show you the archive.'

They again followed their guide across the grained oak floor to the last bay to the left of the large window.

'You shouldn't be disturbed, as most of the students are on vacation at the moment – but the odd person may arrive and obviously, in a library, we would ask you to be as quiet as possible.'

The librarian took a key from her pocket and opened the door of an oak cupboard faced with linen-fold carving. Each 'reading bay' had an identical cupboard built into the shelving.

'This is where we keep all the documents on the history that comes before Glover College was built; your building, Winter Hill. I'll put the items that Dr McLaine wanted you to see on the table. Perhaps, while I do so, this would be a good time to open that letter?'

The girls looked down at the envelope in Polly's hand and backed away towards the light of a window that, had they turned to look, would have given them a view across the green and the front of the college to the decorated façade of the chapel. They found chairs either side of a worktable and sat down. Polly broke the envelope's wax seal, then removed and unfolded a single piece of paper.

'It's a letter. From Dr McLaine.' Polly looked up at the back of the librarian and said in soft tones, 'I'll read it first and then pass it to you.'

'OK.'

Polly, Lucky and Muna,

If my worst fears are confirmed, you have just been given this letter by my good friend at Glover College, Mrs Almer. You deserve to know the contents of the Reverend West message you found. I have made promises to you and I intend to keep them. I cannot tell you everything but if you are clever, read carefully and look around you, it should be possible to follow the decoded instructions Reverend West has left.

The message I started to decipher in the Winter Hill tower room, is as follows;

herneedleshadowatnoon*togas?eofabeastinglass*seekourlordintheto wer*asheisfoundinthebrass*rho firstpointstheway*thenfollowthebeas t*wherethelineofk?himeets*adoormustbereleased

The question mark indicates where West has used an incorrect letter from our alphabet but which is as close as he can get to what he wants. There is no 'z' or 'c' in the Polynesian language. The 'stars' or asterisks indicate where there should be a break in the text. I have replaced them with what I believe is now called a 'forward slash'.

So the fully decoded message reads;

her needle shadow at noon/ to gaze of a beast in glass/ seek our Lord in the tower/ as he is found in the brass/ rho first points the way/ then follow the beast/ where the line of chi meets/ a door must be released.

Here are some suggestions that will help you;

· Look for the needle from the window on the top tower room at Glover College

· Lucky has already found 'the gaze of the beast' though she may not know it.

· You should know where the brass is by now. Find the symbol, then, look for a larger version in the Winter Hill tower

· When you have the tower symbol, extend the right lines and the meeting point will reveal the location of the door.

I must leave you to discover some of what this means because, although I trust Mrs Almer, if anything happens to me, it is possible that this may fall into the wrong hands.

You see, my dears, you are not the only people looking for 'the prize'. Take great care.

I have one more request to make – of Lucky.

For much of my life I have been taught that it was my duty to help those who were good and fight those who were evil. Because of the 'old prophecy' I am no longer certain that I know which is which.

In the Ferrington journal I have left for you to read, he writes of a night when he stumbled on a meeting between the Reverends Angel and West. This was at a time just before West's disappearance from Binghamton. It appears that they may have had an argument. What did they talk about? I would like you, Lucky, to use the journal to make another of your 'connections' and, if you can, find the answer to that question. When you have it, speak to me or Mrs Almer – she will know what to do.

God be with you,
Margaret McLaine

Polly handed the letter to Lucky and waited for her to finish reading it. Each looked at the other. Their wordless and mutual astonishment was softly interrupted.

'I have left everything on the table for you, as I was asked. The cupboard is open and you are welcome to read anything you like but it is mostly accounts of meetings. If you need my help I will be at the other end of the library.'

'Thank you,' said Polly. 'Mrs Almer, do you know what is in this letter? Have you read it?'

'I have not – and I do not wish to. I have followed Dr McLaine's instructions because she was a good friend of mine but I have no intention of becoming mixed up in matters that are not my concern. Now, I will leave you to your reading. Please wear these gloves before you touch any documents. They will help to protect them.'

The librarian took two pairs of small white cotton gloves from her pocket and handed them to the girls. She then turned and retraced her steps across the wooden floor to her desk, close to the entrance.

'Well, what do you make of the letter?' asked Polly.

'I'm not sure I understand it all but what I do know is that we are mixed up in something much bigger than we realised. Doctor McLaine said something like that to me on the night she came to my house.'

'What did she mean about keeping her promises?'

'Well, she made a promise to the three of us in the tower room at school didn't she? She promised she would give us the full decoded message. But there's something else, Polly ...'

'Yes?'

'Well, you know I told you she visited me and set me that test about returning to the past?'

'Yes.'

'Well, when I'd proved to her that I could do it – like I told you, she asked me to visit the college in 1940 and bring back some information. She promised me that if I did this she would not only give us the decoded message but go further ...'

'Go further?'

'Yes, she would tell us everything because she no longer trusted the people she'd been loyal to.'

'Wow! And the 'old prophecy'?'

'That's the first I've heard of it. I have no idea what it means.'

Polly looked at her watch.

'It's already half-eleven, Lucky. We have to get a move on. Dr McLaine wants us to look at this stuff that the librarian has left out and we have to try to make sense of the decoded message.

'The two are connected, Polly. Dr McLaine is pointing us to the information we need but she can't make it too obvious because she couldn't be sure that the letter would reach us. She's doing exactly what West did – trying to make sure that she reveals something to the right people, while still hiding it from the wrong people.'

'Ok, well, the first part is *'her needle shadow at noon'* and she says this should be clear if we go into the tower and look from the window. I don't see how we can see something like a needle from the top of the tower but, anyway, we can do that later.

'Then she says you already know about *the 'gaze of the beast'*?'

'She must be talking about the time she sent me back to Winter Hill. She asked me to look at some windows that were blown out by a bomb in the Second World War. I made a sketch. I'd have to look again but I think there was a bear standing next to a post in one of them. Perhaps that is what West is on about?'

'OK, then there's *'seek the Lord in the brass'*? She says

we should know where that is by now? And what does this mean about 'rho' and 'chi' and drawing lines?'

'No idea. Google might help. Let's look at what she wants us to read.'

Lucky put on a pair of gloves and took the first book from the pile, *'A History of Winter Hill College' by Reverend T.R. Barker.*

'Looks like there are some places marked for us,' said Polly.

Lucky opened the book as indicated by one of two bookmarks. Three quarters of the two pages displayed were filled with closely written text and the rest with a black and white photograph of a stone monument.

'You read it Lucky while I look at some of this other stuff.'

Polly opened an album of sepia-coloured photographs and drawings of some of the people involved in the early history of the college. The subjects were seated in formal poses showing their profiles. They wore black robes and the contrasting white neckbands of their Nonconformist faith. She recognised several of the names; the Reverends Timothy West, James Angel, Thomas Barker but others were unknown to her.

Next, she looked at some drawings of the original plans for building Winter Hill. She recognised that some of these were the same as those copied onto blockboard and fixed to the walls of the long corridor at Winter Hill. Lastly, she came to a booklet with the name 'Samuel Posthumous Ferrington' on the front cover. When she opened the scuffed leather cover she could see that it was a diary and that it contained another placemark.

'Lucky, isn't Samuel Ferrington the name of the Winter Hill student you talked to in the cemetery?'

Lucky looked up from her reading. 'Yes, it is.'

'Well, I've got his diary here and there's something marking a page ...'

Lucky looked on as Polly pushed her fingers into the journal's pages where the piece of paper protruded. The journal opened to reveal the script of the diary and a loose sheet of paper; a drawing of a man in a straw hat against a background dotted with strange trees and native houses.

'William John, the drawing. So, she came here that night. '

'What? Who came here? What night?'

'This is the drawing I told you about. It's the one that Doctor McLaine sent me back to steal. I gave it to her and she must have brought it here to work on the coded message. Then she must have written the letter and organised these clues for us. But look what I've discovered ...'

'What?'

'This piece in the book about Winter Hill is about a tall stone monument. It stood in front of our college building, at the end of a long avenue of trees that ran from the steps to the far side of our playing fields. It's called an obelisk. It says there was an inscription on it, 'Dux femina facti', whatever that means.

'I've seen something like that before.'

'Where?'

'On the telly.'

'No, where was the obelisk?'

'In Washington, in America.'

'Yes, but there's one in London as well, next to the river.'

'And didn't we see some small ones like this in the cemetery? I think they must have been obelisk crazy in those days?'

'What's on the other page, Lucky?'

Lucky re-opened her book to find another black and white photograph. They recognised it immediately.

'It's the same as the one downstairs,' exclaimed Polly.

'Yes, the brass memorial that they brought here from our college. And look Polly there's a strange shape at the top of it, like a capital P and an X joined together. Is that the symbol we have to find?'

'Let's go and look.'

'OK, but before we do, I need to read those marked pages in the journal. Why don't you go and talk to Mrs Almer about the Latin words on the obelisk?'

Polly turned to follow Lucky's suggestion.

'Oh, Polly.'

'Yes?'

'Ask her if we can make some photocopies – I think I'm going to need them.'

'OK.'

'And Polly.'

'Yes?'

'Don't say too much about anything we've found. We still have to be very careful.'

Forty minutes later the girls were descending the wide stone steps that would take them back to the ground floor. Polly's bag, over her shoulder, contained copies of the pages in which Lucky was interested.

'She's been great, Lucky. Copied them for free. And she also told me about 'Dux femina facti'. She said it comes from some old Roman writer, Virgin …'

'I think that's probably Virgil, Polly,' giggled Lucky.

'OK, Virgil. Anyway, I wrote it down.'

Polly paused and withdrew a notebook from her bag. She quickly flicked through the pages.

'It means, '*A woman was the leader of the deed*'. She says they think it's about that Elizabeth Glover, the woman in the picture we saw, in the refectory. She was the one who persuaded the family to give the money to start the college.'

'Anything else?'

'Well, she did say that it is possible to read the Latin words in other ways.'

'What do you mean?'

'There's no verb, you see. So, it could also be read as something that is happening or will happen; not just as something that has happened. 'A woman *is* or *will* be the leader of the deed'.'

By this time the girls had reached the bottom of the steps and turned to pass beneath another gothic arch supported by two stone pillars. Lucky suddenly stopped and her friend looked at her in anticipation.

'What's the matter Lucky?'

'If the words can be read as something that *will* happen – you realise what that means?'

'No, what?'

'That the inscription may not be a memorial to Elizabeth Glover at all – it may be a prophecy!'

Lucky had walked only a few paces along the corridor before she stopped again.

'What is it now?' asked Polly.

'I need to look at something in the room back there.'

'What room? I thought we were in a hurry to look at the brass?'

'Yes, I know. This will only take a minute.'

Lucky walked back past the staircase to a set of double doors. The corridor had now turned through ninety degrees as it followed the ground floor of the library wing. Gilt lettering on a wooden block attached to one of the doors read 'Council Room'.

'This is the room I came back to, Polly. It was 1973.'

'Wow! Where you stole the drawing? The room with the wall safe?'

Lucky didn't answer. Instead, she turned the large brass doorknob, as she had only a few days earlier. The door opened to reveal a gloomy interior.

'Quickly, come inside,' Lucky whispered.

With Polly following her, Lucky closed the door, found the light switches and illuminated the room. She recognised many of the pictures and some of the heavy dark furniture though the colours of the walls and the drawn curtains appeared to have changed. They walked slowly around the room, pausing at several of the paintings, including a full length portrait entitled, 'College Benefactor – Sir W. D. King'.

On the opposite wall Lucky moved one of the landscape paintings aside and felt the surface of the wall behind it.

'I'm sure it was here. The safe has gone.'

A little further on, Lucky stood before a portrait she had not seen before. A white-haired, distinguished man, wearing dark-red robes, with a fur-lined hood, stood with his large right hand curled around the top of a walking stick. His left hand reached out to touch a pile of leather-bound books on a table. The expression on his face was one of calm, confident, authority.

'Look at this, Polly.'

Polly was soon standing beside her. She read aloud the label attached to the ornate, gilded frame.

'Professor George Arthur Fielding, 1903 – 1985.'

'That's him Polly. That's the man who was here with Doctor McLaine. Look, he's even been painted holding his stick. I think he had something to do with this mystery.'

'Well, he can't help us now.'

'No. We have to solve it ourselves. Let's go and look for that symbol.'

As the two girls stood in front of the entrance hall memorial brass, they were unaware of a tall man, wearing a black, academic gown, entering through the open door behind them. Holding a sheaf of books and papers to his chest, he glanced briefly at the two girls and paused.

'May I be of any assistance?'

Polly and Lucky spun round to face the man and were struck not only by his height but also his long, grey hair. His expression, both questioning and authoritative, helped dissuade them from giggling or even smiling at his unusual appearance.

'No sir, well maybe, sir,' said Polly tentatively. 'Could you tell us what this means?'

Polly pointed to the combination of P and X at the top of the brass, close to the point where the two sides of the arch met in a point. Lucky looked a little unsure about the boldness of her friend's request.

'I can. That is a chi-rho. A combination of two letters from the ancient Greek alphabet; chi is the X shape and rho the P. They make a 'chuh' and 'ruh' sound – the first two letters of the word 'Christ'. The 'chi-rho' is an ancient Christian symbol, often found in religious monuments and buildings.'

The girls looked at one another. Polly smiled.

'Thank you.'

'My pleasure, young ladies. And may I ask where you are from?'

'We're with a group from Winter Hill College in Binghamton. Dr McLaine arranged for us to visit just before she ... died.'

'Really, is that so? That is indeed very interesting; visitors from our ancestral home, eh? And what is your interest in the memorial brass exactly?'

'My friend and me, we're doing a project on our college history and wanted to do some research here in Oxford – Dr McLaine was helping us.'

The man stroked his closely-shaven chin. 'I see and is there anything else in which you are interested? We are always pleased to show off our college to visitors.'

The two girls once again exchanged glances and Polly registered the slight shake of her friend's head and her furrowing brow. Encouraged, by the discovery concerning the symbol, she decided to ignore Lucky's wordless warning.

'If it was possible, sir, we'd love to go up into the highest room in the tower; if it wasn't too much trouble.'

'Up into the tower?' The man paused, rubbed his chin again with his left hand and then glanced at his watch.

'Why not? I'm sure it can't do any harm. If you wait here for me, I'll fetch the key.'

The man quickly disappeared into the corridor. Lucky waited for a few seconds then spoke.

'I don't think this is a good idea, Polly. Don't forget what we've been told by Mrs Almer and Dr McLaine – there are things here that we don't understand and some people may not be friendly.'

'You can't be worried about him? He's so funny with his strange clothes and long hair. He looks like a skinny woman. Anyway, how else are we going to get into this tower?'

'I don't know – but I know you and you can get carried away. We were told to be careful, not to take risks ...'

Lucky stopped when she heard footsteps in the corridor. Moments later their guide reappeared, no longer holding the papers but carrying a large black metal key in his right hand.

'Forgive me. Introductions are in order. My name is Playfair. Doctor John Playfair. I'm one of the tutors here at Glover College. And your names?'

'I'm Polly Venables and this is my friend Lukhwinder Ladwa, but we call her Lucky.'

'I see,' replied the man, with new warmth, his face wreathed in smiles that Lucky thought made him appear strangely distorted.

'Well, let us climb the stairs to the tower and you can tell me more about your research.'

The girls followed the flapping tail wings of the black gown back up the staircase to the first floor, giving access to the refectory. On this occasion, however, they continued up and into a narrower staircase passing a number of doors until they came to the last, the point at which the staircase ended. The man, now breathing audibly from his exertion, bent to insert the key in the lock. It turned with an accompanying 'clank'.

Inside, there was a completely empty space, divided into two equal parts; to their right, a room that looked over the rear of the college, where a brick wall below marked the boundary of the college and another building arose almost immediately and, to their left, another room with two small windows that looked out across the circular lawn, gravel path, and the extensive grounds beyond.

The girls hurried to the window to their left. From this elevated position they could see over the top of a low building on the far side of the green to the grassed area on the far side.

'Look' said Lucky. 'Over there, in the middle of that lawn.'

'Ah, yes, the obelisk,' added Dr Playfair. 'Of course, that should be part of your project. It stood originally in a similar position, I believe, in the grounds of your school. Before that student accommodation block was built in the 1960s, you could see it at ground level.'

Polly looked at Lucky and then spoke. 'Yes, but we wondered whether you could tell us where the needle is. We were told you could see that from this window.'

The man's tone now changed, as though his exaggerated warmth to this point had been removed like a mask.

'Indeed you can. You girls are not very bright are you? I'm surprised there is so much concern about you. It's the same thing. The obelisk *is* the needle. Obviously they were called needles because they were tall and thin and ended in a 'sharp' point. Haven't you heard of Cleopatra's needle in London on the Thames Embankment?'

The girls exchanged yet more glances. Lucky spoke first in an offended tone, 'Thank you, Dr Playfair. You're right – we are stupid. I do know Cleopatra's needle – I remember now that I once saw it with my dad. I'd forgotten he called it a needle.'

'Well, since I've been so helpful to you, perhaps you could help me?' the man said firmly, with a new note of menace. 'I'd very much like to know what you can tell me about Reverend West's message.'

'What do you mean? We don't know what you're talking about,' said Polly anxiously. 'I think we need to go now. Our teacher ...'

'Don't play games with me, girl,' snarled the man. 'You have no idea what you are dealing with. We know that you have been assisted by Dr McLaine for weeks now. Without her misguided help you would not have got this far. What has she told you about the letter? Has she revealed the contents? What are you doing poking your silly noses into our business? You would be well advised to answer ...'

'We should go, Polly,' urged Lucky, pulling at the sleeve of her friend. 'We don't have to talk to him.'

The two girls easily avoided the man's half-hearted attempt to grab them as they moved in the direction of the door.

'Go ahead then,' he hissed without bothering to turn round. 'You will soon change your attitude.'

Polly hurried to the door, turned the handle and pulled. It wouldn't open. She twisted the handle more urgently and tried to shake it.

'Is this what you are looking for?' asked the man. They spun round to see him holding the key, his arm outstretched towards them. 'The door is very heavy, several inches of solid oak. The entire room is soundproofed and that includes windows of toughened glass. This room was once used for music practice and our neighbours, to the rear, insisted that we did the job properly.'

He moved towards them, with surprising agility, caught hold of Lucky, and roughly pushed her to the floor. Polly screamed and rushed to help her friend as their assailant unlocked the door.

'I'll return in a couple of hours. By then your friends will have left. I would imagine you'll be feeling frightened, cold, hungry and thirsty. Think carefully about my questions. We do not have time to waste.'

He left the room and closed the door. Then they heard the 'clank' of the key in the lock once more.

Some three hours later the girls were exhausted. They had tried screaming, shouting, waving at and banging on the windows whenever they saw someone below on the gravel path. They had stamped on the floor and tried to force the door. They had even tried yelling into the open hearth and the brick flue above. None of these had worked and they were now, as their captor had predicted, very thirsty and frightened.

'Lucky, look at this,' said Polly standing by the window. 'The others are gathering on the path. I can see Miss Frobisher and Mr Burbidge. They are talking to that Thomas woman.'

'Yes, they must be talking about us and look she's pointing to the gates and looking at her watch. She's telling them that we've already left! Gone to the shops, probably.'

'I think you're right. Miss Frobisher is looking very angry and embarrassed. Look, they are walking towards the minibus. I think they're going without us. They can't do that. What did she say to them?'

'I don't know, perhaps they promised to put us on a train if we showed up later. Perhaps they lied and said we'd decided to go back by bus. Whatever it was, it seems to have worked.'

'Look,' wailed Polly. 'They're all getting into the minibus. Oh no, stop! Please! We're here! Look up!

We're still here!'

The girls continued to shout, wave and bang on the windows until the minibus drove through the open gates, turned left and quietly disappeared from view.

Minutes later they heard sounds coming from the door. The scratching and clicking noises continued but with no immediate result. As they waited, both girls rehearsed the story they had agreed to tell in the hope that it might lead to their release. Then, they would go to the police. Although both kept it from the other, neither of them had much confidence that this plan would succeed.

Now they put their arms about each other, backed away to the furthest wall and watched as the door slowly opened ...

'W happen!' exclaimed the grinning face that protruded around the door, followed shortly by the rest of his body. 'Yuh gals glad ta see me, me tink!'

'Umar!' they cried in unison. 'What are you doing here? You're right! It is so good to see you!'

The girls crossed the room, arms extended to embrace their friend. Umar suddenly looked nervous and quickly retreated.

'Whoah! Nah time fa dat. Me tink we oughta ge' wey from 'ere.'

On the stairs, they descended as speedily and quietly as they could, taking care to move more cautiously at the points where each flight of steps changed direction. They reached the bottom of the tower without meeting anyone. Here Umar paused, moved sideways until his back was against the wall and held out his left arm, before dipping his head and stretching his neck, to peer into the entrance hall.

'Dere's nobody here. De door open but we can be seen easy, so we haf ta run.' He turned his head to look at them. 'Red-dee?'

The girls, breathing heavily, both nodded in reply.

'Ok den. Less go!'

The three swiftly crossed the floor of the hall and went through the open, double doors. In the distance to their left they could see the porter standing by the lodge, in conversation with a tall man and a blonde woman.

'Uh-oh. Folla me!' ordered Umar.

Crouching low, he moved quickly to his left and kept as close as possible to the flower bed running, beneath the windows, along the front of the building. The girls followed him. When he reached the junction with the chapel wing, the shrubbery became dense. He led the girls into the spaces behind so that they could continue to work their way along the chapel wall towards the gated exit, without being seen from the path.

They had almost reached the point where they would have to emerge from behind their screen when they heard the sounds of footsteps on the gravel path. Without speaking, Umar held his extended index finger to his lips and squatted down onto his haunches.

' ... anyway I had no choice Gretel. They were hardly going to volunteer the information. In my opinion we've been far too soft – and too slow.'

'But that is not a judgement for you to make on your own, John. Tell me, what are we going to do with them now?'

'We don't need much time, do we? With the rest of those damn kids out of the way, I'll talk to them and find out what they know. They'll be as frightened as kittens by now. You stay out of sight. I'll pass the information I get out of them to him and advise that our chief moves very quickly. If I can't persuade them to keep their mouths shut, we hold onto them until it's all over – or, if it comes to it ...'

'I just hope you're right about this.'

'Sometimes, it is necessary to take a few risks. And don't forget, Gretel, we still have our powerful friends. They are just a couple of kids and none too bright at that. Who's going to ...'

Through a gap in the foliage, Umar watched the backs of the couple for a few moments as they continued to walk towards the door in the tower.

He sucked his teeth, then drawled, 'Yuh gals doan seem to-a mayed a gud im-presh-on wid dat larng pees o scaffoldin!' He grinned, then added, 'We doan 'ave much time. We gotta ge' wey from here.'

Umar stood up and took a few paces forward, passing the entrance to the chapel on his left. From this position he could peer around the corner and see that the porter had closed the gates and was walking towards him along the gravel path. Turning, he realised that the girls had joined him. He looked to his right and opened the door to the chapel, waving his hand next to his head, in encouragement for them to follow.

Inside, they pressed their backs to the stone wall and waited. Outside, footsteps grew louder then gradually, fainter.

'We betta wayit here fa few minute. Wha' dis playce?'

'It's the chapel,' said Polly. 'Where they pray and worship. Look at those windows.'

As the three of them moved further into the chapel they looked up at the large stained glass windows, dominated by depictions of, mostly male, figures. The windows rose above another series of stone statues set into niches within the wall, to a point close to the junction with the high, wooden, barrel-vaulted ceiling.

The dominant colours, deep reds and black, gave the chapel an atmosphere both warm and sombre.

"Who dese geeezer den?' asked Umar.

'What, in the windows? Look, it says who they are. That one there; him in the black robes; it says, James John Angel, beneath. All these must have been important people in the history of this church.'

'And look there, Lucky,' exclaimed Polly. 'The window with the name Cromwell in it.'

'Who he, den?' asked Umar.

'He was the leader of the Puritans,' answered Lucky. 'They fought the King's army in the Civil War. The woman who met us when we arrived said he changed the history of England.'

'But look above his head, that's amazing!'

All three looked up at the coat of arms in a section of the window immediately above the portrait of Oliver Cromwell. It contained a large heraldic shield, coloured red, divided by a white diagonal band. Within the two sections either side of the band were sets of three yellow crosses, the uprights of which tapered to a point.

Umar spoke. 'We gotta go. Dat fren a yurz will soon find yuh garn.'

The girls followed him back to the door. As they left the chapel, Polly looked up at the tower to see the long-haired man standing at the window. He looked straight at them and instantly, began to wave his arms in the direction of a figure on the far side of the circular green. The porter, however, continued to stoop and brush with his hand at some of the gravel that had strayed onto the grass.

Polly shouted, 'Go!' and broke into a run. The others followed. At the same time they heard shouts from behind them.

They reached the gates, but a heavy chain looped through them and slumped at the point where a large padlock was located.

'Keep going,' urged Polly and they followed her past the gates to the point where the boundary railings separated them from the pavement. The railings were topped, at a height close to head level, with spikes. Searching for an exit as they ran, they continued to follow the boundary until they came to a place where a tree stood just inside the grounds. Umar, now in the lead, noticed that a lower branch had been lopped a few feet above the ground. He reached for a branch above his head and lifted his right foot, then the other, onto the one beneath. From this position he was able to wedge one of his feet between the spikes at the top of the railings and pull himself onto them. Further branches extended over the pavement. He reached forward, grabbed one, swung from it momentarily and dropped onto the other side.

'Come na!' he shouted followed by an urgent, 'Hurry!' spoken without a trace of patois.

First Lucky, then Polly, followed. As Polly bounced up from the ground, sweeping her shoulder bag away from her face and back into position by her side, she turned to look back. The porter had almost reached the point in the railings where they had climbed the tree, his face set in a snarl of menace; the blonde woman was shaking the pendant lock on the chain necklace threaded through the gates and, looking up, Polly could still see the agitated figure at the tower window, open mouthed in anger but out of which, no sound could be heard to emerge.

Running, they quickly reached the end of Glover Road, turned left and a few minutes later arrived at a major junction. They paused to discuss which of the options would be most likely to take them in the direction of the bus station.

'We'll have to ask someone. It shouldn't be too far. It's not a big place, is it?' asked Polly.

As they'd run, each of them had periodically, looked back to check whether they were being pursued. When they had seen no-one, they gradually relaxed, their pace slackened and backward glances became less frequent.

Absorbed, as they were, in the question of their next move, it was Lucky who spotted the porter first.

'Oh, no! Look! It's that horrible man!'

The others quickly turned to look back down the road. The porter was walking purposefully towards them, a large stick in his right hand.

'We shud split up. Lucky, yuh run down dere; Polly, yuh go dat way an' me draw him off, dis way,' suggested Umar, looking up Parks Road.

'But how do you know he'll follow *you*? What if he decides to come after one of us?'

'Doan worry. Me goin' to go real slow, preten' like me have a stitch or sumting. Dat mek it eezee fa him. We meet at de buzz stay-shon. Na, go!'

The girls looked at each other and briefly hesitated. Then they looked back at the angry expression on the face of their pursuer, now only fifty metres away. Lucky turned and ran across the road before heading in the direction of an imposing, red-brick building, the walls of which were covered in elaborate blue-brick patterns, similar, she had time to think, to those on the walls of Winter Hill College. Within seconds she had reached the junction, turned into Museum Road and disappeared from view.

Meanwhile, Polly had started running down Parks Road, as directed by Umar. On the other side of the road from Lucky, she passed the front of the patterned-brick building and glimpsed the notice that informed her this was yet another Oxford College, Keble. As she ran, she looked behind her to see whether Umar's plan was working. He had headed along the same road but in the opposite direction, clutching his side, moving slowly and with apparent difficulty.

The porter had paused briefly at the junction, breathing heavily and uttering unheard curses, before turning to his left. With his stick raised, aggressively, above his head, the man followed the boy. When the porter had almost caught up with him, Polly saw Umar suddenly sprint forward to leave the other frustrated and spent, his arm extended to support himself against a roadside tree.

'Ugh! What ...!!'

Polly looked up as she found herself rebounding from the chest of a tall young man. As she recovered from the shock, she could see, alongside him, a young woman with oriental features, equally surprised and staring directly at her. Though the female wore a skirt, both were similarly and strangely dressed in black gowns over crisp, white shirts with matching white bow ties at their necks.

'Please, be careful, this is newly cleaned,' complained the young man. 'Anyway, what's the big hurry?'

'I'm sorry,' replied Polly. 'I didn't mean ... I'm sorry.'

'Well,' he said, his expression softening, as he brushed at his academic gown, 'no harm done, fortunately.'

'Is that man after you?' asked the young woman, looking past Polly and along the road.

Polly turned. The porter had recovered from his failure to catch Umar and realising that another member of his quarry was still within reach, he was now moving in her direction.

Polly uttered another 'Sorry' and hurried away, though her knee and ankle were sore and she was still winded from her collision with the young man. She looked around hoping to find somewhere to hide but on the wide, tree lined avenue, this appeared impossible.

To her right, set back from the road, she could see another grand building with a central tower, flanked by extensions faced with the now familiar, biscuit-coloured, stone. Both sides were pierced with a series of gothic windows on two floors. A sign informed her that this was a public building, Oxford University Museum, and the passage of a few people into and out of the door inserted beneath the arch at the base of the tower told her that it was open. She quickly decided it looked promising as a hiding place.

Crossing a lawn, in order to take the most direct route to the entrance, she passed through the opening in the wooden screen beneath the patterned and elaborately carved archway. She then climbed a few steps and suddenly stopped to take in her new surroundings. She, like Lucky, had been impressed by Glover College but the scale of the space within this building was extraordinary, cavernous; something that reminded her of a cathedral, or perhaps an old major railway station – but with a glass roof. Her parents often insisted on taking her into churches and other 'important buildings' on holidays but her father's fondness for providing a lengthy commentary invariably left her bored and eager to seek other distractions. For once, she wished that he was with her – and for more than one reason.

With another glance behind, she moved forward into the central court. The entire space was flooded with daylight entering through a latticework of lozenge-shaped, glazed ceiling panels. These were supported by a network of struts, supported in turn by towering, slender, cast-iron pillars that mimicked their stone forebears. Above her, the sensation was one of light and delicate pattern. Interwoven branches of leaf and flower filled the spandrels, the spaces between the arches, in a profusion and variety that left her bewildered.

At ground level, the view was equally striking. The central 'nave' was dominated by a frozen procession of huge, bleached skeletons, wired together and supported by metal frames. To either side of these macabre exhibits were lines of tall display cabinets filled with a variety of stuffed animals, bright geological specimens and intriguing dioramas depicting the Victorian age of enthusiasm for the exploration of the natural world.

Polly, recovering from the initial impact of her surroundings, moved between two cabinets into one of the side 'aisles'. From this new position she was able to watch the door without being seen. Her intention now was to wait. If the porter followed her into the museum's central court, she considered that it would be relatively easy for her to work her way around and behind him and back out through the door to meet up with her friends.

When he eventually appeared, however, her sense of alarm intensified. He was no longer alone. Playfair and Thomas had joined him and the three of them spent a short time in conversation at the top of the steps, devising a search strategy.

Eventually, Miss Thomas and the porter nodded. The two men began to move forward into the court, one to the left and the other, Playfair, in her direction. The woman remained at the top of the steps. Polly knew that she had no choice but to retreat further into the building. Around the four walls of the open court, a gallery was supported by brick walls, tapering between pointed arches, outlined with alternating blocks of dark and light stone, to cream-coloured stone pillars. Many of these columns were fronted by life-size statues of men of science. She scanned and recognised the names of a few; Newton, Galileo, Darwin, but many others were unknown to her.

Retreating into the 'cloisters' beneath the gallery, she moved swiftly from one pillar to another, pausing at each to scan the space behind her. Between two tall cabinets she caught a glimpse of Playfair and moved forward again. She wondered whether to risk an appeal for help to one of the adults she passed but decided the risk of exposing her position was too great. She had not yet abandoned all hope of evading her pursuers and joining up with her friends.

Ahead, she now caught sight of the porter, his faced still flushed with the exertion of the chase. She was trapped between the two men and if she returned to the court, she was likely to be seen by Miss Thomas. Then, to her right, she saw an open archway offering a passage into another room. It had an invitingly gloomy atmosphere, in stark contrast to immersion in the bright light of the glazed court. The choice was obvious. She slipped deftly in front of an elderly man, failing to see the inscription in the arch above the door; Pitt Rivers Collection.

Eager to find cover, she quickly descended a flight of steps and moved into the new space in which she found herself. Here, the display cabinets were reassuringly numerous. Each of them, taller than herself, carried a label describing a connection between the array of varied objects crowded onto the shelves. She paused beside one entitled, Magic, Ritual, Religion and Belief. Without access to the daylight and with low level artificial light, she had some difficulty in reading the smaller hand written labels alongside the individual exhibits.

She was startled when an elderly woman spoke to her.

'You need help to read those, my dear. I am leaving now. If they haven't given you a torch at the entrance, why don't you use mine?' she suggested, proffering a small, silver object. 'It's one of those wind-up things. The beam doesn't last long but it's better than straining your eyes.'

'Thank you,' replied Polly, taking the torch from her hand.

'Just be sure to hand it in at the desk when you leave, my dear. Now, I must go. Good bye.'

Polly quickly, repeatedly, turned the handle on the torch and switched it on. Training the light into the cabinets she could now read the labels describing the origins of the objects and a date. She looked up to see the elderly woman reach the top of the steps just as Playfair and the porter entered the room together. The porter remained at the top of the steps while Playfair, picking up another small torch from a basket, began to descend.

Polly moved further into the room, passing displays of pottery, musical instruments and clothing. Everywhere, she caught fleeting glimpses of distant lands and unfamiliar cultures. She felt as though she had been taken back in time to a fabulous warehouse, filled with objects which, she sensed, were important to the people, long dead, who made them, used them, worshipped them. She knew, too, that she could only dimly understand their meaning and power.

The flickering cone of light that swept around the room told her that Playfair was moving quickly, darting from one passage to another. Polly moved closer to the walls, lined with yet more display cabinets. Trying to stay beyond the range of the quivering beam, she turned the corner of another cabinet, dedicated to the native practice of tattooing. She only just managed to stifle a scream when she found herself confronted by a small figure with a large colourful head from which sprouted two immense horns above huge, sunken eyes and the rictus of a mouth, frozen in a savage grin. The terrifying figure suddenly made a high-pitched, giggling sound, turned and disappeared.

Polly, quickly recovering from the surprise, followed the child to a bench where a small group, all wearing different but equally theatrical masks, were assembling before an adult.

'Now, let's go very quietly, everyone. Do try not to make so much noise, Justine. I think you will surprise more people in the museum if you move quietly and sensibly.'

Polly looked at the bench on which several other paper masks, together with crayons, felt tip pens, card and elastic bands had been discarded. She picked up one and slipped it around her head just as Playfair passed between two cabinets, a short distance away. She saw him turn to look briefly at the procession of children and then, directly at her, before continuing forward.

Ahead of her, the teacher-adult reached the bottom of the flight of steps and began to climb, followed by the crocodile of children. The porter scowled as each of the masked figures turned in his direction as they passed. Polly, at the end of the line, was relieved that by the time she had reached him, he had turned away to scan, once more, the body of the hall, beneath.

Re-entering the brightly lit court, she followed the children to another gathering point, where they began to remove their face masks, amid much giggling and chatter. Polly moved away as the teacher cast a puzzled, then disapproving, look in her direction. Turning to look ahead, she could see that Miss Thomas had moved forward, leaving a space between her and the exit. Using a party of French-speaking visitors as a screen, she removed her mask, dropped down the steps and unseen by her pursuers, slipped through the door.

Twenty minutes later, with the help of a pedestrian, Polly had found the coach station and her friends. They bought tickets for Binghamton and waited nervously for their connection while updating each other on their experiences since separating. Polly had the longest, most eventful, tale to tell. The girls then answered Umar's questions about their discoveries in the college before he released them from the tower and they, in turn, asked questions of him. He told them that while he'd been suspended he'd spent some time with some of his older friends and asked them to find out what the girls were doing. He heard about the trip to Glover College and then discovered that spaces had been saved for two younger girls. He guessed that it had something to do with the coded message. He then decided that he would take a day trip to Oxford as well. Before leaving home, he'd found his stained and shabby school tie and put it in his pocket.

He had also 'borrowed' £50 from the wallet of his mother's latest boyfriend and bought a train ticket. From the station, he'd found his way across the city to Glover College, spotted the minibus and when stopped by the ill-tempered porter had convinced him, by pointing to his tie, that he'd become separated from the rest of the group.

After that, he'd explored the college looking for the girls. Finally, a woman in the library told him that she thought the girls were interested in the tower. When he discovered the locked room and heard their voices on the other side of the door, he congratulated himself on bringing along his equipment for picking locks.

Realising how hungry and thirsty they were, they bought some snacks and water. The bus arrived and they found themselves gradually relaxing as they left the suburbs of the city.

Polly asked Umar about the lock picking equipment and where he had got it.

'Dass a see-cret. But dat tower lock was ee-zee, mahn. Anyway, how yuh tink me get inta de skool dat night me get de tin fing?'

'We didn't like to ask,' chuckled Lucky. 'So what do we do now?'

'Get back to Binghamton and go to the police. Kidnapping is a serious crime,' said Polly.

'Woah, yuh carn't do dat?' stated Umar, firmly.

'Why not?'

'Tink bout it. Yuh wi have ta tark bout me 'n' me already in big trubble wid Wilby – 'n' de lahw.'

'He's right Polly. We'd have to explain everything, including the lock picking and that would mean permanent exclusion – and - we'll never get to find the prize; the adults will take over and look for it themselves.'

'But what if they come after us?'

'There's a good chance they won't. They will have to be very careful, for a few days at least. We now have most of the information we need. If we move quickly, we can find the prize and solve this mystery.'

'Yeah, me agree wid dat. Me wanna be famus, man – 'n' rich.'

Polly looked at Lucky. 'I see what you mean about Umar and ... I want to see this through, as much as you do. My great uncle Arthur would want me to, as well.'

She took another swig of water from her bottle.

'Ok. How about we meet with Muna, tomorrow? It's a Saturday and on Sunday the school will be empty. If we can figure out that stuff about the Lord's symbol in the tower, Umar can get us into where we want to go.'

'Sounds good to me,' said Lucky. 'But there's something else I need to do tomorrow as well ...'

'What?' the others asked together.

'Doctor McLaine kept her last promise to me. I intend to do something for her.'

Access to the grounds of the college the following day could not have been easier. Polly had called Muna and arranged to meet at the corner shop at eleven o'clock. By the time they approached the school entrance Polly had told her friend all about the events of the previous day and answered her eager questions. They found the gates open and a number of vehicles in the car park, alongside the playing field.

Lucky was waiting for them.

'Good news. Apparently, there's a football match about to start, so there are some people around. We won't be noticed. And, even better, the main doors into the building are open. If we need to, we can get inside.'

'Great,' said Polly. 'Did you get into any trouble with your Mum last night?'

'Only a little,' replied Lucky. 'She'd had a phone call from Miss Frobisher. I told her that we'd got bored and went to look at the shops. Then, when we got back to the college, the minibus had already left. She made me phone 'Froby' and apologise. You'd already phoned her by then, so, I just backed up your story.'

'She told me I had to phone Miss Thomas and apologise to her, as well. I said I would, but I didn't and I won't. Anyway, I don't think they will want to stir things up for us in case we make trouble for them.'

'Miss Frobisher says we'll have to see Pearce on Monday, though. That won't be much fun.'

'Never mind,' said Muna. 'From what Polly tells me about the plans for tomorrow we could all be heroes by then. And even if we're not, at least you managed to keep Umar's name out of it.'

'Yes, that's true. Umar was wicked. I never thought I'd say that. But let's get on with trying to make sense of these clues. Should I read it all again?'

Polly dipped her hand into her shoulder bag, rifled through a number of sheets of paper until she found the one she wanted.

'Here it is.'

Polly read aloud the message deciphered by Doctor McLaine;

Her needle shadow at noon / to gaze of a beast in glass/ seek our Lord in the tower/ as he is found in the brass/ rho first points the way/ then follow the beast/ where the line of chi meets/ a door must be released

'So, what's that all about, Polly?' asked Muna.

'*Her needle shadow at noon*', has something to do with the obelisk that's now in Oxford but used to be here, on the other side of the playing fields. 'Needle' is another, common, name for an obelisk.'

Polly looked up towards the field. A group of young boys were emerging from the sports centre accompanied by the machine-gun rattle of their studs on the concrete steps. This sound was quickly extinguished once they reached the grass, and replaced by excited cries as they ran towards a loose knot of adults positioned by the white line marking the edge of the football pitch.

'The book at Glover College says that there used to be an avenue of trees that started over there, where the steps go up to the terrace.' Polly's outstretched arm swung through an arc as she continued to outline the course of the lost avenue. 'It ran across the playing field to the far side, somewhere over there, where that white cricket screen thing is.'

'But why **her** needle shadow?'

'The obelisk or needle has an inscription on it in Latin; 'Dux femina facti'. It means 'a woman was the leader of the deed' and they think it's in honour of Elizabeth Glover, one of the family that gave money to build the college, but it could also mean something else.'

'Like what?'

'A *female*, not *'woman'*, *will be*, and not *'was'*, the leader of the deed'.'

'Is that important?'

'It could be, Muna. It might explain why Doctor McLaine, who, it seems, was working most of the time for people in Glover College, went to such a lot of trouble to help us, just before she died. Remember, she was in a position to follow West's instructions much more easily than us.'

'So, you think she was only pretending to help us to start with?'

'Yes, but then something happened to make her change her mind.'

'But what?'

'That's where the inscription comes in. If it means, 'A female *will* be the leader of the deed' it's not just for an inscription on a memorial, it's a prophecy. It's about something that will happen in the future …'

'Go on.'

'Well, if the inscription was a prophecy, the 'female' could be a girl and not a woman and Dr McLaine would have known this and ...'

'Become very interested in a girl who was able to do some very strange things?'

'You're getting the right idea, Muna.'

Both girls were now looking at an increasingly uncomfortable Lucky.

'Ok, you two. Let's get back to this message. I think there was a reason why Doctor McLaine said she would meet us on the field that lunchtime, as soon as possible after the bell. I think she was going to show us, probably with the help of one of those trees in the distance, how the shadow of the needle would point us towards the *'gaze of the beast'.'*

'It's nearly midday now,' an excited Muna interrupted. If we wait for that cloud to pass over we'll be able to see what happens.'

For what seemed to them a long time they watched the grey clouds moving beneath the pale disc of the sun. As they watched, they walked along the terrace to a point between the large open doors and the steps that descended to the grass.

Within moments of their arrival the sun slipped free of its veil and threw a network of strong shadows from the still leafless beeches onto the playing fields. For a brief interval they could see how the shadow of the tree positioned directly opposite the steps, sliced the sight screen in two and moved silently across the grass toward them. Had it been cast by an obelisk, it would have taken the tapered shape of an arrow.

'There, it works!' cried Polly. 'It points to the doorway there with the inscription above.'

'What does it say?'

'Fear of the Lord,' read Polly, deliberately, from the left up to the apex of the arch; then, *'The beginning of wisdom',* downward to the right.

'Fear', said Muna, 'that doesn't sound good …'

'Never mind that. It's just another scary saying from those days. Look, with the doors open you can see through there to the big window in the long corridor. If this were one hundred and fifty years ago it would still have the original glass and in it the *'gaze of the beast'*. Over to you, Lucky.'

'OK, Muna, you know I told you that, with Dr McLaine's help, I went back to the time just before the stained glass windows in the corridor were blown out?'

'Yes. You had that horrible experience. But I never understood, exactly, how she helped you.'

Polly broke in before Lucky could answer. 'Lucky can't go back unless she has something from the period to help her connect with that time. Remember, to visit Key Park on the day the John memorial was unveiled, she used a newspaper article that man in the cemetery sent to her and some other documents she'd researched. To go back to the night of the bombing Dr McLaine read her that article from the Winter Hillians' archive, the one written by the old head teacher; Goodison, I think it was. His is the first photograph on the wall in reception.'

'I see. And you made that drawing of the designs in the window?' said Muna turning to look at Lucky.

'Yes, and one of the windows, the one in the middle, had a bear standing next to a pole or tree trunk or something and he was looking down the corridor towards the west wing.'

'OK, so that's the first bit sorted. We are now supposed to be looking down the long corridor towards the Head's House. That brings us to; *'seek our Lord in the tower/ as he is found in the brass.'*

'Do you know what this means as well?'

'No, not all of it. That's one of the bits we still need to work out. In fact, that's really why we're here.' Polly looked around her. 'Where is Umar?'

'Late, as ever,' said Muna.

'OK, he'll just have to find us. Let's start by walking round the building and we can explain to Muna as we go,' suggested Polly.

As they walked along the terrace to follow the façade of the building, Lucky responded to Polly's invitation.

'In the entrance hall there was once a brass plaque, where the war memorial is now; the original is in Oxford.'

'So you saw it? You saw the brass?'

Yes, it's in Glover College; in their entrance hall.'

'And how was the Lord 'found' in the brass?'

'There's an old symbol for Jesus or Christ, called a chi-rho. It looks like this.' Polly turned the paper over and showed Muna the combination of P and X. 'We have to find one of these in the tower.'

'And that's why we're walking around the building?'

'Yes, *'seek our Lord in the tower/ as he is found in the brass'*,' repeated Lucky. Thanks to Dr McLaine we've seen most of the inside of the tower and there's nothing I can see at the front … or on this east side. We'll have to go down to get around to the back.'

Because the land sloped at the far end of the terrace they had to descend some steps to follow the wall of the east wing. This gave access to the lower ground floor, the servants' quarters for the original college, now converted for use as showers, changing and weight-training rooms. They reached the end and turned left to arrive at the rear of the building.

An assembly hall had been added to the rear of the central corridor in the 1920s, so the area of the original, open 'quadrangle' had been reduced. To get a clear view of the tower they needed to walk on a little further. Then, emerging from behind the west wing, they saw a familiar burly shape.

'Umar!'

'Whappen? Where yuh bin?'

'Waiting for you, you div.'

'Yeah, well me need me booty sleep, yuh know. Me had a bizzee day, yessurday. An' me bin having a look a' sum-ting.'

'What sort of thing?'

'Polly, gal, sum stuff to do wid doors 'n' locks. Doan worry bout it,' Umar joked before noticing that Lucky had been distracted. 'Wha yuh lookin' fe, gal?'

Umar turned to follow Lucky's gaze directed to the north face of the tower.

'We walk around with our eyes shut!' she exclaimed.

'Speek fa yuhself.'

'No Umar, Lucky's right,' said Polly. 'Look up there, that pattern of blue bricks between the windows in the tower. How many times have we walked past here and never seen that?'

'It's huge!' added Muna

'Wha yuh tark bout?'

'That's it. A whopping, huge, chi-rho,' Lucky replied.

After a moment's silence, Polly read aloud the notes once more, "*rho first points the way/ then follow the beast/ where the line of chi meets/ a door must be released'.*'

'Rho is an ancient Greek letter, so is chi. The code spells it 'k-h-i' but when I looked it up on the internet the correct spelling is c-h-i but 'khi' is the sound it makes. Dr McLaine says West wrote it that way because there were no 'c's' in the Polynesian alphabet, so he had to use a 'k'.'

'But which shape is 'rho'? The 'X' or the 'P',' asked Muna

'The P shape. So, if *'rho first points the way'* we must follow the stem of the 'P' and go down.'

'Down where?' asked Umar.

'Look,' said Polly. 'There's the level of the main corridor, there, where the windows are.'

'Yeah, me see dat, so wha'?'

'The back of the building must be lower than the front because there's another level below that floor. Isn't that where they keep tables and other stuff they use in the hall? It's got a strange name. What do they call it?'

'The undercroft,' said Lucky. 'There's a door into it through the hall.'

'So we have to get in there and head in that direction, following the gaze of the bear, towards the west wing.'

'Where the line of chi meets/ a door must be released', added Polly. 'That's the last bit.'

'If chi is the 'X' shape then there are four possible directions for *'the line of chi'.*'

'Yes, that's right, Muna,' agreed Lucky, 'but only *one* of them can meet with a line from the *'gaze of the beast'*. Two of them go upward into the sky, one goes down to the left; only the one going down to the right can meet up. And where it does, – that's where the door is!'

'Well, I would say …' said Muna holding her arm out with an extended hand at an angle, 'that would be about … where the west wing begins. Wouldn't you?'

All four of them went through a similar process of trying to gauge the meeting point and all agreed.

'So, arl we gotta do – find de door 'n' open it!'

Before separating, they agreed to meet the following day, a Sunday. They decided an early time would give them the best chance of getting into the building without being seen. Once inside they would be safe. They agreed too, that if anyone was late for the meeting time the others would go ahead without them and the latecomer would have to go home. Everyone knew, however, that without Umar they were unlikely to get anywhere

'Don't let us down, Umar,' pleaded Polly. 'We're going to need your help.'

'Doan worry. Me be dere – wid me kit.'

'I've got to get home. I'll have to go,' said Muna.

'But wait a minute, what about the alarm? That's going to wake up everybody.'

'Doan worry 'bout dat, needer. How yuh tink me get in b'fore. Me wotch de caretaker an' me know how ta switch it off - if me qwik enuff.'

Umar and Muna said 'bye' and walked off in different directions. Lucky asked Polly if she could walk with her for a few minutes.

'Polly, I need those papers we photocopied from Samuel's journal.'

Polly looked directly at her friend.

'You're thinking about that job Dr McLaine asked you to do, aren't you? Do you think that's a good idea, Lucky? We've come such a long way on this search and tomorrow is going to be really important. If you must go back again, can't it wait?'

'I want to get it over with, Polly. Dr McLaine wants to know the truth about West and she asked me to find out. Today is a good time to try.'

'But why does it matter? Dr McLaine doesn't *want* to know the truth, she *wanted* to. She's dead.'

'Yes, but how did she die, Polly? Was it an accident or are there people responsible? It all seems too much of a coincidence to me. Anyway, it's not just about Dr McLaine.'

'What do you mean?'

'I'm not sure what I mean. I don't think I understand it, completely, myself. But, believe me, if you can go back in time, there is no past tense. The dead live on. This is about all the people I've met; Angel, Professor Fielding, Goodison, the young soldier who grabbed me. But most of all, Polly, it's about Samuel. He is a real person to me, as real as you, flesh and blood, not just a name in a history book. I have to try and find out what happened to start all this and why.'

'But what good will it do?'

'I don't know, exactly, but Dr McLaine thought it was important. We started on this with your great uncle's letter but it goes back much earlier than that. We've learned a lot about the history stuff - and we've also learned that the past doesn't die. Ideas and lies and 'quests' don't die. We may or may not find the 'great prize' tomorrow but I might be able to find the truth and pass it on to others - just like she asked me to do.'

Polly sighed, took the papers from her bag and gave them all to Lucky. Then she reached forward and hugged her friend.

'Take care, Lucky. Do you need me? I know mum wants me to do some jobs for her. She's still in a mood about the trip to Oxford.'

'No, you're OK. My mum is going out this afternoon. I'll have plenty of time to go back to Winter Hill and Samuel's journal is all I need to get me there on the right day.'

'OK. But be careful - and I'll see you here tomorrow at 7.00 – or else.'

XI
Winter Hill College, November, 1851

Lucky sensed instantly that she was in the library. She had 'arrived' at night but as her eyes adjusted to the moonlight, filtered by a gauze of cloud, she could recognise some familiar features. The tall windows with stone tracery were as she remembered them - but also, she thought, different in some strange, uncertain manner. Then she realised that their entire length was divided into small, leaded panes; a delicate, repeat-pattern of yellow-stained glass. It was now clear to her that in the school windows only the original lights within the tracery remained. Lucky thought she preferred the original design and now she understood what had been lost, knew she would look at them differently when she 'returned'.

As she became more confident that she was alone, she moved further out into the centre of the room and looked up. The dark wood of the mock-medieval ceiling, with the folded-winged angels at the base of the eight vertical hammer posts, was still there. She could also see that there was a greater amount of shelving and un-painted timber than in the library as she knew it. The gallery that ran around two walls was there but with more book-lined shelves rather than blank walls above computer stations and revolving chairs. On the narrower wall the gallery widened and she could see what looked like a large musical instrument with the rounded contours of numerous vertical pipes. She recalled seeing something like it in a church their class had visited as part of the RE course in Year 8. Then she remembered that Dr McLaine had said that the library had also been used as a chapel and music would be part of any service.

Beneath the organ, at floor level, she now noticed the fireplace and could also see that it was matched by one on the opposite, far wall. As she moved closer and under the gallery, she realised that the original fireplace had an elaborately carved, stone surround. At the opening to the hearth the stone was stained a darker colour and above, in relief lettering, she read the inscription, 'Scientia potentia est'. She ran her fingers over the raised letters and the clusters of leaves and flowers. Above this point the stone rose in layers that formed a tapering canopy culminating in the carving of the head of a figure whose name she could just make out, Dr John Pye-Smith. She remembered the name. This was the man pointed out to her by Samuel Ferrington in Key Park Cemetery

Then she heard the faint, splintering sound of breaking glass.

She knew from the extract she had read in his diary that Samuel, returning late to the college after spending an evening with friends and finding himself locked out, had discovered an open window and climbed into the laundry room below the Matron's house. He had dropped onto a table and caused the bottles to fall and break on the tiled floor. Soon he would be climbing the stairs into the matron's hall, finding the key in the door and entering the long corridor on his way to the west wing and the stairs halfway along its corridor which would take him to his bedroom.

Taking great care not to make a noise, Lucky walked through the open library door and into the entrance hall. On the opposite wall, above the dark wainscoting, she could see the outline of the familiar elaborate stone surround and within its perimeter, the glint of light on the original brass memorial. 'The Glover plaque', she mouthed silently. For confirmation she approached it until, in the gloom, she could just make out the chi-rho symbol she and Polly had seen in the entrance to Glover College. She shivered at the thought of Dr Playfair once more explaining the meaning of it. Then she moved to her left and through the opening in the wall. She was now standing in front of the five-panelled, stained glass window she had last seen on the night of the bombing raid. Turning to her right, she looked down the corridor to the point where Samuel would soon emerge through the door that gave access to the matron's house.

She moved back towards the wall. She did not have long to wait before a black rectangle grew out of the wall and then disappeared again to be replaced by the outline of a man. 'Samuel', she whispered to herself before retreating further into the shadows. She knew he must soon arrive at the entrance hall and, intrigued by the glimmer of candlelight he had seen outside on the terrace, that he would climb the stairs to the first floor room in the tower. There, he would overhear voices and hastily withdraw when he realised the risk he was taking.

Within seconds he arrived, entered the hall, paused, turned to his left, passed quickly through the opening leading to the staircase and began to climb. She could see that he was moving slowly to reduce the creaking sound made by the passage of his weight on the stairs. She realised then that these stairs, which in her time led to the teachers' staff room, were, one hundred and fifty years earlier, very different. Not only were they obviously made of wood but the stairwell turned and climbed more steeply, within half the space. She guessed this must be yet another change dating back to the time before the college became a school.

Knowing he must return the way he had gone, she waited, watching the silent shifting in the pattern of shadows thrown onto the walls by the moonlight and light clouds.

Minutes later, she heard the light creaking sounds on the stairs once more. The figure passed quickly through the hall again, entered the corridor and turned left in the direction of the west wing.

Right, Lucky, now's your chance.

She moved through the opening to the foot of the stairs. As she did so, the door in the room above her opened and a new light source entered the stairwell. She retreated once more into the shadows.

'Well, there is no-one here. See for yourself.'

She heard more sounds of movement on the stairs and another voice, 'Perhaps we should leave the door as it is. We can then be sure to hear the approach of anyone on the stairs.'

'I tell you James, the college is virtually empty. Most of the scholars are at their preaching stations and will not return before late tomorrow – but if you insist ...'

Then the sounds of their talking became less clear as they returned to the interior of the Council Room. Lucky knew that any attempt to overhear their conversation would be impossible, now that her approach would be easily detected.

Then she remembered. Dr McLaine had shown her how the door in the corner of the library led into the stone spiral staircase that went to the top of the tower. It connected with all the rooms in the tower except the Council Room. She wondered whether, if she was able to enter the room above, she might then be able to listen to the men without arousing suspicion.

She returned to the library and quickly found the small door in the left hand corner of the room. She turned the smooth brass doorknob. It opened easily. She entered the spiral staircase. It was much darker here than in the library but having found the central pillar and the first of the stone steps she began to climb.

Lucky had already surprised herself by the way she had managed to suppress her fear of the dark but, enveloped by the blackness of the stairwell, she found herself struggling to move forward. Try as she might, she could not prevent Umar's warning of djinns and evil spirits reverberating in her head. Confined by the curving wall, she shivered, then, forcing herself to climb the first few steps, she suddenly felt something light and sticky cover her face. Unable to suppress a small exclamation of shock, she wiped at her face and spluttered the covering from her lips.

'Urgh! Spiders!'

She continued with her head held a little lower, in the hope that she might avoid any further problems.

Turning as she climbed, she became aware of a slight improvement in visibility and soon discovered that this resulted from the positioning of one of the narrow lancet windows in the tower wall. In the moonlight, she was able to see a door on her left which she knew accessed the gallery in the library. She calculated that, although there was still some distance to climb, the next door should take her into the space above the Council Room.

Urging herself on, she reached the door and was again relieved to find that it was unlocked. The Victorian college, she guessed, had less reason to deny entry to the tower than a secondary school full of inquisitive children.

Relieved to have escaped the confines of the stairwell, she detected the low murmur of voices rising, together with some welcome light emerging through an opening in the floor. There was, as she had seen on the plans, a set of stairs from the room below up to this level. All she needed to do was move closer to the wooden rail that served to prevent anyone from falling through the opening and onto the stairs.

She moved carefully around the furniture as she crossed the wooden floor. The walls were lined with glass fronted cabinets and in the middle of the room stood display cases such as those she had seen once before in Binghamton Museum. She looked down through the glazed top of one and could see what looked like a collection of rocks, some dull, others shiny and the regular shape of stony objects that looked like large snails.

' ... but there have been other instances of betrayal.'

'Betrayal? I cannot allow you to use such a word unchallenged. That is a weighty accusation. To what errors of mine do you now refer, James?'

Moving close to the opening, Lucky now knew that this gravelly, weary voice must be that of Timothy West and the other, smoother, more self-assured, that of James Angel. Reverend West was evidently on the defensive, his partner sensing vulnerability.

'Believe me, I do not use the word, betrayal, lightly. For many years Timothy, have we not been close colleagues, striving to lead our neighbouring chapels?'

'We have but ... '

'Have we not also worked together, with the aid of the Elizabeth Glover's generosity, to raise funds for this college and its important work?'

'Of course ...'

'Nevertheless this has not tempered your enthusiasm for political activity which has damaged, and continues to damage, our ability to raise money for Winter Hill at times when we were most in need of financial support.'

'It was a matter of principle. The Tory Government was corrupt ...'

'And not content with bringing the college into disrepute by your association with radical politics you now seek to immerse us in a new swamp of philosophical speculation.'

'But, my dear James, surely you would agree that we are a church ready to celebrate the employment of our God-given intellect?'

'And have you forgotten the words that appear over the entrance to this building? *Fear of the Lord, the beginning of wisdom.'* You would do well to temper your enthusiasm for intellect, in favour of greater obedience to the teachings of the Bible; anything less exposes you and our vulnerable young men, to mortal sin.'

'Oh, come now, James. This is the middle of the nineteenth, not the sixteenth, century. Our church has made a great contribution to enlightened thinking. Many of our community believe as I do …'

'Ah yes, Timothy. Your confederates – the identity of whom you withhold from those who, you evidently believe, fail to merit your trust or confidence. When severed from the teaching of the Bible, Timothy, this 'passion' for 'intellect' serves only to undermine the certainties of faith.'

'I am disappointed to hear you speak in this manner. It is the very reason why I and some friends have formed a fellowship.'

'A closed society, a brotherhood - and you recoil at my use of the term 'betrayal'?'

'We would much prefer it if we had no need for secrecy and our female members give a lie to the charge of 'brotherhood'. But we feel we have no choice but to identify those who are our allies – and our adversaries.'

'You turn away from your brethren. Your arrogance is astonishing.'

'We feel we cannot impose the wearing of some rigid

and ... absurd blinkers to restrict our quest for knowledge.'

''Fear of the Lord', Timothy. I see little 'fear'; in fact I see little 'respect' in you, either for the word of our Lord or the proud tradition, for which we were both appointed guardians. You are a minister, one of the chosen, one of the elect – if you follow God, you are saved. Have you forgotten the duty that goes with such a joyous privilege?'

'I have never shared your enthusiasm for Calvin, James – I would prefer to believe that our destiny, be it heaven or hell, is shaped by the lives we lead and not decided before we are even born.'

'Well, whatever dilution of faith you have permitted yourself, you cannot ignore your duty as a minister. It is a sacred duty not shared by your friends; men such as Lyell and Darwin.'

'They are brave men, James; men of principle. I believe that one day Darwin will astound us all. His ideas about the diversity of life ...'

'Please, Timothy, do not speak to me of 'principle'. I am only too aware of your own shortcomings in that regard.'

Lucky waited for a response but a lengthy and tense silence ensued. Eventually a quieter, more anxious voice was heard.

'James, please, I know my own failings only too well. I have repented of them. I have suffered for them. It is true that I have been weak, sometimes tempted by worldly comforts and idle pursuits. But when will you release me from the debt I owe ...?'

'Timothy, I will do so but you must now be ready to pay a price for my silence.'

'Ah, so, we have it, at last, the price ...'

'I say this with a heavy heart - but my duty to God and our college benefactor comes first. I require that you leave Binghamton and take up a position of pastor, if you can secure one, elsewhere.'

'I see, and if I refuse?'

'I will have no choice but to protect our faith, our church and this college by disclosing the facts of your shameful past to your friends, your congregation, your fellow ministers – and your family.'

Another silence began, during which Lucky, kneeling on the floor at the edge of the opening, began to feel some stiffness in her legs.

'You are a severe man, James. You ask everything of me.'

'Not 'everything', Timothy – if you agree to my demands, you will continue to enjoy the solace of your family, your considerable wealth, your misguided interests.'

'And how shall I explain my departure from Mount Zion chapel and Binghamton?'

'You will say that your health has not been good and that you feel you must retire to milder climes, somewhere to the south, perhaps. I will support your account and you will agree to have no further contact with the college, the Trust or our circle of supporters.'

'I see.'

'There is one thing more,' the voice went quieter as the Reverend Angel placed new emphasis on his words.

'I have reason to believe that, with the help of members of your 'fellowship', you have acquired many 'items' of great value from your friends abroad ...'

Eager to stretch her legs, while, at the same time, lean further out over the rail in order to hear more clearly, Lucky stood up. As she did so, she snagged her bead bracelet on a protruding sliver of wood. The bracelet thread snapped, spilling a stream of dried, coloured seeds and shells onto the top step before they continued their chaotic descent into the room below.

Struggling to contain the panic rising through her, Lucky turned and ran from the room. All thought of concealing her footfall was now abandoned. She re-entered the spiral staircase and, despite the gloom, descended at speed, her outstretched right hand feeling for the wall, while the other swept at unseen cobwebs. Though distressed, one thought concerned her; that she must find somewhere to hide while she composed herself, otherwise she would have difficulty returning to her own time. Solitude, security, calm were everything if she was to get back home safely.

Moments later, she arrived at the door she knew led onto the library gallery. She paused. Her first thought had been to continue to the ground floor but something told her she would be safer at the higher level. She opened the door and entered the room. With her back pressed to the wall, she scanned the space in all directions and waited. Apart from the sound of her own heavy breathing, she could hear nothing. She moved forward along the gallery, past the organ and turned to her left, keeping close to the book-lined wall. She thought she could hear noises now – perhaps from two directions.

Yes, someone is approaching from the spiral staircase - and another from the Council Room stairs.

Lucky quickened her pace, found another door

where the gallery reached the end wall and opened it. She was now in a space, a hallway, she did not recognise. She thought hard about the layout of the building as she remembered it from the plans. There were doors to left and right. The one to her right, she guessed, must take her into the central corridor in the west wing. This would lead to the first floor bedrooms for the scholars. Somewhere on that corridor was Samuel's room but she had no way of knowing which room was his. Uncertain about what she should do next, she tentatively opened this first door and looked along the corridor that ran for the entire length of the wing. Protruding from both walls, beside the door to each bedroom, were a series of brass bells, beneath each of which a small chain with a hand pull was suspended. She was about to move into the corridor when she heard further sounds coming from somewhere ahead and below. She realised then that this corridor must be accessed by another staircase from the ground floor. Once on that staircase there would be someone both behind and ahead of her. She would be trapped.

She closed the door and at the same time heard the sound of bells from the corridor beneath. The noise was growing as more bells were being violently agitated.

Lucky closed the door and reached for the other. It opened and this time she entered a much narrower corridor. She moved along it and found herself on another staircase. Even in the profound gloom it felt familiar. She realised these were the stairs that led to Dr McLaine's room. She remembered that when the building had first become a school, the headteacher used to live in this part of the building. Before then it had been part of the barracks and before that the principal's ... but now she could hear more bells being rung on the bedroom corridor and sounds, also, from the floor immediately below her. She had no choice. She bounded up the staircase onto the first landing and then up again to another. Here, at the top of the 'Head's House', she could go no further. She opened the door to the room she knew as Dr McLaine's office. She guessed that she had only a short time before someone looked in this space, filled with books and packing cases. Then she was relieved to find a key on the inside of the door. She reached for it and the lock turned with satisfying clank.

A little relieved, she settled on the floor, took a photograph of her mother from her pocket and tried to calm herself further through deep breathing. She knew that she needed to enter a condition where she felt able to detach herself from the present fear and disturbance. Without this sense of separateness, she was unsure as to what would happen to her.

Minutes passed. Her breathing grew steadier, her pulse slowed. She began to slip away from consciousness when the door handle began to rattle violently ...

Polly didn't like it when anyone entered her bedroom unannounced. To help her family remember this important fact, she had stuck a large 'PRIVATE. KNOCK BEFORE OPENING' notice on her door. On this occasion, however, as it swung open without warning, Polly's inclination to protest was stifled. Her mother's face instantly revealed that something serious had happened.

'Polly, you need to come downstairs. The police are here and they want to talk to you.'

'The police? What do they want? If Umar …'

'Umar who? It's about Lucky. She's not well.'

'Not well? What do you mean? What's wrong?'

'It seems that she's in some kind of coma. I'm sorry, Polly – you need to hear the full story from the police.'

As she and her mother entered the front room, Polly saw a uniformed WPC seated on the edge of the sofa, her hard bowler hat alongside. Polly's father, turning in her direction, was the first to speak.

'Here she is. Come and sit down, Polly. This is WPC Simmons. She wants to have a few words with you about Lucky'.

'Hello, Polly. I don't want you to be worried about your friend but her mother …'

'What's the matter with her? Mum said she was in a coma. What happened?'

'Well, we don't know exactly. I'm not sure that 'coma' is the right word but she does appear to be in a deep sleep or a trance of some kind - and we can't wake her. We think we should be very careful. Her mother says that you are her best friend and may be able to help us understand what is happening.'

'Yes, I'm her best friend but I don't know what's wrong with her.'

Polly's mum, her arm around her daughter's shoulder, interrupted, 'But you do know something about this?'

Polly turned and looked at her mother. 'Well, mum, you know what Lucky's like. She's different. She's into all sorts of stuff to do with yoga and meditation. I've seen her switch off from everything before. She can even do something like it at school.'

'So, Polly', asked the policewoman, 'you've seen her do something like this before?'

'Yes, but not exactly like this, not for long or in a way that would worry people. What are you going to do?'

'Well, a doctor has had a look at her and at the moment they're thinking about taking her into hospital for observation, if she doesn't wake up soon.'

'I think that would be a bad idea. You should leave her in her bedroom. She won't want to be anywhere there's lots of strange people and noise.'

'Polly', said her father, 'I think we're going to have to leave the medical care to the doctors....'

'Is there anything else that you can tell us, Polly; anything that might help the doctors?'

'Not really – only that she can do things like this and when I saw her do it before she came back safely.'

'Came back?'

'Yes, she said that she wanted to visit her dad'.

'But Polly,' revealed her mum, 'her dad died five years ago'.

'I know mum, but that's what Lucky said. Can I see her?'

'Probably not at the moment Polly,' replied the policewoman. 'But I'll tell her mum and the doctors that you asked. Perhaps, they'll think it might be helpful.'

'It sounds to me as though this is more like a case for a psychiatrist ...'

'Dad! That's unfair. Lucky's not mad! How could you be so ... stupid?'

'Polly, I only meant ...'

But before he could finish Polly had turned her back on him and stormed out of the room.

XII
Old College Home
January, 1919

Lucky looked around her. Something was wrong. She knew this was not her bedroom. Although it was dark she had the sense that she was still in the same room.

The transfer has not worked.

She recalled that she had been trying to meditate, to focus on the return to her own time when she had heard the sound of loud banging. But it wasn't just a sound that she experienced; she had seen a man's fist take shape and appear to strike her forehead. The hand had passed right through her skull and entered her brain. She had felt both fear and pain. Suddenly the sound-image had dissolved and she had opened her eyes. With some difficulty she stood up and steadied herself with a hand against the wall.

What do I do now? I must try to remain calm.

Pushing herself off the wall, she reached forward in the darkness for the door. The handle turned. She moved out onto the landing.

I locked the door. It should not have opened like that.

Moving carefully, Lucky found the top of the stairs and began to descend. The air felt colder than she remembered and she paused to rub her hands vigorously against her upper arms. She went down the stairs to the next landing and heard a new sound; gentle snoring, coming from the room to her left. She descended a few more steps to the corridor she knew would take her back to the point where she had entered the head's or principal's House.

She opened this door and was now back in the familiar hallway, faced once more with a choice; another door to her left that would lead to the west wing bedrooms and the one to her right that would take her back onto the library gallery.

If the scholars are still asleep, I may be able to find Samuel.

She opened the door to her left and peered into the gloom. She sensed that something else was wrong here but she couldn't be sure what it was. She began to move down the passage, reminding herself, as she proceeded, that she must avoid brushing against the bells. She could not afford to wake anyone and raise another alarm.

Then she realised what was wrong. There were no bells. There were metal brackets protruding from the walls but the bells had been removed. She was wondering why anyone should bother to do such a thing when she heard a high-pitched whine coming from one of the rooms a little further down the corridor. It sounded like the whimpering, the crying of a child but she told herself that this would make no sense in a college for men, the very youngest of whom was seventeen and the majority some years older.

She found the door to the room from which the sound was coming, took a deep breath to steady herself and carefully opened it. In the dim moonlight that penetrated the flimsy curtains, she could make out the shape of two large structures either side of the window. As her eyes accustomed to the new light level, she realised that these were bunk beds. She wondered why the room should be so equipped when there should have been plenty of space to accommodate all the scholars. Samuel's journal had recorded the fact that not all the bedrooms and studies were occupied in his day.

The whimpering began again on the bottom bunk to the left. Then a voice reached her from the direction of the upper, right hand bunk.

'Please don't worry, Sister, Davy is a just a little cold. You go back to your warm bed, Sister. I'll look after him and make sure he doesn't disturb you. Now Davy, that's enough. Go to sleep. Good night, Sister Rose.'

Lucky thought the girl's voice managed to sound both firm and anxious. She paused and felt certain that all four bunks were now occupied by people very much awake, awaiting a response from her.

'Can I help at all?' she whispered softly, kneeling to the level of the bottom bunk. She could just distinguish the shape of a small child, perhaps five or six years old with his hands and arms outside the bed carefully aligned with the sides of his body beneath the covers.

A thin voice replied, 'I'm sorry, sister. I couldn't help it. Please, sister, please, I'm sorry.'

As the child began to sob uncontrollably, Lucky leaned forward in an effort to comfort him. Then she registered the pungent odours from memories of her own childhood. She stroked the boy's arm and tried to reassure him.

'It's OK, little one. Don't worry. You needn't be

afraid of me. Let's try to sort you out.'

The girl in the top bunk behind her pulled herself up into a seating position.

'Sister, if you could give him some new pyjamas, he can come in with me.'

Lucky had pulled back the bedclothes and found the cold, wet stain she had anticipated.

'The trouble is, I don't know where to get dry pyjamas and bedclothes.'

'Are you new, sister?' asked a small girl on the other bottom bunk.

Lucky turned to face her. 'I'm not a sister. I'm a visitor and heard Davy crying. Now let's get him out of these wet trousers and then I'll try and find some fresh bedding for him.'

'He can come in with me sister, I mean miss, while you get some for him. I know where it's kept, just along the corridor.'

'Could you fetch it for me while I strip the bed?' asked Lucky.

'I could show you where it is, miss but if I get caught taking it I'll be strapped.'

'What by the college tutors? I don't think ...'

'Not them, miss, whoever you said; by the sisters, miss. They would say I was stealing and stealing is a sin. You can get strapped for stealing – and for wetting the bed.'

'OK, show me where to get the bedding and I'll take the responsibility. Then I want to ask you some questions about these sisters. I am very puzzled.'

P olly looked at the open mouths of her friends. She sensed the moisture in her eyes beginning to blur her vision.

'That's all I can tell you. That's how it was when I went to bed last night. I left the house this morning before anyone else was up.'

'So, she may be awake by now,' offered Muna optimistically.

'It's possible. I'll find out when we get back but we need to decide what we are going to do.'

'I still can't believe it. Poor Lucky. We'll have to call it off and go home.' She looked at Polly and hesitated. 'Won't we?'

'I thought like that, at first,' replied Polly, wiping the corner of each eye in turn, as she struggled to recover her composure. 'But now, I'm not so sure. Let's think about it. We don't know how much more time we've got. The people from Glover College will show up again soon, I'm sure of it. This could be our last chance to find whatever the treasure was that West hid in the building.'

'No teefin' geezer goan' ta get me share,' insisted Umar, thumping the fist of one hand into the palm of the other.

'And think - what would Lucky want us to do? We wouldn't have got this far without her but she'll wake up soon and we'll be able to tell her, *show her*, what we found. If we miss this chance, she may never forgive us.'

The three friends stood in silence for a few moments, then, Muna spoke.

'You're right, Polly. Let's go in. Lucky would want us to.'

'Is that OK with you, Umar?' asked Polly with some uncertainty, turning to face him.

'Shur ting. Me cool wid dat.'

'OK then, let's check we've got what we need,' said Polly with new resolve. 'Torches, tools, bags, and Umar you should have your - special equipment.'

Polly looked at the others as they checked their bags and nodded.

'And did you bring some rope, Umar?'

'Yeah, 's in me bag.'

'Good. Right, Umar, we're following you.'

Umar led them further up the path running alongside the west wing of the college. A dense laurel hedge screened much of the building from the road and was well known to pupils as a refuge for smokers. Long ago, two of the railings had been buckled to provide an exit for those wishing to leave the school grounds without using the gates. The opening led directly into the undergrowth.

They looked around, saw no-one on the road, removed their backpacks and slipped quickly through the gap. Once they were concealed beneath the canopy of the glossy, evergreen hedge they paused while Umar explained the next steps.

He told the girls that the 'recce' he had made the day

before suggested that approaches to most entrances to the building were covered by CCTV cameras. The only one that avoided these appeared to be that leading to the steps giving access to the Head's (or Principal's) House, at the junction of the front with the west wing. To reach the door they would have to cross an open space lying between the railings and the west wing. This area was known as the 'Head's Garden' though it consisted largely of mossy lawn enclosed by the laurel hedge in which they were hiding, the building itself and two further hedges one of privet, the other, yew, to complete the rectangle.

Once they had arrived at the steps leading to the door, Umar told them that he would need to pick the lock on the door, enter the building and switch off the alarm. It would be more difficult for him this time because of the greater distance he had to cover before reaching the control box in a small room off the entrance hall. He told the girls they must wait for him to return before entering. Without speaking, the others indicated their agreement.

Then following Umar, in a crouching run, the two girls crossed the lawn before halting at the bottom of the steps. Until they were inside they could now easily be seen from the road. Umar went up to the door and began to use his lock picks on the main deadlock. Within moments he heard a satisfying snap. He then withdrew a large bunch of small keys and began to try each of them in turn in the second, cylinder lock. Two stone heads, green men, with foliage emerging from their mouths, one either side of the door, looked on as though they found the scene grotesquely amusing.

Meanwhile, Polly and Muna, squatting at the foot of the steps, were alarmed to see two men in uniform, police uniform, appear in the distance from behind the cover of some trees. They were following the pavement alongside the playing field and were headed in their direction. Within a few moments they would disappear behind the sports pavilion, but at the point they reappeared, would be only a short distance from the main gates, giving them a clear view of the doorway and steps.

Polly and Muna exchanged anxious looks.

'Umar!!' hissed Polly as the policeman reached the pavilion. 'You'll have to hurry!'

Umar didn't respond, but having glanced around and seen nothing, he continued to make his way methodically through the bunch of keys.

'Umar, police! Hurry!' added Muna.

'Wait now! Doan rush me ...'

Within what seemed like only a few seconds, Polly could now see the policemen emerging from behind the brick wall of the pavilion. Fortunately, they were absorbed in conversation, but might look in their direction at any moment. The girls climbed the steps and stood behind Umar their limbs agitated, their heads turning to and fro, urging him, from both sides, to hurry.

'Umar, come on!'

'Quickly!'

Polly and Muna heard the door open and rushed forward propelling Umar before them into the small, tiled, lobby.

'Wayit!! Geroff! De alarm,' grunted Umar as he fell

forward and knocked his head on the stone surround of the small fireplace with the girls on top of him.

Umar was momentarily dazed. Then he remembered the problem they faced and shaking his head shouted, 'It wi go off ... geroff me!'

In a fresh frenzy of activity Umar pushed Muna to one side and struggled to get to his feet as his bag became snagged on Polly's jacket. Despairing, he wriggled out of the straps and reached for the door that would give him access to the corridor.

Then, with one hand on the handle he stopped.

U mar exclaimed, 'De alarm! Dere's nah alarm beep!'

He turned and closed the outer door and picked up his bag as the girls got onto their feet. He stood still once again and gestured to the others to do the same. Then he spoke.

'We was lucky, mahn. Nah alarm. Muss be broke or sumting.'

Polly got to her feet, checked to see that the policemen had passed out of sight behind the laurel hedge and audibly exhaled in relief.

'Boy, that was close.'

When they had all recovered, Polly led the group through the Head's House and out into the long corridor. Moments later she paused beside the large window with the five leaded lights.

'There, Lucky's sketch showed the one in the middle had a bear on it looking that way,' she said indicating the direction from which they had just come. But we've got to go down first, into the undercroft. Come on.'

A little further along the corridor they came to a flight of steps to their left. They descended and with Umar's help passed through another locked door and into the assembly hall. Polly had read in a book she'd found in the school library that this hall had been added to the back of the college soon after the move to

Oxford. A wealthy Binghamton businessman had bought the building and grounds in the 1890s and converted them for use as a hydropathic baths and botanical gardens. He had installed a swimming pool to one side of the quadrangle and covered it with the hall that linked to the east wing. Years later, in 1914, it was this hall that served as a canteen or 'mess' for the soldiers and then, from 1923, as a place for school assemblies and indoor sports.

At the rear of the hall they found the door leading into the passage that ran beneath the long corridor. Umar began work once more.

Ten minutes later the door yielded and they entered the undercroft. Umar had attached his headtorch and the girls carried their hand-torches but the combined illumination did little to dispel their growing sense of claustrophobia as they slowly made their way in the direction of the west wing. To either side of the passage they passed stacked furniture, mostly damaged chairs, desks and tables, but also cardboard boxes, outdated classroom equipment and other assorted items. All had been stored in case they should one day be needed or repaired and then long forgotten.

Each of them was struggling to maintain their resolve as they travelled away from the door and further into the darkness. Eventually they reached the point where they could go no further. Ahead of them was a wall of stone and to their right, where the corridor turned to run under the west wing, they could see a girder running horizontally across the wing with the space beneath filled by a brick wall.

'That girder must help support the new lower floor in the west wing,' Polly conjectured, 'but the part we can see is only a few feet long.'

'So the rest of it must be hidden by this stone wall,' added Muna.

'*Where de line a khi meet/ door muss be release'.* So, where's de meetin' a de line?'

'It must be about here. Behind this wall there must be a room.'

'We know there is,' said Polly. 'That's probably one reason why Doctor McLaine wanted us to look at the plans of the building in Oxford. Under the Head's House there's a cellar. I think the caretakers use it now to keep their cleaning supplies but there may be more than one room. Look.' Polly pointed to some wrought iron grills, located at head height in the stone wall.

'Air vent,' muttered Umar. 'So wha'?'

'But why are there two of them, only a couple of feet apart? Perhaps if the cellar room reaches only so far then the other vent could be …'

'Another room!' added Muna.

'But where de door?'

'I don't know. Shine your torch over here, Muna. Look for anything unusual in the stone.'

'Like what?'

'I don't know. Just look.'

Thirty minutes later they had carefully explored the entire face of the wall several times and could find nothing that would suggest a hidden door. The frustration and tension was beginning to show.

'They didn't make it easy, did they?' lamented Muna.

'If they had made it 'easy' it would have been found by someone else, long ago,' Polly replied impatiently.

'Well, we don't know for sure that it hasn't been found anyway.'

'Dat stray-inge,' said Umar, who, unwilling to join the exchange between the two girls, had sat down on an old wooden chest and pushed his fingers idly into the space between two blocks of stone.

'If it had been found, Muna, I don't think that creep from Glover College would have gone to the trouble of kidnapping Lucky and ... Umar. What are you doing?'

'Wha' d'wit look like?' replied Umar, pushing with all his strength at one of the blocks. ''S goin'. 'Elp me den!'

But before the girls could reach him, Umar felt the stone block move forward and a small irregular section of the wall, about three foot square, swung open at ground level. All three looked into the opening in astonishment.

'Umar, how did you know!? That's it. You've released the door.'

''S nutten. Dere was no mortar roun' de block a stoan, so me tort me try ta push it. Dis whole seck-shon mussa move on sum sorta counterway't.'

All three got onto their knees and shone their torches into the pitch-black space. Stone steps led down before reaching a wall, returning and continuing down to a point directly beneath them. Where the steps ended there appeared to be an opening in the wall to their right.

'Umar,' said Polly, 'one thing's for sure,' she beamed at him and although he couldn't see the expression on her face, he could still sense the delight and excitement in her voice. 'You've earned the honour of going first!'

When Lucky had stripped and remade Davy's bed and given him the clean pyjamas she had found with the help of the older girl, Martha, she began to question the children.

'Martha, I know the college as a place for teaching young men how to become ministers or leaders of their church. What are you doing here?'

'Dunno about any church people apart from the Sisters, miss. Sisters of Bethlehem. This is where we was moved because of the war.'

'Moved from where? And what war?'

'Great War, miss. You must know about that. We was at war with the Germans. There was soldiers here first, before we came, but they went to fight in France.'

'Great War? You mean First World ... No, I see. Of course the Second World War hasn't happened ... Look, I know you might think this is a silly question, but what is the date?'

'27th January - or maybe 28th now.'

'Yes, go on ...'

'What do you mean, miss? Oh, I see, Monday, 27th January?'

'And ... the year?'

The small girl from the bunk alongside Davy spoke, 'That's easy for me. I know that. 1919. How old are you, miss? I'm nearly five and I knows more than you.'

A time-slip of some kind. The knocking on the door must have upset things ...

'Don't be rude, Beth,' said Martha. 'Miss knows what year it is. She's just testing to make sure we're not stupid. We were in Shortbridge House first, miss. Our father died in 1915 and Mam was too ill to look after us so they took us to Shortbridge. Me Mam died then and we was proper orphans then, like all the others.'

'Orphans? This is an orphanage? But why were you moved here?'

'They said our home was needed for women who were going to work in the big motor factory in Shortbridge. So, we had to come here.'

'Moon-shins workers,' Davy added helpfully.

'No Davy, munitions – like ammunition, ammo, weapons for the war,' corrected Martha with a kindly smile.

'And now the war is over?'

"Spect we'll be going back. I hope so, 'cos this place is even worse than Shortbridge. At least it was a bit warmer there.'

'Do you know, I don't think that even Doctor McLaine knew this building was used as an orphanage.'

'Who's Doctor McLaine, miss? Are you a nurse? Will you stay with us, miss? Will you be here tomorrow?'

'I'm afraid I must go very soon. My mother is waiting for me. What time is it? Oh, look it's nearly three o'clock. I have stayed too long.'

'Oh please don't go yet, miss. Stay until Davy and Beth go to sleep, otherwise they'll get upset again.'

'Yes, please stay,' pleaded Davy.

Lucky reached into the bunk and rubbed the boy's arm.

'If you promise me that you'll try to sleep, I'll stay a little longer. You, close your eyes now and dream about nice things.'

'Thank you, miss', said Martha, as she, too, lay down and pulled up the covers, leaving her arms like the others, outside the bedclothes.

Lucky decided to wait another thirty minutes to be sure that they were sound asleep before moving from her position on the edge of Beth's bed. When Beth began to moan in her sleep Lucky lay down beside her and stroked her hair. She felt very tired. Beth's breathing acquired a reassuring and pleasant rhythm when she briefly closed her eyes.

Umar went through the opening head first, pushing his back pack before him. When he was on the other side he went down two steps and turned to watch the girls follow him. Together, they descended the steps. At the bottom they found another opening to a passage that appeared to stretch as far as their torches could reach.

'Me go furz' – but doan rush me.'

The passage was narrow and brick lined. Though it smelled musty, it was dry underfoot. All three were both nervous and wordlessly excited about the prospect of finally unearthing the mystery of 'the prize'.

'This must be running directly under the west wing,' said Polly. 'I can't see anything ahead can you, Umar?'

'Nah, mahn. It look like dead en'.'

As they moved further along the tunnel, they passed a small recess carved out of the wall to their left. When they came to a second of these, close to the end wall, they paused to discuss their purpose.

It was Polly who came up with an answer.

'It's like the time I went to Scotland with mum and dad. They have lots of narrow roads there. Only one car can get past at a time.'

'Case yuh noh notiss, dis not a road.'

'No, I know that, Umar. But on those small roads they have passing places where a car can pull in to let another one go past if it's travelling in the opposite direction.'

'I see what you mean,' said Muna. 'When they built this passage they needed places where workmen could get out of the way and let someone else get past.'

'Well, 'ere's de end a it,' added Umar suddenly eager to change the subject.

They were now at the end of the passage and faced with a blank brick wall. To their right, however, they could see that it continued through a turn of ninety degrees.

'This makes sense of something else on the plans Dr McLaine wanted us to see,' said Polly.

'What was that?' asked Muna.

'Apparently, when they first planned the college the idea was to have four sections, not three. There should have been another wing, running parallel to the front, so the quadrangle would be enclosed on all sides. The Barker book says they ran out of money. Lucky and me thought this might have something to do with those stories about Reverend West stealing some of the money.'

'You mean, because he stole the money, they didn't have enough to build the fourth wing?'

'Something like that. If that's what happened, it's possible they started work but then had to stop.'

'Yes, perhaps they laid the foundations and even dug a passage for cellars and stuff. Reverend West would have known about it, wouldn't he?'

Umar had been preparing to enter the new section while the girls had been talking. He interrupted their conversation.

'Sumting wrong here. De passidge blocked!'

They followed Umar in and with the combining of their torch beams could see that the wall to the left had collapsed inward. Bricks, soil and timbers lay in a tangled heap, obstructing their path.

'Oh no!' moaned Muna. 'What happened?'

'I think I may have an idea,' replied Polly. 'Above us, we must be close to the spot where we saw the chi-rho in the tower, yesterday. When the Germans dropped those bombs in 1940 one of them must have fallen about here because we know it blew out all the windows in the long corridor. That's how Holbrook was killed when he was grabbing Lucky. Perhaps at the time they just filled the crater because they didn't know the passage was here.'

'Yes, that would make sense. But look, is there a way through, under that beam?'

'Where? Oh yes, I see. You may be right but we have to be careful. Umar, you know it doesn't look very safe to me. Umar, what are you doing?'

Umar had taken off his back pack, handed it to Muna and began to climb over the rubble. He quickly reached the gap and directed his torch into it.

'Dere spayss ahead. Me goin' ta try 'n' get tru.'

'Go slowly, Umar. You mustn't move that beam or the ceiling could collapse.'

Umar looked up and understood the wisdom of Polly's warning. Carefully, he reached forward to position his hands on the other side of the opening then, hunching his shoulders, lowered his head and tried to squeeze through the gap. He felt his shoulders wedge between the timber prop and the brick wall to his right. He sensed a slight movement in the beam, then, felt his head being peppered with pebbles and soil. Behind him, Polly flinched as she saw a small shower of dust fall from the ceiling on her side.

'Umar, you're moving it. Come back.'

But Umar either didn't hear or he chose to ignore her. Instead, he wriggled his upper body in an attempt to ease his way forward. After dislodging further quantities of soil, his shoulders were finally through and the rest of him followed without further alarms.

''S no problem. Now yuh, gal.'

Polly and Muna, both considerably slimmer than Umar, were soon through to the other side. All three stood up, brushed at their soiled clothing and exchanged relieved smiles.

'OK, we must be there soon – I hope,' said Polly. 'Lead the way, Umar.'

The party fell back into their single file formation and moved cautiously forward. Within a short time, Umar stopped again.

'Me tink dis it,' he said, wide-eyed and in hushed tones. 'Dere's a door here.'

The passage widened a little at this point and gave the girls the opportunity to stand alongside Umar and direct their torches onto the wall to their left. From floor to ceiling a section of the wall appeared to be clad in something dull and metallic. A handle protruded from it at waist height.

'Me tink dat lead cuv'ring de door 'n' dere's nah lock.'

Umar took hold of the handle and pulled. The heavy door creaked and moved a little. Then, after further effort it swung open noisily until it blocked the passageway ahead. The three friends stood in the doorway, their torches moving over the contours of the contents within.

When Lucky woke, she felt cold. She got up from the bunk very carefully and in the grey light, looked at each of the four sleeping children with a heavy heart.

A few moments later she had gathered the wet bedding and pyjamas from the floor. Her arms full, she entered the corridor and quietly closed the door behind her.

They had not discussed their expectations of what they might find if they ever succeeded in reaching 'the great prize'. Having met with so many 'blind alleys' and delays, they had learned to contain their wildest hopes in order to avoid further disappointment. If they did enjoy any private fantasies of wealth then they would probably admit to imagining scenes like those of Ali Baba's descent into the cave used by the forty thieves, Bilbo Baggins's first sight of Smaug's treasure in the Lonely Mountain or any number of discoveries made by a cinematic hero like Indiana Jones.

None of them would ever have predicted the sight that now confronted them.

As their torch beams moved haphazardly over the contents of the room, they compiled an impression of the scene before them. On stone plinths they could distinguish a collection of upright shapes some of which were of adult human size, others the height of children and a few, smaller still. All were covered with hessian sacking once, no doubt, tied tightly but now draped loosely above the scattered strands of frayed rope that had fallen to the dusty floor.

Polly was the first to move forward. She reached out and slowly pulled the sacking from the figure closest to the door. As she did so she uttered a shriek and leapt backwards, colliding with Umar.

'Ow! Dat me damn foot.'

Umar, in turn, now hopped backwards, cursing as he did so until he felt himself propelled forward by what felt like two small hands.

He turned quickly and the beam of his headtorch fell on the figure of a slender, smiling girl.

'Whoah'! Who dat?!'

Polly gasped. 'Lucky! Lucky! How did you get here? You scared us!'

'I know, I'm sorry but Umar was about to crash into me. Soz Umar.'

'Me shud tink so.'

'Never mind that! Are you OK? How did you get here? What happened to you? How did you find us? Am I glad to see you.'

'I know, I know and there isn't time to tell you the whole story but yes, I'm OK. I got back safely, just a little later than I'd hoped. There'd been a lot of fuss and mum wouldn't let me out of her sight for a few hours but when she saw I was ok, she went next door to tell the neighbours about it all and I slipped out to look for you. I knew you'd be here of course and I didn't want to miss out. But listen, where's the tall man? I thought he'd be here, with you?'

'Man? What man Lucky? We're on our own.'

'No, you're not. Just after I found the open door into the Head's House, I saw a tall, thin man in the distance, on the long corridor. He quickly disappeared down the steps and I followed him into the undercroft. When I reached the door in the wall it was closing behind him but I could see how it worked so I waited a little while and then opened it. When I reached the passage I couldn't see him any more, so I guessed he'd met up with you.'

'No, we haven't seen any man. Tall and thin? How could *you* get to us before he did?'

Muna interrupted, 'The recess!'

A familiar and authoritative voice broke into their conversation.

'You are correct, young lady! Well done!'

They turned in the direction of the voice.

'Mr Wilby!'

'Sir!'

'We are so pleased to see you, sir,' said Polly.

'You are?' replied the man, sceptically.

'Yes, sir. I was worried that Lucky had seen someone else.'

'Someone else?'

'Yes, sir. We haven't told anyone at school about it yet but when we were in Oxford, on the trip last Friday, we were kept in a locked room for a while by a horrible man called Playfair. I thought that you might be him.'

'You thought that I might be Playfair? He wouldn't have the intelligence, or the gumption, to follow you down here.'

'But, sir, if you know him … ' added Lucky.

'Yes, that's right, my dear. I am the man who claims this prize.'

With an unpleasant smirk the man took out an old army revolver from his jacket pocket and pointed it at the four young people.

'Move into the room! I am impatient to feast my eyes on what has taken so many years to find.'

'You're from Glover College. You're one of them!' exclaimed Polly.

'My dear girl,' the man sneered, 'all the head teachers at Winter Hill have been men and women from Glover College. Ours has been a long wait and now, at last, thanks to me – and you, of course - it is over. Now, be quiet and let me examine ...'

Mr Wilby turned the beam of his torch momentarily into the store room.

'What on earth?'

He moved forward, still waving the barrel of the gun aggressively in their direction. He shone his torch on the figure that Polly had already uncovered and emitted a low groan. He tore another piece of sacking from the nearest shape.

He swore loudly and continued to hiss intermittently, viciously, as he moved through the room in an escalating frenzy, ripping aside each piece of sacking in turn.

The four friends watched in horrified silence, fearful that any movement on their part might further upset their captor. Before them, there stood a collection of dark, wooden figures. Some were evidently male, others female, and all, unashamedly, naked. Some were shaped from flat, angular planes that reminded Polly of visits to art galleries where her parents would talk excitedly about the paintings and sculptures of artists like Picasso and Braque. Others, in contrast, were composed of smooth and rounded forms with exaggerated, unblinking eyes made from a bright shell-like material that reflected the light from their torches. Some had large mouths lined with white whalebone teeth fixed in fearsome grins.

Grouped together, in the confined space, confronting human eyes for the first time in more than one hundred and fifty years, the figures made for an intimidating sight. Their human audience, unknowingly, mirrored the gaping open-mouthed expressions. The head teacher was the first to cast off the blanket of wordless amazement.

'My God,' he cried, lifting his head to the ceiling, 'have I given much of my life for this? This mess ... of primitive, ... disgusting, ... rubbish. Damn that man, West! He said the great prize was of inestimable value; that it would bring glory and prestige to the church and the nation. Why bother to conceal something so utterly worthless? The man was a fool! He has made a fool of Fielding, Goodison, McLaine, me! We're all fools!'

His shoulders slumped and he held his forehead with his left hand, in evident distress. His right hand, holding the revolver, began to relax and fall to his side.

'I've seen things like this before. In that museum ... in Oxford,' mumbled Polly.

Lucky moved forwards, her arm outstretched, in the direction of Mr Wilby.

'Sir, I think Reverend West thought that these statues, idols, would be of help, give people a better understanding of different cultures. He was a good friend to William John. These must come from the South Seas. They were both worried that Reverend Angel wouldn't understand.'

'Wouldn't understand?!' shouted the man, spraying spittle in his fury.

'Careful, Lucky,' whispered Polly. 'He's mad. Stay away from him.'

'What's to understand here, eh? Tell me! A ragbag of crude, naked ... OBSCENE ... figures. Why should a man like the Reverend Angel, be worried by such worthless trash?!'

'Angel thought that people would lose their faith if his and other churches were challenged by the new interest in science, art and the beliefs of different people in other parts of the world. Perhaps he was afraid that different religions and different denominations would be seen like different species of animal, each one adapting to its environment, each one of them, no better or worse, than another. He hated the new ideas that men like Darwin were discussing. That's why Angel got rid of West and then spread false stories about him stealing the college funds.'

'And when did you become so knowledgeable about our affairs?' spat the headteacher, staring intensely and malevolently at Lucky.

Lucky backed away, disturbed by light reflecting from his wide eyes, the ferocity of his words.

Then, in a low whisper, she replied, 'I can go back – I heard them talking ...'

'Lucky, shut-up, please don't talk like that,' Polly pleaded, close to tears.

'Oh, yes. The girl with special abilities,' he sneered. 'Well, what use is the prophecy now when all it has brought us is this 'reward'?'

'Sir, the idea of the prophecy was yours, Dr McLaine's, the church ...'

Lucky's voice trailed away. All of them were greatly alarmed by the threatening and erratic behaviour of Mr Wilby.

Muna sobbed, 'Why can't we just go back and we can forget about all this ...?'

But Mr Wilby responded to Lucky.

'McLaine didn't even know who I was until ...'

'She didn't know that you were a watcher? Until when? Until that night she came to my house? It was you she was going to meet just before the accident? Or was it murder?'

'And that young lady,' said Mr Wilby, now speaking in more measured tones, 'is the answer to your friend's question, the reason why we can't just forget all this. I have gone too far. Fielding, Playfair and others; we have all gone too far. It doesn't matter what you know because you will never be able to tell your story. Give me those bags!'

Reluctantly, the girls held out their bags for him to take. He turned out the contents onto the ground.

'And yours Hussein! I know that you're the housebreaker here. Let's have the tools of your trade.'

Umar cursed, took off his backpack and kicked it forward.

'Pick it up, girl, and empty it.'

Muna bent down and did as instructed. Screwdrivers, a crowbar, the lock picks, cylinder lock keys and other tools clanked as they hit the ground. A coil of rope followed.

'Put everything in one bag and give it to me. Give me the rope separately.'

'I left a note for my mother telling her where I'd gone, if I didn't return,' said Lucky calmly.

'I don't believe you! You obviously have not told any of your parents about your quest so far. Why should you behave differently today? Good try, but it won't work.'

Umar suddenly lunged forward in an attempt to grab the gun. Mr Wilby sidestepped and brought the handle down forcefully on the boy's exposed head. Muna screamed. Umar grunted and fell forward, heavily, onto the floor.

'This was handed on to me from Colonel Goodison himself. I'm not about to give it to you, you fool. Now, all of you, go right to the back of the room, amongst those gruesome statues. You can keep your torches, for all the good they'll do you. But if any of you come out of the room before I'm through the gap, I swear I'll shoot you.'

The girls and a still-dazed Umar retreated into the spaces among the wooden statues. Wilby closed the door, kicking the crowbar into place as a temporary wedge. He then returned to the gap in the rubble. He threw the bag containing the tools through to the other side, tied the rope several times around the wooden prop and threw the remainder of the coil after the bag.

He faced the way he had come, knelt down and began to shuffle his way backwards through the narrow opening. He used his left hand both to support his upper body and to hold the torch, the beam of which was intermittently directed into the passage ahead. If any of his captives were intent on attacking him he would still have the gun freely available in his right hand.

Slowly, awkwardly and at the cost of some pain to his knees, he inched his way back through the opening. Tired and frustrated, he failed to sense that his foot had become entangled in the coil of rope, as he moved over it. Seeing the door to the store room begin to move and the crowbar slide backwards, he fired two shots and made one last, major effort to squeeze through the gap. The reverberation from the gun, within the confined space of the tunnel, released a torrent of stones from the passage ceiling. At the same time, he, unknowingly, jerked the rope that tightened and pulled on the wooden prop.

With a soft squeal the prop went sideways bringing down several tonnes of brick and soil with a sudden, brutal and final, 'whump'. Richard Wilby instantly disappeared beneath the rubble. When the worst of the dust settled, only his hands, one curled limply above a broken torch, the other still carrying the revolver, would have been visible, had there been any light to see by and anybody there to see.

Inside the lead-lined room the three girls clung to one another on hearing the gunshots closely followed by the collapse of the ceiling. Umar, who had just pushed at the door, instinctively crouched and covered his head with his hands as the walls shook. All four were instantly fearful that the rest of the passage ceiling would collapse but as the seconds passed they began to look around and then explore their position.

They hesitantly moved towards the door and then out of the storeroom into the passage. Polly had dropped and broken her torch when she threw her arms around Muna and Lucky but the beams of the others carved what looked like solid yellow cones in the dust-laden air.

Periodically coughing and holding a hand over mouth and nose, Umar and Polly approached the site of the collapse. They saw the protruding hands and quickly returned to the others.

'Wilby is d-dead - and we're com-completely cut off. We can't get through,' stuttered a distressed Polly.

'Oh no! We're going to die here, in the dark!'

'I don't think so, Muna,' contested Lucky. 'When I told Wilby that I'd left a note for my Mum, I wasn't bluffing. After what happened at Glover College, I knew we were taking a big risk in coming here.'

'So, someone should start looking for us very soon?' reasoned Polly.

'I think so. But it's possible that there nothing obvious to see above ground and Wilby may have gone back and closed the door after I passed him, so we must also try to get away from here.'

''Ow we goin' ta do dat? We trapped.'

'Maybe not. Polly and me looked at the building plans in Oxford. This passage is part of the fourth wing that was never built. It was meant to connect the west to the east wing.'

'Yeah, we arlreddy know 'bout dat.

'OK, so perhaps if we go on we'll find a way out. We've got some torches but it may be a good idea to only use one at a time.'

'Lend me yours a minute, Muna,' Polly demanded. 'I've thought of something else that might be useful.'

Polly retraced her steps and returned a few moments later, carrying the revolver.

'I thought this might help attract attention.'

'Good idea,' said Lucky

'Wish me tort a it!' added a disappointed Umar.

'OK, let's go on then. You lead us Umar,' said Lucky closing the store room door and revealing the passage beyond.

Polly moved forward and placed the gun in Umar's hand.

'You should have it, Umar, if you're in front.'

Umar uttered a soft *'Tanks'* and guided by the beam of his headtorch, began to walk forward.

Within a few minutes they had reached the end, another plain brick wall with a recess to the right but with no further progress possible.

'Looks like all we can do now, is wait for someone to dig us out,' said Muna.

'Unless ...' Lucky's voice trailed off as she began to explore the space to the right of the end wall. 'The passage is very dry ... yes ... I think there's one up there.'

Umar squeezed into the space and followed Lucky's line of sight to a spot in the ceiling above.

'Can you see how there's a lighter patch in the ceiling? Angle your torch into the corner. Yes, there, another grill.'

'It's too high to reach!'

'But there's some light above. It must lead into a room in the east wing. What's the lowest level in that wing?'

'The changing rooms and loos, under the gym.'

'No Polly, there's another level. If you go outside there are those steps, remember, the ones that go down to a door. I was pushed down there once by some girls in Year 11. I tried to get through the door at the bottom, but it's always locked.'

'Of course, you're right, Muna, the boiler room! It's the boiler room and the caretakers must go down there.'

'So, we'll have to wait until we can hear people moving about and then use our torches, our voices – and if necessary ...'

'Me gun!'

Umar never did get to use the revolver. An hour or so after they arrived at the end of the passage, a solitary policeman approached the school grounds. He was responding to a call from a concerned parent. One of the caretakers had also been contacted but by the time he arrived, the policeman had already found a way into the grounds and the open door in the west end corner. Through the windows in the long corridor, he had also spotted a strange depression in the path that ran along the rear of the building.

The caretaker, Eddie Ray, was unable to explain why, if a break-in had taken place, the alarm system hadn't worked. He said he had set it on the Saturday, after the football match. He was confident that he'd done so because he could clearly remember demonstrating, at the time, how the system worked to the head teacher, Mr Wilby.

After examining the sunken hole in the tarmac the policeman called for further assistance and enquiries were made about Lucky's friend, Polly. Before long the school was the focus not only for numerous policemen but also some school staff who'd been summoned when the head teacher could not be located, a knot of anxious parents and even a local journalist who happened to be passing.

The building was cordoned off and a thorough search ordered.

It was Eddie Ray, switching on the lights as he checked the boiler room, who heard the muffled calls coming from one corner. When he had cleared away some old machinery blocking his access to the location in the floor, he could see light coming from the other side of a ventilation grill. Then he heard Umar.

'Raas. Me almost shoot yuh, mahn!'

Miss Frobisher leaned back in her teacher's chair and beamed at the small group of Year 9 students.

'Well, here we are again. A new term ...'

'A new head teacher,' added Muna.

'Yes, or at least there will be very soon. But where is Lucky?'

'She'll be here in a little while, miss. She had another appointment this morning with the psychologist ...

'Yeah, me arl-ways say dat gal a men-tal kayss,' grinned the boy perched on one of the classroom desks.

'Psychologist, not psychiatrist, Umar,' countered Miss Frobisher. 'Now, on the other hand, an Asian boy who tries to speak caribbean patois, that's a serious matter ...'

The girls laughed until Polly changed the mood by asking, 'How much money do you think the idols will sell for, miss?'

'I've no idea, Polly. I don't think that even the experts know the answer to that question. My guess is that, with the city council saying they will only sell in one lot, so that they stay together, the price will be less than if they sold them individually.'

'Why, miss?'

'Because only a really big organisation, like the British Museum, could buy all of them together, so there won't be much competition. Even so, I've read that they may sell for as much as half a million pounds.'

'An' we get nutten,' added the boy, miserably.

'No, Umar, but you understand why that is, don't you? The idols count as 'treasure trove' and belong to the owner of the land and that's Binghamton City Council. If the council had given you permission to search for 'the prize' that might have made a difference …'

'I heard that the South Sea islanders want their idols back,' Polly added.

'Yes, what we now call the South Pacific islands of French Polynesia. I believe that if the British Museum can raise the money then they have agreed to lend the collection to the islands for long periods.'

'But will the school get some of the money, miss?' asked Muna.

'I think we'll have to wait and see. Those councillors you met in the Council House said they would find some way to help the school, didn't they? If they do as they promised, you'll be the heroes of Winter Hill!'

'The Binghamton Mail has already called us 'the Fab Four'. They want us to go on the radio soon with some professor who'll be able to explain all the history stuff; the first college, the guy who built the baths, the First World War barracks, the orphanage and the school.'

'Yes, we know that it's a long story but we still don't know how much money the school will get or how it will be spent,' added Polly.

Miss Frobisher smiled. 'Well, the new head teacher will have something to say about that – when he, or she, is appointed.'

'I wonder who it will be?'

'Well, Muna, at least we know that this time it won't be someone working for Glover College!'

'Yes, you three, four with Lucky, had a close escape from those awful people.'

'Was Mr Wilby an evil man, miss?'

'That's another very difficult question, Polly. He was certainly guilty of bad or evil acts. But I hope that one thing you might have learned from your project is that 'good' and 'evil' are not always easy to separate. Doctor McLaine thought she was doing 'good' by working secretly for her church …'

'But she changed her mind,' Muna interrupted.

'She did. And Reverend West was known as a 'bad' man in the same church for many years,' added Polly.

'That's right. Even the people who killed William John …'

'An' ay-ut 'im!'

''And ate him', thank you, Umar but we now know that their island had been attacked by Europeans earlier in that same year and many of their people had been killed. They thought they were defending their land from another attack by white men.'

'So are you saying, miss, that if good and evil are all mixed up, we can't tell which is which?'

'No, I don't think I'm saying that. What I am saying is that sometimes we need to understand, to be able to see things as others see them, in their own time. But the taking of innocent human life is always wrong and all religions are agreed on that … ah! I see I'm about to be rescued!'

Miss Frobisher broke off to stand up and turn towards the classroom door. Through the glass panel she had spotted the approach of Lucky. As she entered the room, Polly and Muna rushed to exchange hugs with her before firing off a salvo of questions.

'How did it go? What did they say? How are you feeling? Are you OK?'

'I'm fine, really. I'm fine. They've decided I'm not crazy.'

'Den dey mus' be!' Umar countered with a smirk.

'I'll ignore that, Umar. If only you'd stop trying to hide your true feelings for me ...'

Everyone laughed, even Miss Frobisher, even Umar.

'Instead they've told me that my,' Lucky crooked, then waggled, both forefingers to either side of her head, "so-called ability' to time travel, is nothing of the kind. Apparently, I am just a 'particularly imaginative child', able to absorb a great deal of information in a short space of time and then use it to create ... what did they call it? ... 'incredible scenarios' that I believe and persuade others to believe, are real.'

'I think,' said Miss Frobisher, 'that was probably 'credible scenarios' Lucky. In other words you imagine believable pictures or scenes.'

'Yes, that's right, ... when I'm in a 'self-induced trance'.'

'Hang on a minute! Let me get this right,' said Polly. 'You didn't time travel – you just thought you did and if you 'brought back' information ... it was just a coincidence that it was correct.'

'That's right, Polly, I'm as ordinary as anyone else.'

Lucky smiled and winked at her friend.

'OK,' said Miss Frobisher suddenly, 'well that's a relief to everyone, I'm sure. But look, I need to get some work done before the rest of the class return after break, so I'm going to have to ask you to leave me in peace.'

The four friends began to walk towards the door.

'But I do want to say that it's good to see you all again. Let's make this a good year, shall we? It's May, 2001 and whatever happens about the money, I think you four have made a priceless contribution to the whole school. You are definitely part of the history of this place now Umar – and the rest of you, too.'

The four friends looked at each other with smiles. 'Yeah man'.

'Yes, miss.'

'Bye.'

They moved towards the door and opened it.

'Inshallah,' added Muna.

Outside, Umar and Muna agreed they would fetch some drinks from the canteen. Polly and Lucky found an empty bench on the perimeter of the playing fields in the shade of a large beech tree, part of a group planted for the college when it first opened. Lucky turned to look at Polly.

'I had another surprise this morning.'

'Oh, what was that?'

'I had a letter from Jenny Almer.'

'The librarian at Glover College?'

'Yes, it was a really nice letter, inviting us to return there whenever we want to.'

'Go back there! No thanks!'

'No listen, Polly. Things have changed. Playfair and Miss Thomas have gone. Others like them, people we never met, have gone as well. The people in charge are saying that they want to apologise for things that happened in the past.'

'What do you mean?'

'Well, Jenny explained the story to me. It starts with the link between William John, Elizabeth Glover, James Angel and Timothy West. They were all great friends once and worked together to help their church. Timothy was the man with the ideas and imagination, James Angel the organiser and William John the practical one, 'a man of action'. Elizabeth's part was to use her great wealth to support, not only the building of Winter Hill College, but lots of other charity projects as well.'

'Like what?'

'Like alms houses for old people who had nowhere to live, Sunday schools so children could learn to read and write because they didn't have schools like we have today and supporting missionaries in different parts of the world.'

'Like William John?'

'Yes, especially William John. But Jenny says that with what Dr McLaine and I told her they now know that there was a big bust-up between them.'

'A bust-up? Between who? Why?'

'Well, like I said, Timothy West was interested in ideas and in the first half of the nineteenth century there were big changes taking place in understanding the world and how it worked.'

'Science?'

'Yes, but Jenny thinks that West was a man also interested in exploring different ways of living. In other words he liked the 'good things in life' – I think that means money and all it brings … food, drink, fine clothes, a posh house …'

'Women?'

'I don't know, maybe. She didn't say and, unfortunately, I interrupted the Reverend Angel when he was about to say more. Anyway, this behaviour of West's didn't go down well with people like James Angel who was very strict in his religious views, so he turned Elizabeth Glover against West and together they tried to get rid of him.'

'Where do the idols come in?'

'Well, William was first inspired to become a Christian missionary by Timothy's preaching and for this reason, wanted to help him with his interest in other cultures and their beliefs - but he didn't want to upset Elizabeth. He couldn't afford to if he was going to do the things he wanted to do in the South Seas, like building churches and schools ...'

'So, he sent the idols to Timothy, in secret?'

'That's right. There was a small group within the same church who knew about the cargo and who were willing to help. Jenny thinks Timothy West would have known all the members but because of the secrecy the others may not have known who else was in the group. She says that the design on the tomb and the tattoo on William John's arm are the same and may have been the way they recognised a fellow member.'

'So, why were the idols hidden in the college?'

'Who knows? Don't forget, though, that Timothy West was the man who first had the idea for a college. He would have known about the fourth wing and may have thought, when the pressure was on, that this was the best place to hide them – right under the nose of Reverend Angel. You have to admit it's probably the last place that he would think to look for them.'

As Lucky spoke, a group of girls, all from their class, strolled past. They turned to look at the girls on the bench and smiled.

'Hi, Lucky, Polly. See you in Science. We're in the same group, this term.'

'Hi, Charmaine,' Lucky replied.

Polly added, 'Yeah, see you there.'

'Seems you're not so much of a snob as you used to be,' suggested a smiling Polly. 'Anyway, you didn't finish telling me about the idols. After West hid them here, they stayed undiscovered for more than one hundred and fifty years?'

'Yes, James Angel knew that something valuable had been sent to Timothy from William but didn't know what it was or where it was hidden. William John was killed by natives on Erromanga in the New Hebrides islands ...'

'Cannibals!'

'Yes, on some of these islands they believed that by eating part of the flesh of an enemy you gained his strength and his skills.'

Polly grimaced.

'I know. Froby explained to us why William John was seen as an enemy even though he wouldn't have hurt them ....'

Lucky paused before continuing.

'Anyway, so John was dead... and then Timothy West disappeared when he left Binghamton and Samuel Ferrington died very suddenly. When the others who knew something were also dead, the tales of a treasure or 'prize' became just another rumour. As their church got smaller, some thought that finding it would change their fortunes. Then Fielding was given the Ferrington journal and he began to send secret 'watchers' into our school.'

'Yes and the strangest thing of all is that what Wilby thought was useless and disgusting, turns out to be worth a lot of money.'

Polly looked up and waved to Muna, who, with flattened hand raised to her forehead like the peak of a cap, was scanning the field and playground in search of her friends. Polly could see from the bulges in her blazer pockets that she had been successful. Umar, a few paces behind, was already piercing a fruit juice carton with a plastic straw, indifferent to the very public violation of the school rule that said all food and drink must be consumed in the canteen.

When they were reunited on the bench, Muna was the first to speak.

'I wonder whether there'll be any more adventures for us this year?'

'Well, I know of at least one,' said Polly with a smile.

'What's that?' asked an eager Muna.

'My dad went bananas when he found out that I had 'borrowed' his uncle's letter. Later though, when he calmed down, he spoke a lot about how he wanted to visit the battlefield where Arthur died in France and a memorial - it has Arthur's name on it.'

'Sounds like an adventure for him,' said Lucky.

'Yes but he wants us all to go with him and mum.'

'It sounds interesting but I couldn't do that, Polly. My mum can't afford it,' said Muna miserably.

'Me needer,' added Umar angrily.

'But you don't understand,' said Polly. 'He wants us all to go with them as a special 'thank you' for helping him discover more about Arthur. He's paying for everything!'

'OK - that's different!'

'Cool!

'Wow. I'll have to ask my mum but it should be OK if yours is going,' added Muna.

They spoke excitedly for a while about Polly's news before Umar raised his voice to interrupt their exchange.

'Me know me 'ave a nudder ting to tell yuh. Me startin' back in arl lessun.'

'Yes, I heard that. That's great and I think I know who helped. Maryam says that she was in Pearce's office when 'Froby' told him she thought it was time you went back to a normal timetable and not just her lessons. She said you deserved it. She likes you, you know. According to Maryam, she said that you may act like a 'gangsta' but that deep down you have good 'emotional intelligence'!'

Umar spluttered as he drank from the carton through a straw.

'Wha?!'

'Eeargh, Umar don't spray that stuff all over me.'

Muna began to wipe her blazer with her hand, then, looking up, saw Miss Frobisher approaching them. The teacher was smiling at her and carrying a shoulder bag that looked very much like Polly's. Muna realised that their teacher was about to return it in person and tried to gesture a warning to Umar.

Umar ignored Muna's signals. He was far too interested in giving vent to his outrage.

'*Mo-shun-al een-telly-jense.*'? Wha' she tark 'bout? Dat 'Fro-bitch-ur', she one crazy wum-an.'

Umar felt a single sharp prod to his shoulder. He spun round to see a black woman, hands on hips and head thrown back in an exaggerated expression of anger.

'Chaw man! Wha feh yuh tark like dat – yuh no bleck. An' how many time me tell yuh, *'Doan cuss de crocodile afore yuh crass de rivah'*? Ya unnestan'? Yuh-a too facety bwoy, now hush yuh mout'!'

Then Miss Frobisher handed the bag to Polly, winked at her, turned and, head held high, strode back in the direction from which she'd approached. She left behind a small group of girls whooping and crying aloud in admiration and delight and the slumped shoulders of one burly boy, his mouth open, unable for once, to find any words at all.

Acknowledgements

Thanks are due to the many friends and family members who have encouraged this project and agreed to read early drafts but particular mention must be made of Judy, Gerd, Jenny, No'omi, my son Stephen and my daughter, Claire.

Thanks also to Dave Etheridge for his invaluable assistance with formatting and all things technical.

Thanks to Keith Townsend for being a long-time, research-buddy and to Richard Cobb and the archive group of the Moseleians Association.

Thanks to Keith, again, and Jude Davies for proofreading. Having lost, as a result of their input, all confidence on what to do with a comma, all remaining, errors are, entirely, their responsibility.

A final thanks to Keith for help with executing the front and back cover design.

Thanks too, to all those kids I taught, or tried to teach, over the course of thirty-four years; I learned a great deal from them.

Finally, my thanks are due to my wonderful wife, Diana. Without her enduring support and encouragement it is unlikely that the manuscript would ever have seen the black ink of print or the light of cyberspace.

About the author

Born and raised in Norwich, the author has lived in Birmingham since university days. While waiting for the right job to come along, he tried secondary school teaching.

Starting a young family, shortly thereafter, instilled the necessary financial discipline.

Some years later, supported by a working wife, he thought he might better enjoy the life of academe. He completed a Master's degree and then embarked on a PhD. Having already faced problems with his own personal development, he had worked for some time as a volunteer counsellor. Now, failure to 'follow through' with his PhD and a new personal crisis led him to offer his services as a teacher-counsellor in a tough, north Birmingham, neighbourhood. This was a period in which schooling was freer to experiment than was, perhaps, appreciated at the time.

A new relationship and a new post in a school with a unique educational and architectural heritage prompted further effort at poetry and other forms of writing, the culmination of which is this novel for teenagers aged between thirteen and ninety-nine years.

There are other writing projects warming on the hob.

Is it possible that the right job has finally arrived?